THE COMMON FRIEND

For Colin Edwards and Emma & Julian Skinner

Erika
from Jim
Nov 99

THE
COMMON
FRIEND

James Willis

Arkst Publishing

First published in Great Britain 1998 by
ARKST PUBLISHING
LONDON

Copyright © James Willis 1998

British Library Cataloguing in Publication Data
A catalogue record for this book is available from the British Library

ISBN 0 9525243 1 7

Printed and Bound in Great Britain by
Whitstable Litho Printers Ltd., Whitstable, Kent

CHAPTER ONE

INCIDENT ROOM

'Where is the man then? Everyone said the scouse git was going to deliver; he was the man who was going to raise the siege, wasn't that it? He was going to get it all sorted so we can all be home for Christmas, and now, where is the bloody man? That's all I'm asking. Doesn't seem all that much to ask, now does it? Don't tell me your darling laughing boy did a runner on us, and went down home to whatever her name is; that's all we bloody need. Leave it out. Christ what a total absolute shower. Who needs it?' A pause, then, glaring, 'All right someone tell me, straight up, where is the bloody man, where fucking is he? That is all I am, in actual fact, bloody asking.'

There was little doubt about it, DCI Len Manson, head honcho of the Anti-Terrorist Unit, well, he really had a way with the words when you came down to it.

Newly-joined members of the Unit who knew no better, sometimes asked why it was that he was referred to as 'Stiffer'. It was soon made clear to them that while it might be that he was *known* as Stiffer, you didn't call him that to his face. That would have been well out of order. And in any case he knew bloody well where the scouser was for Christ's sake.

Like many good coppers, Manson looked rather like a villain, dressed like one, that is your actual conservative style with just a hint of flash, plus he had the right, beat-the-shit-out-of-you-if-you-don't-come-across-my-son look in his eye, the muscular body build, the whole bit. You wouldn't want to mess with the Stiffer unless you were team-handed. Like too many policemen he drank more than was good for him, from time to time; smoked too much all the time, never ate the right food and looked exhausted, strung out and bad tempered.

Unlike most policemen however, he was humourless, never a good sign. He had little time for the man he had just referred to as 'the scouse git', his junior colleague, DI Edwards whom he perceived as a jumped up tosser who was soft on drugs, blacks and gays, a bleeding hearts liberal, a closet do-gooder who probably voted Labour and, for all he knew, read *The Guardian* or worse. As far as he was concerned Mister bloody Edwards and his sort, epitomised a breed of smartarse, college-educated cleverstick coppers that he hated and could never understand. Perhaps he was a colleague to be regarded with something that was not too far removed from fear. And why not? *'A College educated prat. Your Edwards and all his lot if you ask me? One of your wet-behind-the-ears coppers, that's your bloody Edwards and the like. They dial nine-nine-bloody-nine for someone to wipe their backsides half the bloody time,'* as he'd frequently said. Too often, many of his colleagues would have added.

He gazed aggressively, possibly with a shade of uncertainty at his exhausted colleagues in the incident room which had been set up in haste in a schoolroom in Kensington, next door to the Royal School of Needlework. Where else?

And so he lit his twelfth cigarette of the morning and coughed for a while and said, to no one in particular, 'Right, this is it. I'm giving up next week.' And laughed, in case anyone chose to notice, let alone comment.

The incident room was smoky, stuffy, overcrowded and more than a shade frantic behind the studied calmness and measured tones. Trestle tables were covered with monitors, surveillance equipment, word processors, half finished sandwiches, food cartons, coffee cups and papers. The chairs were hard, yielding little support to Metropolitan Police haemorrhoids. Coaxial cables snaked across and around the floors. And above it all there droned the unrelenting replay of monitored phone conversations with the people, the police, the SAS, the Intelligence, all the punters who were watching the Embassy and waiting. All the while the sounds of crackling intercoms and the low buzz of the talk of a watchful group of people who were getting a shade near to meltdown after four days of continuous observation of an Embassy siege on the boil. Tough shit.

All this was in sharp contrast to the real purpose of the infant schoolroom but no one was aware of this except for the Officer who had been deputed to feed the pet rabbits who had been left behind when the place had been evacuated to make way for the anti-terrorist squad which had arrived four days before. They had started off in the Royal School of Needlework but the possibility that cigarette fumes might rot the priceless tapestries had caused two committee members to faint away and the President to have an attack of the vapours at the prospect of having to confront the Royal Patron with such dire possibilities.

'Nice one Guv.' retorted DI Dave Johnson, 'We all know you're going to pack it in, honest we do.' He couldn't think of much else to say. His chief lit another cigarette and edged nearer to the widow-maker that lurked inside his anterior descending coronary artery.

'Leave it out sunshine. Just tell me where the Scouser is.'

'The last call we had located him coming up to the site in Range Rover Echo Delta, and he was on line to the contact in the Embassy, Mohammed Ibrahim.'

'Who's he again? Some bloody raghead as per usual.' Why did Manson have to go through this elaborate ritual of pretending not to know that Fizzer was the negotiator dealing with the Embassy contact? What sort of a bloody stupid game was it? Why did everyone have to sweat it out in the middle of this bloody feud and act as if it wasn't going on? He'd only been negotiating with him for four days for God's sake.

3

'No Guv, it appears this Ibrahim, well he's not your average raghead; he's an educated guy and, with respect, I mean, you know very well Guv, Fizzer has got to know him over the time they've all been in there.' He nearly added 'and all the time we've all been out here in case you hadn't noticed', but thought better of it.

Dave was becoming weary of Manson and his infantile day-in day-out act of pretending not to know the full SP and all because Manson hated Fizzer's guts because he wasn't a real Met man and all that crap. If he heard the story one more time he'd do his nut, all about how Fizzer was little more than a soft copper and how he hadn't done his bird with the Met, jumped up bastard and stuff. Jesus it would give you a right pain in the arsehole while you were sweating on sodding retirement, promotion or even a bloody holiday and you're obliged to spend your time buttering up the old man who's jealous of the young hero, while no one gives a toss about the forty hostages in the Embassy with a load of nutters waving shooters at them. Ragheads too; bad enough if it was just Micks. Christ alight.

'All right' replied Manson 'I read you. So our laughing boy is talking to our dusky chummy in the Embassy. As long as he doesn't do a Stockholm on us and want to get into bed with him, we're laughing, but will someone tell me why the Scouser, sorry I mean your darling Inspector Edwards, isn't on the line to me for once. I am in charge of this operation in case you'd all forgotten. I mean he reports to me you know.'

'He spoke to you fifteen minutes ago,' suggested Dave gently. Jesus, we had noticed, in case anyone should ask you; you only tell us every fifteen bleeding minutes, that's all. What's the bloody use?

But now there was no more time for day-dreaming as Manson's personal mobile started beeping rattily. He answered, for him, unexpectedly quietly. He had a good idea what was in the pipeline anyway, and said as much out of the corner of his mouth. Well stuff it, he would, him being in charge, thought Dave. A major big deal he'll make out of it. It's time I quit this job, I didn't used to be like this. Who is? Why does he have to

4

use a mobile for Christ's sake? No one else does. He's a copper, not a bloody futures dealer.

And Dave thought, I know it they've authorised the heavies in the black kit to go in. I bloody know it. Jesus I just hope it works this time. I'm going soft, that's it. Has to be.

Silence. All eyes are now on Manson. Manson click folds his mobile. Looks round. *Look at my mobile you prats – I'm not some wally from Thames Valley. Got me?*

'Right lads, this is it. The word is the boys in black are going in to kick ass, just as we expected, in fifteen minutes, as per. The drill is known to all of you. We are all on listening mode as of right now. Let's hope Mr, I mean DI Fizzer doesn't screw it up for us.'

'He won't Guv.' said Dave 'He won't. Not Fizzer,' and he thought, he's been watching too much NYPD Blue. I can always tell it when he bangs on about kicking ass. Why can't he speak English?

At that moment four hundred metres from the Embassy building, DI Robert 'Fizzer' Edwards was sitting in the Range Rover talking on the phone to Ibrahim, the terrorist spokesman inside the building. Once again Fizzer had the ball at his feet. He'd been stringing Ibrahim along, nicely thank you, for the past four days and had sort of got to know the guy; he even vaguely liked him at times but it wouldn't do to let on about that now would it? Hang on, that sort of thing might give Manson a few ideas for a start.

Funny thing about Ibrahim though, he seemed, well different from your average toerag. Educated chap, what was it he said, Baghdad University? Keeps going on about it. Still some of the Provies were educated when you came down to it.. Yes, in a way, he had quite got to like the guy, no doubt about it. He sensed that things would start moving quite soon; no point in getting soft on the Ibrahims of this world, but all the same he had... he had what? Bugger it, they'd killed two hostages so far and must know by now that this was the acceptable limit. Soon enough and sure enough the siege would be raised and maybe a lot of people would qualify for the wooden overcoat and they could all go home. Just keep Ibrahim on line till the lads with the shooters arrived.

In any case he felt pretty good at the moment. This would be another notch cut in his Glock, another rung in the promotional ladder. His track record of hostage negotiation was faultless and soon, if he kept on like this, he'd be able to get away from the envious Manson. He knew too well what Manson thought about him, he'd made it plain enough and often enough from the start. Every time they spoke he could feel Manson eyeing his gear with sweaty shiny-arsed disapproval. Poor old Manson and his M and S double-breasted flappers. He looked more like a double-glazing salesman to tell the truth. But not Fizzer; no way. Always well turned out was the Boy wonder. Why go around looking like a sack of shit tied up in the middle was how Fizzer saw it? Manson thought Fizzer was too flash, that was double obvious. So what? If a copper wants to go around looking like a sweaty collar feeler with his pants full of shit, all baggy arsed and looking as if he'd been on the black stuff all night, well tough shit as far as Fizzer was concerned. Apart from that, wearing decent gear helped him pull the odd bird. Imagine Manson pulling a bird? Don't make me laugh sunshine. Birds sort of reminded him of home and Sylvie. He rubbed his crotch as mild stirrings reminded him that like too many coppers' marriages, his was badly stretched. Things were not going right with Sylvie, well lately, she laughed too readily and glanced at the gin bottle a bit frequently. Also he wondered if she might be getting a little bit extra somewhere. You never knew. No one's perfect.

He was roused from his thoughts by Ibrahim's voice on the phone.

'*Yahallah!* Mr Fizzer. We all are awaiting the news of your government's decision. I don't need to repeat that one. All we need to know is that we may have the safe conduct to the Heathrow airport with our Freedom Fighters falsely imprisoned in Pentonville and all here will go free. Inshallah.' He paused, breathing heavily with fear.

'Now I am hearing some strange noises here Mr Fizzer. What is going on? No tricks if you please.'

'I hear no noises Ibrahim. I don't know what you're talking about. Go on.' replied Fizzer. They'll be drilling holes for the charges, he thought. Surely they used silent drills for Christ's sake. For Christ's sake don't let them blow it in the last few minutes.

'I trust you Mr Fizzer.'

'No noises Ibrahim. I don't know to what you refer in this instance here,' he replied in his best flat official negotiator tone. It was now time to switch to authoritative mode, 'Listen up now. We wait on the final clearance from Heathrow as of right now. So just be patient here. You read me? That's all I'm saying.'

That should hold him, he thought.

Ibrahim replied, 'Noises I tell you I'm hearing some noises here. What it is going on?'

'Calm down man, there's nothing going on. It's the radio. It's a bit crackly my end.'

'No tricks please. Don't try to fool me. You forget my friend I am Ibrahim, a man of education, unlike I think, yourself. Remember Mr Fizzer I am a graduate of University of Baghdad unlike yourself, who, I suspect went to a poor school in your Liverpool where you learnt nothing except to drink and to shout at your Anfield isn't it? I don't want the Christian lies.' He paused.

'Again I hear a funny noise. What is going on Mr Fizzer. I have the right to hear the truth from you I think by now.'

'What's that supposed to mean?' said Fizzer 'What are you on about?' What does he mean 'poor school'? Good enough for Paul McCartney wasn't it?

'I mean that *foot and eye should not lie* you understand', Ibrahim sounded as if he might just be cracking up thought Fizzer. What was the bloody man talking about, foot and eye?

'What are you talking about Ibrahim? I don't read you.' said Fizzer. He wondered was the guy freaking out or what? You could never tell with this lot. All that religion, just like I got at home from me mam.

'Is from Nietzsche – "Also spracht Zarathrusta." A German Philosopher Mr Fizzer he was...'

But Fizzer never got to hear the rest of the sentence for at that moment Ibrahim's quotation was cut short by a half-second burst from a Heckler and Koch as forty four slugs ripped into his chest and belly.

But Fizzer had already heard the stun grenades and the shouts and heard it all and heard it again and he knew that the SAS had arrived, he knew it. He smiled.

In the Incident room tension erupted into wild yells of laughter and cheering.

Fizzer had pulled another stroke. He'd held the coon on line while the shit hit the fan. Bollocks to the CARD.

Nice one Fizzer.

Manson sat back. He was relieved, no question about that. Bugger Fizzer for the moment. The only catch was that the scouser had done it again. Never mind, next time, and there would be a next time, he'd see to it that Mr Darling Poncey Edwards dropped himself right in the shit. No mistake. He was so pleased at the idea that he quite forgot to light another cigarette for at least five minutes.

CHAPTER TWO

EMBASSY

But outside the Embassy Fizzer was now thinking, well that's it, the boys in black did it again then didn't they, as soon as the stun grenade echo stopped bouncing around his teeth and faded while the automatic weaponry stopped crackling and ripping the air, and he heard the silence come down like a fast curtain. After the initial silence, there were scattered shouts and cries, even a few rounds of quiet applause mixed with some quickly squelched laughs, and then, in an instant, a stream of people started to come quickly out of the building.

At the head of the line was Ken, the cop from The Diplomatic Protection Unit; poor sod he'd been in the building all the time, from day one thinks Fizzer. He looked pale and in bad shape, he had obviously been given a fair old whacking, but at least he was alive. Enjoy it while you can, Ken my old son. You'll be forgotten in six months, that is if you haven't been suspended or accused of unprovoked police brutality by *The Independent*. A reporter called out 'How you doing Ken?' Ken made no reply, he just walked on. Then, the hostages, they came out astonishingly quickly, that was the thing that amazed him on these occasions. They always come steaming out double quick, except for the poor buggers who get carried out. And they never look back either, he'd noticed that, not one tiny glance over the shoulder. Poor sods are probably afraid the SAS or someone might shoot them, as an afterthought, just to tidy things up. You never know.

There was another subdued burst of applause from the bystanders beyond the security cordon, then police car rooftop lights started to revolve, sirens growled and took up the chorus of wails as the cortege of ambulances drove off with the sick ones. In one month's time no one will give a shit about the hostages, he thought. It's always the same. Everyone gets debriefed, and for a week or two the hostages get interviewed by the press, and then off they go and that's it. For all anyone knew they probably got a load of stick from their families too. *'Where the bloody hell were you, and what were you doing all the time when we were worried stiff about you?'* Maybe that was a bit over the top, but you couldn't help wondering. It's amazing what happens to people who get caught up in things, he thought, like the poor bloody Mick we sweated a few days after the bus got blown away, and it turns out he was just a dumb Mick who was in a bloody bus. Then he gets busted by us for being an Irishman in a bus that got bombed, and next thing is, he ends up a dead heroin addict after he'd been taken into hospital to dry out. That's what they used to call dramatic irony, when I was at school.

Otherwise it was almost anticlimactic. The sun came out as the waiting column of garbage vans and street cleaning trucks edged slowly forward to harvest the MacDonalds containers, paper cups, crisp packets, cigarette butts and dogshit. A few demonstrators who had supported the Freedom Fighters had managed to remain hidden amidst the scattering remnants of the spectators. As Fizzer edged slowly past in the Range-Rover, one of them spat on the windscreen cursing him in Arabic as two policemen pulled her away. Who gave a shit? The spooks had probably planted the demonstrators anyway. He noted the two US black-windowed support vehicles, motors running, everything tightly shut and no sign of the heavy mob inside. What was it to them? Muscling in and giving unwanted advice. They call it advisement.

Already most of the Press were on their way, and the TV and film crews were packing up. Coaxial cables were winched up and away, camera boxes banged shut. The show was over. And in the sky above, the aircraft on the flight path to Heathrow had already been allocated to a higher approach level now that things had chilled out. Aircraft noise was of no importance and no further use to the boys in black. Then they started bringing out the bodies, all bagged and tagged. Sensibly, the Police made sure that this didn't go recorded on film or TV, as being not suitable for the viewing public. Next thing you get the bleeding hearts brigade banging on about uniformed murderers and all that crap.

Which one was Ibrahim? Fizzer wondered about that. He also wondered if the rabbits were all right. He wondered too, if he might slip down to Heathrow to watch the bodies being loaded on the aircraft when they sent them out of the country in a couple of nights. Better not to maybe. But he would have liked to have followed up on the rabbits.

CHAPTER THREE

MEETING

Fizzer had often wondered how it was that he had strayed into casual intermittent promiscuity instead of say, surfing the Internet, or fly fishing. As in so many instances, it was a case of letting fame go to the head and instead of letting it stay there, where it can do no harm, permitting it to travel to the balls, where its capacity for harm is boundless.

At the same time, he often wondered how it was that he had ever got into a relationship with a politically active lawyer. As far as his mates in the police were concerned, that was bad enough; after all it is only comparatively recently that a civil servant who bought *The Guardian* regularly, would be regarded as a security risk, as a matter of course, and subjected to checks, even deselected, until clearance had been established. In the police such a variety of unacceptable behaviour was reputed to merit decontamination.

But Fizzer not only went around with a *Guardian* reader, he bloody married her. Worse still she was black. The fact that he had married a black woman ensured that he was suspect, and that he immediately acquired a cohort of unrelenting enemies who would be after his ass for ever. It was as straightforward as that, and no amount of pious denials would change it.

He first met Ms Sylvie Woodhouse LLD, at the Police Staff

College, Bramshill, when he was attending the Inspectors' course, a key event in the promotional ladder of an aspiring copper, and a good deal more important than membership of the right lodge, no matter what the tabloid press may claim. This early meeting remained long buried in the archives of Sylvie's selective memory loss, as she was later to acknowledge. In truth the first encounter had been so dire that ever after it had to be jolted back into her recollection. Perhaps it was because, having been invited to lecture at the College, the experience had turned out to be so humiliating for her that she nearly ran away, crushed and defeated by hostility and prejudice.

Until that time her acquaintance with police bigotry had been second hand, and confined to stories told by clients. This time, she was in the middle of it. If anyone had told her at the time, that she would end up marrying a copper, she would have confidently dismissed the idea as fanciful nonsense.

As far as Fizzer was concerned, any meeting with someone who appeared to be a sworn enemy of the police raised many problems, not only because of his job, but because of his own ambivalent feelings about being in the force at all. He felt unsure of the appropriateness of his being in the police, mainly because his family had always opposed it. His mother was a superstitious Irish woman, whose mental state was fuelled by living on paranoia clouding at six hundred metres.

Naturally she had never liked the idea of his becoming a copper. She would have preferred him to be a doctor or a priest, preferably the latter, since it would have made him, what she called 'safe', that is immune from the sexual clutches of designing women seeking her pet lamb's prick. Since she was married to a fellow Irishman who was perfused by the sexual guilt peculiar to his priest-ridden heritage, it would be hard to know how she had dreamt all this up. But Catholic families in Liverpool tend to think and act like that when sober. His brother was a Physician who was well up in the consultant ladder in the NHS. He had made it up and away, out of the poor Catholic scouser role to the achievement of better things and for Jaysus sake, here was Fizzer, in the police. Woe city. The family wouldn't wear that at all and, as a matter of principle, were no help to him.

But he did well in the Merseyside force, and rose quickly. He liked his home town and had an encyclopaedic knowledge of the natural history of its crime and criminals. Liverpool was his manor.

So naturally, Liverpool had assumed a greater significance for Sylvie.

It had to be so, for it had become, by a process of psychological condensation, the place in which they first met, and as such, had acquired an almost magical significance. But there was no magic attached to the Police Staff College, where their previous meeting had been too threatening and plain nasty to be thought about. So she blanked it out, no nonsense for her about repressed memories. She just chose not to remember it. And this is how she was obliged by her experience always to claim that their first meeting had occurred in her home town.

The encounter in Liverpool had been about as unpromising as one could ask for, since it had occurred during the aftermath of a weekend riot in Toxteth, at a time when major disturbances were over, but regular weekend upheavals remained unreported by a grudgingly compliant local Press who had cut a deal with the Merseyside force, by agreeing not to report any disturbance that involved less than a hundred and fifty people.

At the time every Friday evening, groups of two, three, even four policemen and sergeants carrying drawn staves, were to be found on street corners of Smithdown Road, waiting for potential troublemakers. This was at the gates of Toxteth within sight of Sefton General Hospital, the old Toxteth workhouse, separated from the cemetery by a long wall running up from the road. Half way along the wall was a bricked-in doorway, through which, in the past, the workhouse paupers had been carted off to their dishonoured graves.

On the other side of the road there was a line of scruffy buildings, a tacky mixture of newly-built Barratt Homes, boarded-up shops and grim pubs, Chinese fish and chip shops. Dead opposite the hospital gates there was a stark funeral

14

parlour, 'Low Cost Our Aim. Your comfort Our Privilege,' where small kids liked to stand and shout obscenities at the women attending the ante-natal clinic. At the foot of the hill was the gloomy Royal Hotel, gaslights, games room and all. Hardly worth asking why two streets nearby had been barricaded for months. There wasn't a great much else to do, if you were permanently unemployed, and lived in a town hated and despised by the mean-spirited Superbitch from hell who ran the country at the time.

That's how they saw things in Liverpool and that's how things were.

As to the prevailing state of affairs, riots or no riots, no one could say what would happen next. The latest riot had caused worsening of a bad situation on all sides. The Police had come along to cool things down on that hot summer evening, after ten doctors' cars had been vandalised for radios that, when sold, could buy shit downtown. It was a hot evening, and everyone was angry about everything. The police arrived in black cabs, so as to avoid the stones and petrol bombs which were usually thrown, as a matter of honour, at recognisable police vehicles. The discovery of this unconventional mode of transport for the force caused the usual protest from the rent-a-sociologist cadre. For their part the police handled their public relations side with all the diplomatic finesse of a Conservative Member of Parliament found in a whorehouse in a pair of French knickers and a Maggie Thatcher mask. Definitive action was called for, and it happened that Fizzer was in the right place at the right time.

At this stage, Fizzer was already a promising young DI in the Crime Squad, and was therefore a natural choice for the task of meeting Sylvie, the feared political activist, in order to chill her out. 'He's a good looking lad and you never know, she might fancy him,' an anonymous DCI was reputed to have said. It was a more or less genuine attempt to establish some area of common ground during the mean-spirited aftermath of the riot. Chronic insults and anger smouldered and flickered. As it turned out his partial success in this respect was better than anything that anyone had dreamt of hitherto, and more-or-less overnight, he became an expert in chilling people out. From that day on, he was cast in the role of mediator. His success was taken up enthusiastically by his superiors who were only too pleased to find someone who was willing to cope with difficult situations, get trouble off their backs, and, best of all, someone who could be dropped if he screwed up, since he was relatively junior.

With the passage of time he graduated to siege negotiation; here luck was on his side, since his first assignment was to deal with a group of incompetent psychopathic bank robbers, borderline retardates in need of counselling and attendance at schools for people with special needs, e.g., how to rob a bank properly. Next time round it was sharp-witted terrorists, a different proposition, but Fizzer did well once again. But the first foray into negotiating the seemingly impossible, after the Toxteth cock-up, an undramatic opener, was not easy.

For a start he felt that he had been sweet-talked into a task for which he had no particular skills, but his chief had come back with the unanswerable and irrelevant statement that as he, Fizzer, had a Masters in Criminology for which he had studied at the taxpayers' expense at the Liverpool Polytechnic, then surely it was time that the public had some return for their money. All this was said with calculating *gravitas* to the ambitious young police officer. He realised that he had no choice and, that all he could do was go along with what he had been ordered to do, as best he might. When preparing himself he decided that the best plan was to give Ms Woodhouse no chance to put the boot in, but to attack, using any tactic available, even to the extent of acting the helpless male confounded by her brilliance, using appeals for sympathy, any bloody thing to stem a tide of politically correct verbiage that he would find difficult to deflect. At the same time he knew well that it would do no good to talk in the way he carried on during laddish chats with his mates in the police. That would go down like an all-time lead balloon. In any case, he told himself, I'm an educated chap and can hold a rational conversation. And he was. Where's the problem?

So he waded right in, on the first phone conversation with, 'I'm here to tell you that being a copper, is much of the time, about one of the most awful jobs in the world, in case no one had ever told you'.

And all this before Ms Woodhouse had said a word.

And he went on, 'You see your trouble is, people like you, you bang on about stereotypes and prejudice, and the next thing, you know what, you're talking slogans as well as thinking in them,' which was a brisk start, and which was how he meant to continue, but somehow, as he was inexperienced, he lost it, tailed off, and then thought, sod it what's the use, I don't really know what I'm on about, she'll have my card marked in no time there's no point in going on, she's no more likely to listen than anyone else, and he wondered, why should she? Who ever listened to a copper? As far as she was concerned, she was convinced that she was right, all coppers are bastards and over the wall we go. He was unlikely to shift that lot in a hurry. Entrenched? But then so was he, so are most of us, he thought. But he was wrong.

He saw this as soon as she said slightly earnestly but amiably enough, in an appealing telephonic voice, 'In what way the worst job? Don't kid yourself. I don't hear you telling me why it's so awful for Christ's sake. You get good pay, job security and a pension, plus you're a member of an elite that looks after its own, and you can beat the crap out of anyone you like, which is what you seem to like doing anyway, what more do you want? Convince me.' But she laughed as she said it, nonetheless.

Fizzer replied 'OK, I hear what you're saying.' Ordinarily he would have said, try this for bloody size you tiresome bitch, but sensing that he had made some sort of impression, he held his tongue and said 'For a start, it's dangerous and I'm not talking about going knowingly into a house on bloody fire, dangerous, jump you fucker, *jump down into this here blanket what we are holding out here for you,* dangerous, *and you will be all right,* dangerous'. She laughed at this, maybe he could make a point with this bigoted cow, for once in her life. 'I mean dangerous,

17

like breaking down a door in a crack house in some shithole estate at five in the morning, not knowing if you're going to get a sawn-off up your ass, or a chain across your face or what. It's dangerous or nasty, like telling someone their kid's just been found in a bin bag fucked to death by a nutter with her genitals torn to bits and her tits bitten off, bloody dangerous, that's what I mean, Miss clever ass bloody lawyer.'

Jesus I've ruddy blown it this time and, now that I come to think of it, why did I call her bigoted and stuff? Maybe it's me. No doubt about it, she's getting to me. She listened to him and said, 'Now I know why they call you Fizzer.' He paused and thought again about his outburst, and thought, I've played straight into her hands, just like they warned me not to do, and then he sensed that she smiled as she replied, 'Perhaps we should think about telling each other something about ourselves. People do that, you know.' Fizzer thought, Jesus she's a social worker in disguise, hesitated and said, 'Well, since you put it like that, I'd give it a shot.'

It would be convenient to be able to report that, from that moment on they had developed a firm and lasting relationship which was based on mutual respect, on a firm subsoil of caring attitudes, in a setting of trust and regard for the other, but that would be a travesty.

Their relationship was turbulent from the start, since they were both difficult people in their various ways. Fizzer was also an unhappy man. Being on the force doesn't generate happiness. Marital breakdown, too much booze and fags, living on junk food and fry-ups, all these do wonders for one's life.

'Well' she said, 'if it's all that important, I'd be happy to meet you, and discuss the matter, though I have to say that, given the hitherto entrenched attitudes of the Merseyside Police in an affair which has stirred the conscience of the nation, I feel quite strongly that your attitude, and that of your colleagues in the Merseyside Police appears to be extending insensitivity and plain disregard for common humanity to a degree that leaves me practically speechless, to say the least.'

Jesus, we should be so sodding lucky, her speechless, that'll be the bloody day; she's reading this from a prepared statement, it's got to be that. How can any one churn out crap like that with a straight face and she's supposedly intelligent?

'I quite appreciate that,' he replied, thinking, well I would, if you weren't talking a load of pretentious bollocks, 'but it is important that we can hear your people's side of the problem, in a setting of informed neutrality.' Stuff that for a game of soldiers, I can talk crap too, it's dead easy once you get into it. Instantly she became angry 'What do you mean, my people? Is this another racist slur?'

Holy Christ, what's going on here? Is she putting me on or what? Never mind, we've established one thing, she's got a much shorter fuse than I'd have expected, and that's worth knowing. Maybe she's not as invulnerable as they reckon. Keep calm they'd said. Don't let her get to you. It's all a bloody act. If you blow your cool, just remember that she's probably got a bug on the call, so she can get it all down on tape, and on the front page of *The Echo* that night. String the black cow along and get the full S.P.

'Can I take it that then, you'd be agreeable to meet, in a non-professional setting of mutual parity, of a non-discriminatory nature?' he said, still in conciliatory mode, then changing tack he came on a trifle strong with, 'Because, if it's OK with you, I thought, well, I've booked a table for lunch in the restaurant of the St George's Hotel for one fifteen today and we could maybe meet in the bar if that's all right with you, Ms Woodhouse.'

She was so stunned by the speed of his delivery that she agreed.

He parked his car in the grimy underpass below the hotel, and went in via the dungeon-like entrance up ramps that looked like entrances to the world's largest public lavatory. And he thought, it's just like a fortress this place, still perhaps with the likes of her on board, I'll need body armour anyway. He made his way to the lift and wandered into the bar past prints of the docks. He thought, it's true, they really do have special air in places like this, it's not just the music and the funny foody smell which they squirt around in cans every morning, they mix it with something else, air freshener, stale booze and smoke in the air conditioning or something, with sweaty waitress perfume on top.

He looked around, the bar was full of the noonday baggy suit squad, dragging on their Marlboros, all talking away about sales figures and profit margins over their pints of John Smiths and packets of cheese and onion.

Then he spotted her, standing at the window, looking out across to Lime Street Station. She was listening to the buses hissing along the wet road surface as they came up and around the corner toward the station from the tunnel. They had been right by Christ. She was one striking looking person all right. Next thing was that he recognised her as soon as she came into the place. They could have started off by exchanging hostile glances or recognition, but he realised immediately that she didn't remember having met him before. He'd forgotten about her astonishing physical presence. Jesus Christ, don't even have thoughts like that, or she'll read my mind, and carve my dick straight off. Thank you waiter yes I think I'll go for the Carvery, five slices of thinly sliced policeman's dick, medium rare. Be careful right from the off, she's a looker. Don't let that get to you. Remember, that's what they said at the briefing. Forget about her tits and remember, all you have to do is find out where she stands. Don't get into anything, repeat anything, that she can use against you with the Press, anything like that. Just sus her out, and what ever you do, don't touch her or even look at her, too hard, or it'll be date-rape before you can say, are you handy darling? You're not Special Branch, don't get any ideas above your station, and don't offer her a smoke. As if I would sir. No matter what she's said about the police, and she's said a lot, erase it from your mind. Your job is to get yourself on her side or sound as if you want to be totally impartial. Mr Honest DI Nice guy, doing his job, that's you. You are there to find out what she knows about the story. Remember too she's a highly thought of lawyer. Great, he'd said, I'm just the guy for the job. Well they'd said, you've got a Masters in Criminology so where's your problem? She'll respect you and think, hello, at last you might be the decent cop she'd always hoped to meet. Bloody likely thought Fizzer, if she's as bright as they reckon, she'll have picked up on that one.

'My name is Detective Inspector Edwards of Regional Crime,' he said, 'You must be Ms Sylvie Woodhouse.' She smiled coolly, conceded that she was, and that she knew who he was. 'May I offer you a drink?' he said and she accepted a glass of white wine. He wondered if she was putting him on when she asked for it and thought, now I'm the paranoid one here, it comes to us all, sooner or later.

After the drinks had been set down she said, 'Well now Mr Edwards, why don't we cut the crap, I'm told you're the new breed of educated copper that I keep reading about in *The Guardian.*'

She smiled disdainfully at him as he handed the drink to her from the table. Nevertheless, at the same time, he felt comfortable with her, yes that was it, comfortable. 'Though I'd often heard that they existed, I could never really believe it.' She added that, and she wasn't joking either. 'Educated policemen, I mean.'

Straight for the bollocks thought Fizzer as he parried this one easily enough, 'They taught us how to hold our knives and forks properly at the College,' he said, 'you see I did quite well there, me being a scouser and all.'

There was a long pause. 'Ah yes, the Police Staff College, I've heard of it,' she replied, 'That's where they give you lectures on "The Nature of Prejudice and Drugs and related problems in Today's Society" and then, I understand that you all go off and get laid by the domestic staff, when you've sobered up after guest night in the Mess, isn't that it?'

Fizzer wasn't going to be side-tracked by this one, so he said, 'You did your homework didn't you Doctor? I'm surprised that you forgot to mention the seminars we attended on how to bash a poofter after he's given you a blow job, that is before he admits to being a serial killer.'

She smiled, 'I asked for that didn't I; that's what you want me to say isn't it?'

21

He smiled and said, 'That's down to you. All I do is buy the drinks.'

They had been right, he is sharper than the average cop who's been to college, plus he has a sense of humour. Sometimes they're the worst because all the time they make the jokes they're looking for your weak spots. Sod it, don't forget he is a cop though. Why does he keep looking at me like that? Don't say he's trying to, I don't believe it, he is. Next thing he'll be asking me to have dinner in a restaurant where he won't be risking loss of promotion by being seen with a black, if such a restaurant exists. Hang on we're meant to be having lunch, so that can't be right. Now I'm getting paranoid, or is it that I just know that I'm right?

She noticed that he was looking at her and smiling, and then he said, 'You still think I'm trying to chat you up. Please remember that I'm here for a different reason.' She was astonished by this directness, but wasn't prepared to let on, 'I'd heard as much.'

No I'm not going to give an inch to the cheeky sod. It's the way they think that just because they're good looking, that's all that counts, not that it does anyway. That's what pisses me off.

So Fizzer, tiring of this, said 'Look Ms Coploather, could we cut out this shit actually. In case you'd forgotten, we have met before this. At Bramshill you see. Last year. Perhaps you chose to forget it or maybe it's a bad day for you. It certainly is for me so far.'

How dumb can I get, thinking I could get that one past him. After all he is a copper and spends his life amongst liars. I do remember him. He was the one who had been deputed to take me down to dinner on guest night in the college. That's right, and he didn't blink an eyelid when I said, 'You poor sod. You drew the short straw then?' To be fair, he was no worse and no better than anyone else on that occasion.

She had been invited to lecture at the Inspectors' course on 'The Nature of Prejudice,' and, at the end he had proposed the vote of thanks to a chorus of sniggering grown men looking her over, whilst the women gazed at her uncertainly. No doubt they had felt like she did when they were exposed to crap men of this sort and, if it came to that, they were in that state all of the time probably, but they had the added protection provided by white skin. The men leered on at her. You could smell it, mixed lust and hatred; tasty bit of black meat. Cop those knockers Ted. Pffhaugh. They say she fucks like ten men.

Fizzer said, 'Excuse me. Do you suffer from a minor form of epilepsy by any chance? I asked you a question and I'm still getting no answer.' She replied, 'I'm sorry about that, I suppose I should say, well I had a late night and I'm a bit wiped out.' If you believe that copper you'll believe anything, she thought. So he laughed and she noticed that he had an attractive laugh and seemed friendly enough and not quite so guarded as this lot usually do.

No weakness Sylvie. Hold on, this will not do.

'I'm sorry I forgot what was the question,' she said and thought, maybe now I'm being over-sensitive, and I should just sit back and enjoy the ride.

And so their meeting had proceeded.

She listened to his arguments carefully and politely, but at the end of two hours they had reached the impasse that they had expected and it was time to pack up and go.

When he had left, she felt an odd twinge of unexpected anger and, to her indignant surprise, an element of regret. And then she remembered details of the evening of their first meeting, quite clearly. As they had walked into dinner at the college, she had been overwhelmed by the pretentiousness of it all. The officers and their guests emerged from the bar, an oak-panelled room in the Jacobean manor house; she had been amazed at the way in which they were required to line up and walk in solemn procession to the dining hall, and through a walled garden, at that. She was on Fizzer's arm. To give him his due, he seemed to view it all as, at least slightly ridiculous, but he was too loyal to let it show.

It didn't take her long to realise what the pantomime was all about. Here were the Police with their very own Staff College within farting distance of the Army college at Camberley, the

RAF college at Bracknell and the Military Academy at Sandhurst. And all with the object of educating men and women for promotion, in a purpose-designed college, a creditable enough ambition to provide further education for people who had missed out.

But being the English police, it was not public school, nor anything much really, but an institution that sniffed sycophantically around, trying to ape others in every respect. This was something that you couldn't explain to anyone who was unfamiliar with the arcana of the class system. Senior officers spoke of *our sister colleges* down the road. As if anyone cared, the 'sister colleges' particularly. And the dining rituals were the same as in the Army with the loyal toast, 'Mr Vice, The Queen.' and all the rest of the boring crap that preceded dissolution into the public-school idiocies of high-cockalorum, no doubt. When she saw all this, and it was laboriously explained to her, she realised what she might be up against. And all this before she had even brushed up against the canteen culture which she ran into during the remainder of that week.

She still had a lot to learn.

Anyway, that was it, back to the here-and-now and the problem of dealing with him as he looked at her, was he still looking her over? Hard to say, but it seemed like it. She wondered if he was married, as if it mattered. In any case why did she wonder? He looked like the sort who would tell her soon enough, or did he? She noticed that he was not wearing a ring.

The next time that they met was in an Italian restaurant opposite the Trade Union HQ on Hardman Street, just down from Hope Street below the Phil, The Philharmonic Dining Rooms, England's most ornate pub. Fizzer had just come from the Police Station on Hope Street. The restaurant was empty except for Sylvie who had been visiting a client in the Women's Hospital in Faulkner Street.

It was a restaurant that was usually empty except at Christmas and at graduation time, when fledgling graduates lunched with their parents, all decked out in graduation kit and

24

best parental gear, before the degree ceremony in the Philharmonic Hall. Fizzer knew the proprietor, Mario, a solemn looking Italian who spoke Italian with a scouse accent and English with an Italian accent. He was surprised to find anyone there at all, and even more surprised when he saw that it was Sylvie. He liked the place. It made no concessions to the visitor. Bare floorboards, a few Chianti bottles strung here and there, and at the back, a spotless kitchen where Mario's parents continued a lifetime's squabbling and fretting. He said, 'May I join you Ms Woodhouse?' And she said 'Why not?'

And that was their third meeting.

CHAPTER FOUR

MORTUARY

In the chilly mortuary air the two bodies lay on two tables, all around them shone the white enamel tiling and steel guttering, all running into clean hosed hissing drains and the echoing clangour of receiver dishes and instruments. A radio played Capital FM in an office somewhere – Capital Eff Em; the smell of Dettol and Nescafe Gold Blend. Strip lights and big operating room lights on the ceiling. On the wall there hung large scales for weighing the body bits and pieces, and there were plastic bags all folded clean and ready for bits that were to be disposed of, rather than returned to their points of origin. On the tables the scalps had been pulled down ceremoniously like cap brims forward over dead guardsmen's peaked caps pulled straight down over guardsmen's tops of skulls neatly sawn off like the tops sliced off boiled eggs, revealing shiny pink brain tissue below. Chests and abdomens lay sagged and open, rib cages neatly sawn like unrolled crown roasts. Running water and gurgling sounds that made you wonder where they came from, and the farty smell of dead guts. Wet hair hanging down over dead faces.

The Professor of Forensic Pathology was as breezy as they tend to be, and clearly on good form, as he dictated, 'Body one is that of a young well nourished middle-eastern male of about

26

twenty seven. There are about fifty gunshot entry wounds commencing in the maxillo-facial region on the right side and proceeding in linear oblique descending order through the neck, anterior thoracic wall, abdominal wall and left femoral region. I note that in the majority of instances the projectiles have caused extensive soft tissue damage as they tracked from the points of impact. No doubt related to high velocity impact.' A young constable stood staring straight ahead 'All right are you, lad?' said the Coroner's Officer, 'It's his first I reckon,' he said to no one in particular, as he turned to say a ringing, but ambiguously respectful, 'Good Morning Sir,' to DCI Manson who informed anyone who might be listening, that he was sorry he was late, as he nodded to the professor. *I speak to him man to man.*

'The trachea has been severed by projectile wounds and there is extensive damage to pulmonary tissue and a large haemothorax on the right side. There is extensive laceration of the liver consistent with projectile injury and widespread similar damage in the large and small intestine. In the...'

No one was listening, apart from the Coroner's Officer who hung on the words of his favourite forensic pathologist, every now and again smiling around at the members of the group, giving his respectful seal of approval to everything the Great Man was saying, words dropping like stones into a dull pond of inattention.

That would have been one half-second burst from a Heckler and Koch. What was that Ibrahim had said, on the phone, about foot and eye should not lie? What foot? What eye? What the hell was the bloody man on about? He knew what he was on about, well enough. Was this him, Ibrahim, on the table? Yes it was, it had to be. What was this one here, was this his foot, his eye? What was that all about? Nietzsche. The German philosopher, an unread book, another one among many. Perhaps I should get on to it. Rubbish, coppers don't read that sort of stuff, or maybe they should. Maybe I shouldn't be a cop, perhaps I've got it all wrong. Hang on. Maybe I'm stressed-out, or something. Anyway, why the hell do they always call it, stressed- out? What do they mean, stressed out? What's wrong with plain knackered? Or just stressed? Pissed off even? Well set up, by the look of it. Big tool too, still these Arabs did, didn't they? Hang about, show a bit of respect for the dead, after all if the lab techs can, so can I. And then, he thought of one of the first inquests he attended, and how everyone reacted to the evidence given by a green young constable who had found the dead man, hanging in a bedroom. He was asked 'Now tell us constable, did you cut the deceased down immediately?' The young man, eager to please, had replied, 'No Sir.' The astonished Coroner said 'And why was that?' Came the reply, 'Because Sir, he wasn't properly dead at that particular moment.' Funny the way some things stick in the mind.

The Professor droned on, 'and so my conclusion is that death was caused by multiple entry gunshot wounds.' Bloody load of pervs, tin gods, if you ask me. Wouldn't last five minutes in your average nick. Playing at cops and robbers. 'Thanks Prof, as per usual, you did a good one and professional with it, if I may, so to speak, gild the lily as I believe it's called. I note that the aforementioned deceased had a large tool. Hand reared I believe. Old jokes still the best in my humble...' Manson remarked, in all probability unaware that he was being no more crass than usual, and as patronising as ever to the pathologist who, fortunately wasn't listening to him since he was already half an hour late for a meeting at Guy's. It really was a typical post mortem, even down to the pathologist getting his rocks off in the corpse's guts, police gallows-humour and no one listening to anyone.

Fizzer, forcing out an embarrassed laugh, said, 'I wonder which one of these guys is Ibrahim.' More to stop Manson banging on than anything else. Manson wasn't having that, thank you very much, as he lit another cigarette,

'Come on Edwards, I reckon you mean, you wonder which of these two recently deceased heaps of shit was formerly the late chummy on the blower to us then, that one that you were so chatty with. That's what you wonder. What was it then? Fancy him did you? Was that it then? It's all right I was only joking.' The trouble was that he probably seriously thought that he was joking.

Fizzer drew breath, thinking how could anyone be so straight up, bloody awful? For Christ's sake, best to forget it, he's just a tired old copper who's trying to be clever. You'll be one soon enough. We all will. He doesn't mean much harm. It's just the style he's grown up with. Remember that. This man has been at this bloody job for years, probably bloody good at it too, in his day, though you'd never guess, and now he's to the point where he knows that the whole world is either villains or toerags. We all get like it, they reckon. He probably started in Carter Street, dealing with all the toffs from the Old Kent Road and all that lot. It's not Mayfair, none of your gentleman villains to be found in the Walworth Road. Nothing is going to change the likes of him, probably me too, in the end. He's seen the lot, he's burnt out, ausgespielt... Is that it? Whatever you do, always remain calm at all times, that's what they say.

So he held back and said quietly 'Oh no, it's not like that Chief, and you know it. After all I did speak with the man for four days and nights. Or hadn't you noticed?' And then thought, Jesus what a self-righteous prick I must sound.

Manson thought, right, I've got the sod bang to bloody rights; he's as soft as a virgin's cracker, as expected. And they say he's a hard man? Forget it sonny. Getting shirty over nothing. What's wrong with him? Let's try putting the boot in right now. He continued, 'Listen Mr Edwards, I think it's time I got a bit personal here, and I hope you'll take this in the spirit in which it's given.'

I really didn't know people spoke like this, I really didn't thought Fizzer.

'Frankly your sort of copper gets right up my throat, and always has done, in case you didn't know. Too flash by half, that's what you lot are. College education, and all that. Your lot don't have any idea what the real score is, do people like you.' He paused, wondering if he'd gone off too quickly, then carried on anyway, 'Listen, everyone's always going on about how no one has any respect for the Force nowadays. That's a right load of old bollocks in my view. In the old days they never had any respect either, and don't you forget it. I'll tell you what they had, just in case you didn't know.'

Fizzer did know, only too well as it happened, and he could have written Manson's script for him. Next, he'll say he supposes we think he's old-fashioned. And, in case Fizzer ever forgot, Sylvie reminded him about it most days. Home and away, I get it. Funny to think that Manson and Sylvie shared some common ground. Unbelievable, when you thought about it. Other sides of the coin, you could say. Aren't we all?

'Examination of the second body reveals multiple gunshot entry wounds, all on the posterior chest and abdominal wall and on the occipital region of the skull, with exit wounds partially removing the entire maxillo-facial region on the right and left sides,' continued the professor.

Why can't he just say he's had his sodding face blown off from behind and be done with it?

'What was that then Guv? I'm not sure I know what you meant there, for a minute,' said Fizzer. Best to string him along, as if I'd never heard it all before, as if I didn't know, as if none of us knew what was coming, as if he'd just discovered the wheel or something. Why do we coppers persist in repeating ourselves all the time? Is it that we need to reassure ourselves that we're getting it right? But, by now, Mr Manson was getting well into overdrive, there was no holding him.

'I thought as much. Double simple. In the old days, it wasn't respect they had you see, it was fear. Straight bloody unadulterated fear. Right? Anyone who got pulled in for anything, parking offences, pissing in the street, you bloody name it, drunks, any bloody thing, they bloody knew they were in for a good whacking.' He laughed in fond reminiscence. 'We loved the Saturday night pissheads best of all. Everyone got a bloody good whacking. We still had the six foot rule in those days, and we could break all the heads we wanted and we bloody did. Blood on the walls, round the clock. No tapes and no briefs sniffing around. That's what I call thief-taking like it ought to be.'

'Why don't you get it typed up and send it to the *Guardian*, they're always looking for the personal view from the copper on the beat I'm told?' said Fizzer softly. 'I mean I knew about that.' No need to crowd my luck just yet he thought. But for all he knew Manson didn't even mean all that stuff, perhaps he was just whistling in the dark. Wouldn't do to bet on it though.

'It's nothing, I'm just thinking aloud you see.' Manson added. It was obvious he hadn't heard nor listened to a word, and didn't intend to.

It's amazing, I never knew the man could think. I still wish that I knew which one was Ibrahim though. Perhaps Manson is right, maybe I did fancy him. What does it matter? I certainly don't fancy Manson. But then no one does, not even his wife, from what I've heard. Perhaps that's his problem. Or one of them.

And then Manson said, 'And while we're at it, I'd like to see you later, say about twelve in my office. Sort of a second debriefing, you could call it.' Fizzer had endured enough by now and said 'Right chief, I'll be there.' And left quickly. As he was going out the door, Manson called after him, 'Yes and another thing, in my day, a hundred years ago at the Elephant, we didn't have time for ethical policing and bloody workshops on the community, we just bloody got on with it.'

But Fizzer knew well that, for DCI Manson, there was no way he was going to give up and even if Fizzer had said 'Is it true you're having problems at home sir, I mean is that why you seem to have certain concerns and are so fucking pissed off about things?' that it would have counted for nothing. He would have answered politely, saying that he was not aware of being upset, in any way shape or form, a favourite phrase of his, he'd have you know. And then he would have said, perfectly calmly, that now was neither the time nor the place, to discuss matters of a personal nature, and any way it was none of anyone's business, that is, even if there was some problem, not that he was, for a moment, conceding that there might be. He would have then dealt with the enquiry in the same methodical detached way that he would have used in coping with a group of militants demanding to know the truth about the death of a black suspect in police custody. Using exactly the same measured tones and with the same total lack of concern, beyond mildly outraged astonishment, coloured by impatience with anyone who presumed to question the unquestionable. No, there was no point in having too many cosy chats with Mr M., if he could help it. He knew that Manson would never let go. He never let go when he was dealing with a villain, so why should a mere bloody copper be made an exception?

After Manson had finished, Fizzer had felt angry but less so than he'd expected. He was struck by the fact that the man was in far worse shape than he had realised. Being a policeman is bad for the health. Too many coppers look ill or near-ill, tired, pale and pasty-faced for much of the time, he knew that well enough. Most people who have to work hard, look crappy except when they are on holiday. He'd noticed that the only punters who look the picture of health, around the clock, are the Royal Family and the extremely rich. Such people are cleaner than everyone else; their clothes are spotless, rarely wrinkled and never smelly. Fizzer had picked up on that when he'd been on Royal visits, when he'd seen them close to, all pink, clean and well-dressed talking about people who lived in hices. That was it, it was down to the job, it had to be. The harder you work and the less you earn the more ill you get, plus you die sooner, at least, that's what the Chief Medical Officer of the Department of Health had said, and he ought to know.

Not to worry too much though, promotion had to be in the agenda, even Manson couldn't stop that. Sylvie's new appointment; more than a cut above a job, that was something that loomed, something that couldn't be ducked, because it was dodgy. She knew it was dodgy but wouldn't let on. Why?

When she first told him about it he'd tried to act pleased, but there was no way he could be pleased. It wasn't a job, it was something that he'd always feared she could too easily fall into with her background and stuff, a bloody political minefield. Worst of all, she not only knew it, but appeared to be revelling in it. If she took it up she would waltz him straight into the arms of Manson and those around him who wanted to get rid of a copper who was married to a black lawyer, and now they would be unable to believe their luck that she had been selected as the European President of an organisation that every copper believed to be at best a bunch of wets, at worst, a terrorist front. How could she be so dumb?

He had tried asking her, and met with total refusal to acknowledge the possibility of it being even a problem. As far as she was concerned, it was none of his business. If he and his fascist colleagues were unable to see that the Front for the Liberation of Kurdish Women, was an organisation dedicated to freedom and justice for victims of political persecution, and nothing more, that was their problem, not hers. End of discussion. It was as simple as that.

From his point of view, Sylvie had to drop the whole idea, no ifs, no buts. That wasn't going to happen. Any attempt to talk it through, met with flat refusal. He'd not seen her like this before and was unable to handle it. And she'd say that sometimes she wished that she'd never married a copper. And he'd answer that all police wives said that, sooner or later, and that for God's sake, didn't she remember that he had warned her about this. But she would look straight back at him and she'd say, 'But,these police wives, they aren't a black married to a white.' And one thing would lead to another, and there'd be a fight. Unanswerable, when you thought about it. And the more he thought about it, the worse it all became. It was the sort of problem that would be reinforced by the, not-so-well-intentioned, comments of friends. If there was one thing he couldn't stand it was those smiling uninvited comments about the durability of their marriage, usually from those who should have known better. It was bad enough having to deal with prurient, poorly-disguised enquiries about the supposedly exotic nature of, what it's like to have sex with a black woman. But these could be handled, as opposed to the tolerant voices, the half-apologetic smiles and the 'caring', knowing sentiments associated with the production of nuggets such as, 'Amazing really, when you come to think of it, if you don't mind me saying so, you know, there being no problems in, well, you know being married to...' and he'd say 'You mean you can't understand how I've stayed married to a black woman, and remained in the Police?' and then, they would come on with the, 'You can tell me all about it, I'll understand,' bit that made the stomach churn. And it wasn't just the more entrenched colleagues in the police either, as he'd said to other friends in moments of ire. It could be anyone. He learned soon enough that liberalism and tolerance slip away when drink takes effect and lets people say, 'Well, after all this time you must know what's it really been like. You can tell me? I'm a good listener.' He supposed that they wanted him to reply, 'of course there are problems in any marriage that crosses cultural lines, but nothing's insoluble.' But as soon as you start, their eyes glaze over, and the listening ends. You aren't telling them what they want to hear, something that will confirm their expectations of what they hope to hear. They want to hear that you're in shit, and they fall back on understanding smiles that are meant to say, 'I really understand. You can't tell me. One day you will. Poor you, I, we that is, we understand.' Jesus. In the early days, he could hack it well enough, but if things should ever go really sour with Sylvie, it would be different, and he knew that was something he could never bear. She knew him better than anyone. She could pick up on dialogue from the other side of the room. Just as she could spot him glancing at another woman from four hundred yards. And say 'I suppose they were asking you what a piece of good black ass is like,' and laugh. But that was in the days before the Front. And she wouldn't change her mind about the Front.

What the hell does Manson really want to see me about?

As he walked to the door of the mortuary, the coroner's officer looked up to say goodbye and said, 'Funny thing that, one of those two punters back there, the one... you know... well, I couldn't help laughing in a way, know what I mean? Reminded me a bit of your good self, no offence intended.'

CHAPTER FIVE

VAUXHALL

Among the architectural sights of London, the concrete ziggurat of Vauxhall Cross should get a special award for Vaubanesque flakiness. Its postal address is P.O. Box 1300, and the police call it, 'The Box,' which is as good a name as any. Its central features look as if they have been cloned from Senate House in Bloomsbury, and plonked on top of the De la Warre Pavilion, after which the architects, having run out of E's, left it to a young lad, temporarily employed on work experience in Costain's Head Office.

Here squats the temple of furtive bureaucracy, and big boys' games-playing, a heavy-arsed monument to the seedy funkiness of the secret world; always striving for unattainable cool. A world that is about as uncool as the *Daily Mail*, and you don't get much uncooler than that. It is respectable however, that is beyond question, even though its respectability is said to have been dented by the discovery of a drunken Irish meths drinker, who was found, sodden reeking trousers and all, sleeping it off in the main lobby, on the morning of its official handover to the nation. Remain calm however, British Intelligence guarantees that we will never knowingly be undersold. Not only that, but responses to an encoded advertisement in *The Guardian* will be treated in the strictest confidence, and remember, don't tell your friends that you were up for a job creation scheme which gives sheltered employment to the otherwise unemployable.

Perhaps this is a good reason to wonder whether it is likely that, one day someone might mount a mortar on a truck and, having parked it on the north side of the river in the early hours of the morning, lob a cluster of bombs into the MI6 headquarters on the south side of the bridge. Such an appalling act of urban terrorism might comfort those who think that the grisly pile, a vulgar outgrowth of Thatcherite delusions of post-imperial grandeur, has little relevance to the security of a nation that could conceivably be duffed up by Israel, perish the treasonous thought. Provided that it was empty and that no injury nor loss of life occurred, its destruction could enrich the aesthetic life of the Capital, save money for the taxpayer and do a favour to anyone who remembers the Thames-side skyline before it became a tacky monument to the fuck-you-I'm-rich brigade.

This was the unlikely scenario that was running through the mind of Mr Francis X Sarno on a Monday morning exactly one week after the siege had been terminated. It was a bright enough morning, but not at all bright enough, as far as he was concerned. He sat peevishly in one of the most prestigious offices, which was frequently called the Philby suite by some of the more seditious employees. Despite the upgrading of the Secret World from tweedy games-playing and silly-clever Oxbridge jokeyness, it must have been reassuring to note the preservation of the rigid allocation of Office furnishings as laid down in cast-iron Civil Service schedules. Bare floors at one end of the scale, hat stands in the middle, and Japanese prints at the other. But everywhere the walls bore the Civil Service notice boards, dealing with sick leave, holiday facilities and social clubs, just like the BBC.

Sarno sipped at his cup of Lapsang and snapped at a biscuit like an angry turtle. At that moment he was so ratty that he would have welcomed any treasonable suggestion for the future disposition of a building that he despised, that is if you can despise a building. And who might this oddly named person be ?

F X Sarno could have been described as the eccentric doyen of an elite anti-terrorist cadre, and that would have been that. But this would have sold him short; he was a shade too complicated a person for such a simplistic biopic, let alone job description. The Francis X Sarnos of this world do not need job descriptions, they are above them. He was simply a man with a keenly developed appreciation of the ridiculous who had talked himself into the centre of things, and who was able to stay there fulfilling his role, even though no one quite knew why he was there in the first place. In this respect he was a good example of the person who has acquired a place in a large institution by manipulating the system to their own advantage, so that no one knows why they are there, and everyone assumes that it is somehow all right, because someone in another department is reputed to have said so at a meeting which was unminuted, and a matter for congratulations all round for having displayed excellent judgement in selecting someone who is clearly and indisputably, 'one of us.' In Sarno's case, entirely wrong, as he wasn't one of anyone's. This happens more frequently than people care to admit, in fact the best examples are found in the armed services where Senior Non-Commissioned Officers have been known to inhabit offices for years without working, until the day of retirement, and no one knows they are there or why. They usually do no harm, and play a good game of brag.

F X Sarno was in a much bigger league however. For instance he knew a great deal about *zeitgeists*, Postmodernism, Noam Chomsky, Comparative theology and the history of every subversive organisation that had ever existed, plus inside his head there was a database of names and addresses of the people involved going back over forty years. Not only that, he was a card carrying minimalist with little time for expensive clothes, cars and materialist baggage. He was a humorous man, and had a tendency to overdose on irony now and again. He was a pragmatist who discharged his duties to his line of command with commendable style and *brio*, but he was able to view the whole thing with a detachment that raised the collective blood pressure of his senior colleagues, leaving his cohorts in a permanent state of slightly baffled wonderment. Which is what he liked to do. His place in the administrative structure covered international counter-terrorism, and Irish and other domestic terrorism. He was definitely an unusual person. His origins were obscure, inviting puzzled discussion and speculation. How had he got where he was, that was the question? A question that is not confined to his particular world. He didn't seem to fit into anyone's stereotypes, all of which were way out in left field, as he would never have dreamt of saying. Some claimed that he had previously held high rank in one of the services, but could be no more specific beyond such a vague assertion. Others had wilder ideas, and spoke darkly of connections with the CIA, but even they couldn't be certain. Certain unusual details were spoken of. Some said that he was an excellent baritone sax player, and insisted that he had once sat in with Stan Getz, at the Blue Note. Hardly an obvious qualification for the job in hand. He was a curious mixture of the secretive and the flamboyant, a polymath and something of an intellectual snob, a Gore Vidal of the secret world, who knew shit from shinola and didn't care who knew it. One smart cookie, one of his most important assets was his empathy with and knowledge of Israeli intelligence which, characteristically, he respected above all others, because of its toughness, dedication and possession of a level of power unknown in most democracies.

His Chief Assistant, Ted Blunger, was a former avionics whiz kid, a graduate of Halton and Cranwell, who had, in his spare time, made it as far as the world poker finals in Las Vegas, where his ultimate defeat at the hands of Jed Larsen of MIT in a sixteen hour game of Hold 'Em, is spoken of to this day among the cognoscenti that patronise the smoke-filled world of burgers, chocolate fudge cake, shakes and dyspepsia.

This interesting and unlikely duo were having their mid morning meeting, the first of the week. As usual Blunger sat and waited for Sarno to start. Sarno put down his copy of *The Tablet*. 'I see that the woollies are in trouble again,' he said quietly to a Lucien Freud on the wall. Sarno was quite well off and liked to show off his arty farty treasures, mainly to infuriate people. No one knew exactly why he read *The Tablet* either, but that is no big deal since no one knows why, or indeed if anyone, reads its constipated pages anyway.

Jesus Christ, thought Ted, I know it, this means he's going to start straight in on his favourite diatribe about the uniformed branch or something, first thing on a Monday morning too. God give me bloody strength. He said nothing as Sarno continued, 'Come Teddy, don't be such a slyboots.' Christ, now he's doing his camp act as well, I can't bear it, thought Ted, as he replied 'I don't know what you're saying Frank. Too early for me. Why do you have to talk like that?' Ignoring him, Sarno continued, 'You know perfectly well what I'm saying. The papers are full of it, and it's been on the Telly all week, quite apart from our watching it together over the monitors. I don't see why you have to be so bloody coy. You know that I'm referring to the siege at the fucking embassy, and it barely a week gone.'

'So, what's new about that?', and he longed to add, there's no need to be so foul-mouthed, you public school ponce, but let him continue, 'That's more like it. Well the question is what are we going to do about this man Edwards?' said Sarno, as cool as you like.

'I'm not reading you.' Christ I know what's coming. He can't be serious. Maybe he fancies him,' he thought desperately, yes perhaps that's it. At last he's going to reveal himself about something, anything, we can pin him down to, for once in his life. But he realised that there was little likelihood of that.

'I don't know what you mean,' he paused 'and in any case how do you mean in trouble? What trouble? They only raised the siege. That can't be trouble surely, and what's Edwards got to do with it once it's over?'

What's the use, don't tell me, here we go, he's going to drag us into it somehow. Sarno continued 'One could say much

more, but I have to repeat that the person, Fizzer is of interest.'
At this Blunger said irritably 'Well you would, you always had
a soft spot for the working classes. Like rough trade, do we, is
that it?' Sarno hummed a few bars of Harrison Birtwhistle, who
else? He knew that Blunger was merely showing his irritability
here, it being a Monday morning. And so he continued, 'Sticks
and stones; don't crowd your luck sonny, keep it for your
leprous associates at the Colony Club where, if my information
is right, you may need it in the barren days that lie ahead. I hear
you dropped a bundle two nights ago.' There was a pause
while calm returned and he went on. Ted Blunger was not a bad
loser, but he had taken a beating at blackjack, it was true, and
needed no reminder.

'Blunger, I believe that you're trying to irritate me. You
know perfectly well that Edwards has been, so to speak, on the
tip of everyone's tongue since the bloody siege ended.' He
paused.

'Every time one turns on the Telly, he's spoken of as being
the siege negotiator of the century, and I therefore feel that he
should be of interest to our people; for a start he's not gay and
that's a novelty as far as they're concerned. Also he's not a
sodding dummy. He did that last one very well. He's too good
for the collar feelers. Most important of all, I have something in
mind for him that he will carry off perfectly.'

I knew it, thought Blunger, he's losing his marbles, that's
what it is. He often wondered if he took funny chemicals, now
and again, but he knew that it was not the case. The chemical
hadn't been invented that would unhinge Sarno, worse luck.
Maybe he just has straightforward delusions, next thing he'll be
hearing voices telling him he's the greatest, that's it. But he
knew that wasn't like that at all. Behind the intellectual drag
queen act Sarno was too sharp, he was merely testing the water.

'All right Chief, supposing you're right,' he said
cautiously. Good, thought Sarno, I've convinced the ruddy
radar lab tech, I know it, he called me Chief, that's always a
good sign, 'I usually am.' He continued, 'In any case his
antecedents are irrelevant. He's a bright lad, we need him

40

sooner than I had thought. A high flyer too, originally from Merseyside, and I gather, not too popular with his immediate senior, a spiteful little baggage called Manson. He has a natural gift for negotiating hostage situations as the illiterates call them. And I think that he deserves better than spending the rest of his life releasing shitty-panted tourists from charter flights to the Maldives so that they can return to the care of their loved ones in Rochdale.' Blunger interjected, 'not the Maldives, they don't allow tourists there, it's strictly lardies only,' Sarno ignored him, and continued, 'And that's why I want him. Also he interests me because of his personal life, which is more important. He has one unusual characteristic in that respect, for an officer in the anti-terrorist shower, that is.'

'And what might that be?' asked Blunger. 'For a start, I gather he's not on the bloody square, it can't be that surely.'

'His wife is an Afro-Caribbean of unruly temperament and I'm told, an arresting physical presence. She's a non-smoker and, amazingly, she has never suffered from an eating disorder, I'll have you know, and she's a highly thought of lawyer to boot.'

'Jesus' said Blunger 'now you're talking. A lawyer, I bet Manson loves that last one, the ethnic bit. I bet they all do.'

Ignoring him, Sarno continued 'I have no doubt that this latest stroke will have Mr Manson green with envy, him being a tad on the maritally-dysfunctional side, as I learn. That's why I think we should try and buy him out. Unfortunately for us, he's an angry unpredictable fellow at times, and that could be a problem. Did you catch him going on at Manson last week on TV, and did you lamp his face at the Press conference? I thought, heavens above, those two will tear each others' eyes out in no time. We'll need to calm him down a bit if he's to be of use to us.'

Jesus thought Blunger, how do I bear all this crap? It's like a comedy thriller without the comedy.

'Easily said Chiefy, but the Met don't care for spooks like us, you know that, and why should Edwards be any different?'

'For God's sake Blunger, the Mansons of this world and the

Edwards for that matter, don't like anyone or anything, and aren't interested in anything much beyond their ingravescent pensions. But there might be a way. We should put a tap on Edwards' phone for a start. Find out if he has any other weaknesses we could use before he joins the club.'

'Its already done, we put one on two days ago.' Blunger replied, 'to be on the safe side. Anything else while we're at it?' he paused, 'He's as clean as a whistle apart from a young woman here and there, and one or two police groupies hovering.'

Sarno thought for a while and said, 'Well yes, you could call his department and find out if he's accepted my invitation. You see, I've invited him to come over here for a chat.' he said, smiling contentedly. 'This morning.'

'This morning? Isn't that a bit previous?' said Blunger.

'I think not. The man is in trouble with his wife, mainly on account of a disagreement over her new job, a job which will embarrass Mr Fizzer, then there is the matter of an abortive mesalliance with a blonde policewoman at a party the night the siege broke. This has been relayed to his wife. I took care of that, and finally there is his chief who has always wanted his bum in a sling. So, he might be pleased to hear about my ideas for the advancement of his career and, may I add, the enlargement of our interest.'

Now he's on to the pompous bit thought Blunger, Christ this means he really is serious. 'What did you have in mind?' he asked, as casually as possible.

'Simply that we ask him to do us a favour, in return for which we get him off the hook with the oaf Manson, and earn his undying loyalty. And who knows we may save his marriage. Thereafter, he is our property. We need some new blood in the place, wouldn't you agree?' Blunger pretended to think about that and said solemnly, 'Some people might comment that what you're really doing here is something that you've tried before but never pulled off.' Sarno nodded 'Careful Mr B.'

Blunger continued,' They might say that this was just a

personal game on your part. It's called manipulating people for your own ends, I believe.'

Sarno replied, 'I choose to ignore your tasty nuggets of homely wisdom from the *Readers Digest* school of personal psychology, thank you very much, and prefer to point out to you that he is probably on his way up here at this moment.'

'Well, that's bloody great, that is,' said Ted, 'I mean we can't totally ignore departmental procedures regarding supernumerary recruitment and its impact on fiscal rationalisation. There's been a spate of memos about it...' but he trailed off as the door opened and Fizzer came steaming in, ready it appeared, to fight the house.

It was obvious that DI Edwards was not best pleased as he stood just inside the door and looked around as if he was inspecting a blocked sewer. He looked the two of them over and said coldly,' Right which of you two gentlemen is F X Sarno?' Ted Blunger looked as if he was ready to make a matching retort but, before he could start, Fizzer cut back in with, 'OK, so it's not you. Then it has to be you, as if I didn't know. And before I start, and you can minute this, tape it, do what you like with it, as long as you hear it and remember it, and it's this. I don't have too much time for you lot as it happens. I'm a policeman, a thieftaker. That's it. Don't forget.'

'Perhaps,' said Sarno, 'Inspector Edwards, you'd care to join us for some coffee, or would you prefer tea?' If Fizzer was at all disarmed by this, he gave no hint, but agreed to come in and join in the fun, as Sarno afterwards described the incident.

'I'm not proposing to waste my time here exchanging epigrams with your lot,' said Fizzer calmly 'You people probably think that I'm just another woolly, another plod thicko, come along to get the piss taken. Be warned,' and added, 'I'd like to know what's going on. Who do you people think you are anyway? Your people have been after me for over a week. You've had four pavement artists on my back for the last forty eight hours, my phone's tapped; it can't be the Special Branch they're too busy chasing Micks, so it has to be you. Am I right? Plus I'm confident that if certain people get to hear about your people persecuting a member of the anti-terrorist squad, your lot could be in the shit. No one's invulnerable, you know.'

Despite Fizzer's anger, his words made sense. His story of being under surveillance, coupled with the fact that he had picked up that it was some extracurricular activity by Sarno, when relayed to Sarno's superiors, could be embarrassing, since Fizzer's department was the flavour of the month at the moment. It just wouldn't cut the mustard. Sarno knew this well enough, but was unconcerned; as far as he was concerned it merely added more *pazazz* to the whole thing. So he sidestepped into his haughty high church voice, 'You can stop that Mr Crosspatch Edwards. None of your high and mighty ways here, if you please.'

Jesus thought Blunger, watch it Chiefy, this guy is major league, he's liable to tear your head off. Sarno went on, 'You aren't dealing with a shower of bloody paddies from the RUC, you know. We'll sit down and talk shall we? There's no need to be so hot-headed. You surprise me. An excellent track record in dealing with explosive situations all over the place and you come in here like something out of Pulp Fiction. What's the matter with you? I can see why they call you Fizzer.'

Christ, thought Blunger, comparing him to Pulp Fiction, that's going it a bit, even for Sarno, next thing he'll be calling him Squire. But Sarno was not to be deterred, he knew that already Fizzer was interested. He looked interested, that was the point.

'After all,' as he said later, 'it isn't often a poor fellow like that gets a chance to talk to anyone with half a brain, now is it?' And he continued, 'Shall we, perhaps discuss what I have in mind for you, and, more important, why? I have the impression that you need a change of direction. The details are no concern of mine. Maybe a change of scene might do you good. Had you thought of that?'

At this stage Blunger was thinking, what is he up to this time? Going to buy him a birthday present are we?

Fizzer replied, almost meekly, 'Well that's what I had

wondered about. You see the way things are, perhaps I need to get away.' Blunger started, what a damn stupid thing to say, trying to play the I'm the, evening all, simple copper on the beat, act. Sarno will eat him without salt at this rate. But Sarno merely went on, innocent as you please and said 'How nice, wouldn't you agree Blunger? Not exactly getting away, in that sense, Mr Edwards. We have something more interesting in mind for you. First of all, Blunger why don't you lower the screen and we can show Mr Edwards the film.'

As the lights dimmed he thought, Jesus the old man is in one of his piss-taking moods. I hope he isn't going to freak out and give us one of his Monday morning porn movies, and remembered the time when Sarno arranged for one to be screened at a key presentation to a group of CIA visitors. A diplomatic incident had been averted on that occasion.

They watched the film in silence. As the lights came up, Sarno said, to no one in particular,' Well Mr Edwards and what did you think of that?' If he expected an angry reply from Fizzer he was to be disappointed, for he replied, 'Which one? The first one or the second?' Jesus he's cool, thought Blunger. He's just seen a movie of his wife, as one might say, in the company of one of his mates, and he doesn't even bat an eyelid.

Sarno said 'Well I thought the first one might do for a for a start.' Fizzer replied 'Well I thought everyone knew that chummy on camera had a few question marks hanging over him. And so I'm not surprised, I'd always had the idea that the man was a villain, even if he is what he is, I suppose your lot would call him "a Senior Treasury Official in line for higher echelons." The word we had, was that he was into kiddie porn. But all right, so it's cocaine as well. What's the difference? Someone has got his card marked and he's going to buy out, is that it?' Sarno nodded. Of course he's going to buy out, you stupid woolly, thought Sarno, as he smiled agreement and then said. 'What else would one expect? But there's more to it than that. This is where we might need your help.'

'In the first place this man is over-involved with a Middle Eastern Power. His activities could embarrass our allies, such as they are, and ourselves, particularly in regard to the Israelis. Good connections or not, the tiresome little man has been selling us out, and using his impeccable credentials for cover, we all know where. He mixes with unsavoury people, and this won't do. He is off to Rome and will need to be followed and diverted or retained. You take my point. I can't go further than that. What do you say to that?'

Fizzer laughed, 'This isn't in my manor, and you know it. This sort of thing isn't for the Met. Most people would say it's a straightforward drug bust. Maybe it's for the US Narcs. I'm a cop, not a spook, remember that Mr Sarno. And no one's going to get me to do a spook's work. I don't like spooks as it happens.' Unruffled, Sarno, changed direction, 'No one said anything about you becoming a spook. We want you to deal with a delinquent Old Etonian whose taste for young lads, acquired at that benighted place, has become an embarrassment to us. More important, he happens to be a VIP whose meddling in matters that don't concern him has to be curtailed.' He paused, and suddenly said, 'But you never said anything about the other news item we screened?'

'You've got someone there who looks like my wife, with someone that could be Dave. Everyone knows Dave likes black women,' said Fizzer icily.

'I do too, in case you hadn't noticed.'

'Perhaps you should choose your friends more carefully' said Sarno softly. Fizzer ignored this. 'What's the use? What should I say after seeing a movie of my wife, apparently getting stiffed by one of my mates? You buggers have a great life don't you? You must think I'm bloody thick.'

'Not quite. What a sensible young man you are. You picked up on the fact that the film is a contrivance. But you are wrong about the man, chummy, as you call him. As he's a Brit, he's on our turf and we've had enough of him. For obvious reasons, it's important that our department doesn't get involved in case it blows anyone's cover. He is a government favourite. They love him.'

Fizzer cut in. 'I don't give a toss if he's Clare Short's

toyboy. Favourite nonce more likely. You lot specialise in that, don't you?'

Sarno smiled and went on, 'Ah, a homophobe too, how predictable. Never mind, I'd like you to think it over. Private enterprise would then triumph again, one might say. Could do you a lot of good. And stop worrying about your wife so much. You're not exactly a fucking saint Mr Edwards.'

Fizzer brushed that aside and said 'I think it's time you came to the point. You could tell me what you want. It's not just a question of me stopping some old ass-bandit on the run. So far it sounds like a job for any competent copper. Why me? Unless, that is, for some reason I don't have too much choice.' Sarno replied, 'You don't actually have any. I think all we need now is to discuss the details.'

'And what am I meant to understand by that?'

'It's all down to your wife, Mr Edwards, you see. Do I have to spell it out? I think not. Her future plans are of interest and, as you know, apart from their intrinsic lack of good judgement, they are not likely to enhance your career prospects. I imagine that your superior Mr Manson will not be best pleased about her proposed change in direction. I refer to the Front and Mrs Edward's recruitment to its committee of management or what ever it's called.'

Fizzer thought, and unsmiling, said, 'In that case Mr Sarno, as to the details; the details perhaps, you'd better tell me about them. I'll have to shoot for that Guv.'

'How wise. Here, Inspector Edwards, is the pitch. It is, as you might say, "double handy". I want you to join Sir Jocelyn on the flight to Rome. If you can find out what he has planned in Rome, so much the better. The main thing is that he comes to a full stop. And by the way, he will have people with him.'

'Mr Sarno, I'm a copper, not a killer.'

'Then you'll have to overcome your squeamishness I fancy. It's your job that's on the line, Mr Edwards, not mine.'

'These people with him. Foreign Office gorillas I suppose?'

Sarno replied, 'Good. I'm glad you changed your mind. They don't have gorillas. No, just unofficial minders, provided by his unsavoury associates. You see, that is the sort of company he keeps these days, another reason for losing him. As to other details, Mr Blunger will give you the paperwork. Passport, in the name Edward Robinson, Architect travelling to Islamabad to consult on the building of a new Teaching Hospital, funded by the Pakistani cricketer with ideas above his station. It doesn't matter what you do or where you go, as long as you don't lose him. If possible, find out about the Rome connection. Mr Manson will continue to believe that you have gone on holiday. He will receive a message from you confirming your presence on a Jules Verne trip, down the Rhine, in one of those ghastly boats, with your wife. You'll need to square that with her, or better still, leave it to our people, they love secrets. It might help if she went with a friend, if the worst came to the worst. Your flight departs, London Heathrow one week tomorrow at 1600. The flight should leave at 1300 but it will be held up. You should make arrangements soonest and whatever you do, please don't screw up. You have a week to get ready.'

Fizzer replied 'I won't screw up, and by the way Mr Sarno, don't you screw up either or I'll have your bollocks for a necktie, before you know it, you may depend on that.'

'And you won't be telling anyone about this.'

Sarno said this so innocently, it wouldn't have fooled a boy scout. But that's why he had said it like that, thought Fizzer. What was this guy really on, that was the question? He thinks I'm a fool, hold on, he thinks all coppers are fools, not just me, so where's the problem? He replied, straight in the eye, no messing, giving him the – yes, by Jove, public school ex-Sandhurst bit – you-may-rely-upon-me-at-all-costs, Sir – look,' Of course, that's perfectly understood Sir.' He near enough said, Never fear, I'll never crack, no matter what they do to me. But he looked as if he might. Impressive.

Good, this bloody man is taking the piss, thought Sarno. That's a point in his favour.

Just as he was about to go through the door, Sarno said,' Inspector Edwards I'd like to ask you one question. Are you happy in your work? It appears that your wife isn't, from what I hear.'

Fizzer turned and replied, 'Foot and eye should not lie...', and he walked out.

And he turned and said 'You know something, about you lot, you're all fucking mad you are.'

Sarno looked pleased with the way things had gone, and said, 'Well thank God he's out of the way for the moment. A hard man is Mr Edwards, harder I'd guess, than his acts of bad temper pretend, and he could be a difficult person. I'm pleased we got him Blunger. He can think on his feet, appears to be totally unafraid, and he will do the job for us. I'm sure of that. Heavens, it is nearly lunch time, hunger alert! I feel that we need a collation, nothing elaborate though, we are not decadent sybarites as yet. But for the moment a bottle of something at Connie's place and a morsel. You will join me?' Blunger nodded, 'Anything you say Chief, you know that. What's Connie's place for God's sake? I can never follow you.'

I don't know why I said that, he thought, I know perfectly well, it's just that I want to break into the cycle somehow, some day. Perhaps one day we could just go down the pub, like everyone else.

Sarno sighed, 'You are so bloody predictable, and that could cost you know. The Connaught of course. Good food never hurt anyone, though the clientele is as dull as ditch water. We can have a bottle of Krug to celebrate.'

Jesus he must be crazy, 'bleeding Christ what do I say to that?' asked Blunger.

Sarno paused and said 'Perhaps you could start with thank you?'

He paused, 'Blunger, after we've enjoyed our lunch, you will make sure that we set up a meeting with Mrs Sylvie Edwards after her husband has gone away. I need to talk with her you know, I mean we don't really want her going off on a boat trip on the bloody Rhine. Though from what I hear she is not the most likely person in the world to do anything that we might suggest.

CHAPTER SIX

LET'S DO LUNCH

Manson was unsettled and uneasy. He had come down from the shared high that had followed the end of the siege, and now, here he was, fartarsing around in his office fretfully pretending to look at files, faxes and memos, highlighting unread paragraphs and examining paperclips. What to do next? He gave up, and looked out of the window at the river. He was waiting for Fizzer; he was sweaty and he felt out of sorts, his mouth was dry, and his pulse raced with anger or, it might have been apprehension. He was sure that it was more than likely that if Ulrika Jonnson had walked in bollock naked, he couldn't have got a hard on in a thousand years. He'd always liked Gladiators, if it came to that. Good decent family entertainment, healthy stuff and of a manly nature and nothing poofy, thank God. Sod it, he was not looking forward to this interview with any relish. Not that he was afraid of the likes of your Edwards, it was just that he was feeling a shade below par, what with everything, but it was important to settle things with the scouse git once and for all. He needed to straighten things out with him, but knew it would be hard going. He stood pensively with a cup of coffee in one hand, looking intently at the cigarette smouldering in the ashtray on the window ledge. He picked it up and put it in his lips, as carefully as an asthmatic using a Ventolin inhaler, sucked the end, inhaled deeply and blew the exhaled smoke on to the tip, all the while carefully watching the end redden and glow. Another smoking ritual successfully completed, thank God. He often did that, it made him feel better, for some unaccountable reason. But perhaps they were right, he really ought to try and give it up. These bloody quacks nowadays, they thought they knew everything, it was all a load of balls really. After all, you have to die of something, but those heavy feelings in the chest of a morning, well it was the crap food in the canteen, more likely than not. That's probably why it went up into his neck sometimes. All those chemicals they put in the food these days.

On the other side of the office door, he could hear the chat, snatches of laughter, the bustling activity of the rest of them, but his rank protected him from all that rubbish, thank God. They could clack away on their word processors, piss around with their websites, and chatter on the bloody phones till Kingdom come, without disturbing him, thank Christ. Jesus, but he could do with a drink. Maybe a good stiff Smirnoff from the bottle in the drawer, just before Edwards arrived. That should do the trick. Just the one mind you. More to settle his upset stomach, if the truth were known. Irritable bowel syndrome, whatever that might be, the quack had called it. What did they know? A good belt of vodka would settle it in no time, bloody sight better than those Valiums the wife was on. In any case, the sun was over the yardarm, or was it under? What a good idea, I'm glad I remembered, he thought, as he pulled out the bottle, filled a pint cup with ice, poured in a third of the bottle, topped it up with orange, and got it down his neck, all in one, just like that. That felt good. Warm inside and a rush of relief. Not a trace of shakes in the old hands now. Look at that, steady as a bloody rock. The old Vodka really hit the spot, when you needed it.

When you thought it through, it was dead obvious, this meeting with Edwards would be a doddle. In any case, stuff it, there was too much communication nowadays. Edwards was late as per. Typical. And there again, to be fair, he had to admit, most of the chaps liked him, scouse or not, and the women bloody lapped him up by all accounts. Perhaps he'd had, what was it, a rush to judgement, that's what the DCC was always on about these days, not making rushes to judgement. All part of sharpening the corporate image of the force, and quantifying decision-making at an executive level. Jesus Henry Christ, what had the bloody Met come to? Nice morning and here I am stuck in the bloody office. Killing time, doing what? The river looked really good this morning though. There was even a stern-wheeled steamboat, motor driven, of course, for the tourists. It looked pretty in the sun there, for a moment, like things used to. A helicopter flew overhead, riverboats moved slowly up and down the river. It was sunny; he could see the light dancing off the water, and it reminded him of holidays and that, at Bognor Regis in the old days before Margaret started having her headaches and the lad had gone away. In the Embankment gardens he could hear one of those tinkling Malaysian bands playing, or were they Bali?

Outside, it all seemed more like a holiday really. Everyone in the world was having a good time except him; he'd begin to feel like that sometimes. He was convinced of that. He didn't want to go to the bloody party tonight, that was another pain in the ass, plus having to endure seeing Fizzer getting the conquering hero treatment, with all those WPC's sniffing round his balls. Bloody load of groupies in a way, in a manner of speaking. And there again, after the words in the mortuary, he had felt angry, even a bit ashamed of himself, still did, up to a point, though he wondered if he could ever be freed from the sort of resentment, yes that was it, the man caused him. Anyone would think he almost fancied him; that's what that cheeky sod Dave had said, more of a joke amongst good mates mind you, but it had hurt at the time. What a bloody nerve some of these youngsters had. But it was hard to get rid of the idea that Fizzer might go on getting the better of him. Why did he dislike him so much? It wasn't just the educated bit, he could handle that. Coppers with a good education, they were two a penny these days, and would probably take the force over, sooner or later. Good luck to them; his job was secure, his retirement and pension were well within his sights; everything should be all right. All he had to do, was coast along for another eighteen months. But, at the heel of the hunt, he could never handle it; why should he? The man had gotten to him from the day he first joined the Met; say no more Squire.

Fizzer had come from the Merseyside Force with excellent reports and a perfect track record. People at all levels seemed to like him. In theory he was the ideal man to have on the squad, but there it was, he just didn't like him. Somehow he was a bit too good to be true, knew too much for his own good. Soft on drugs and full of poncey ideas that made the blood boil, but there were quite a few around like that nowadays, you got used to that. Most of the new recruits had smoked dope at least once, for God's sake, so there had to be more to it. Edwards had never mucked in with the other lads, stand-offish attitude with it, as if he was above the rest of us, like when he was asked if he'd join in the snooker, and sporting activities and all. He just said he wasn't really interested, didn't want to mix much with the lads, never had. That sort of thing gets noticed. And, as for his bloody wife, what could you say? A ruddy brief, for Christ's sake. Nothing against coloured people or anything like that, but after all, it is our country, not theirs and never will be. No point in going over all that. No one really understands. If you do say anything people get the wrong idea half the time, and call you a bigot or a racist, or something like that, when all you're doing is facing facts. People are different, chalk and cheese.

Then, unaccountably, he found himself flushing. He remembered something that might have a bearing on it; a recent exchange with his wife after yet another mess up in bed. Well, they'd been like that for years, hadn't they? It wasn't that simple, anyway, all this fuss about sex was a load of rubbish, and when he'd tried to do his business, she had said, 'Why don't we just call it a day Jack, you never were much good at it anyway,' and she'd turned tearfully away, before he'd hit her, more to bring to her senses than anything, and she'd cried, and said, perhaps he should find a younger colleague who could give her a proper seeing to, before it was too late. One or two of the wives did that, when their husbands weren't up to it, or so she'd heard. And she sort of moaned in a way, more of a cry and he'd hit her again, more to calm her down, than anything else really, and found he'd come in his pyjamas. Christ that had been awful, and she'd tried to hit his face, and said things. He'd never thought she could think about things like that, especially things she said he ought to do, wanted him to, which was worse. One thing leads to another. Maybe they could go away, and have a holiday together, and start again and try even counselling. She could have that even, if it would help her. Because he had feelings, in that sort of way, like everyone, it was just that being tired and sort of, well maybe, not as much vitality there nowadays. And anyway wasn't all this counselling lark, a load of bollocks, at the end of the day?

And then Fizzer came in. Manson greeted him with a sullen pretence of welcome and sat him down. So far, so good, but they both knew that it wouldn't last more than a few minutes, it wouldn't work, the way things were between them. Manson cleared his throat for no reason, offered him a drink, which was turned down, leaned forward, and thought, I got it wrong again, I should have leaned back in the bloody seat and tried to look nonchalant.

Error number one. The boy wonder is on to that one already, I'll bet. And of course, straight up, he was too, 'The old back playing you up is that the problem?' said Fizzer looking about as sympathetic as the late-lamented Albert Pierrepoint in a hurry on a February morning in Strangeways.

Manson smiled uneasily, shuffled some papers and thought, this guy has my arse in a sling already, and knows it.

'Right Fizzer, now that the dust has settled a bit, let's have the full debrief on your version of the ending of the siege. I'm hearing things I don't like, you see.' He'd put much emphasis on the 'your version', as he started off, officiously as ever, but knew it wouldn't make any difference.

'Such as,' said Fizzer calmly, and smiled. 'Or perhaps I should have said, how do you mean? It's the first I heard Chief.'

'Well I'd heard, not that I gave it total credence, admittedly, but I'd heard that you felt unhappy about certain things these days, I mean operationwise in a more general sense?'

'Meaning?'

Christ, the bloody scouser isn't going to give much away. Sod it.

'Well I wondered, and I have to be double frank here Fizzer, I just wondered if you might be going a little bit soft in the middle. Some of us had the impression that you didn't have the edge that we like to see more of, especially, in an up-and-coming young officer. Know what I mean? Surely you can see that.' That should wind the scouse bastard up, surely.

But it didn't. Fizzer seemed as calm as anything and said evenly, 'I'm not sure Guv, that I like what you're saying here, not sure I like your tone on this one. Soft, me? Not enough edge? You must be joking.'

'Since you ask scouser, yes. I mean that was the word I was getting here and there.'

'Sorry Sir but I'm a bit particular about who calls me, scouser, and you ought to know that. There's a waiting list and, if you'll forgive me, you're not on it Sir.'

Christ, he is a cool one.

'Suit yourself. OK, so you're not going soft. If you say so, that's quite good enough for me, but, see, I have to consider the team as a whole. I mean, for instance, and I'll take a particular case, since you ask. Some of us didn't like the way you seemed to be getting a bit too friendly with the dead Arab, what was his bloody name?'

He knows bloody well what his name was, he only heard it for bloody days didn't he? Half of bloody the United Kingdom must have heard it, after some prat leaked it to ITV.

'You mean Ibrahim I suppose.'

'Yes, well, Ibrahim, what do you say to that?'

'Nothing really. When you're carrying someone along, you get to know them, that's what it's all about. You know that Guv.'

But he's right really perhaps I did go a bit soft on him, a bit involved, in any case, what does it matter? It worked, held him cool till they blew him away. Manson's not a fool, he's a tired man. Maybe I should remember that. Jesus don't let me get like that. Burn out, is that what they call it?

'Well as long as we know, that's what I always say in these cases,' said Manson and added, almost blurting it out, inconsequentially, 'Look we're all under a lot of pressures here. I mean the bloody media, for a start. Maybe you need a rest or a bit of a holiday. Perhaps we all do. I know I do.' He was trying now to be jocular and failing badly. Fizzer thought, you're breaking my heart. Maybe he is.

Manson looked out of the window, 'Looks bloody good out there doesn't it? I sometimes wonder, on a day like this,' he paused. 'Excuse me. I don't know about you, but I feel like a drink if you don't mind.' Fizzer nodded, as Manson poured himself a vodka and orange, a modest one this time, and having lit a cigarette, continued, 'Just the one, more to settle the stomach than anything. Yes. I mean, has it ever occurred to you, all this crap, negotiating hostage release and all? It's a load of old bollocks when you come down to it? Have you thought about that? I mean your terrorist, he's scum really, and I sometimes wonder if maybe we'd be better off going in and getting things sorted, as quickly as possible. A few dead hostages, I mean, what's one or two more or less?'

Fizzer said nothing, he didn't feel there was anything to say at this stage. Manson looked a tired man, and the funny thing was, the more he went on, even though you knew what was coming, you couldn't help thinking, well after all, he has been around for quite a time. Poor sod, maybe he's knackered.

But Manson went on, 'Take the American Embassy in Teheran for instance? Right? They paid the ransom to get them off the hook. Right? And Lima, well they went in and blew them away, right? I know, I know what you're thinking. You think I'm an ignorant bastard, well let me say this, you can negotiate till the cows come home, but at the end of the day, someone has to cull these people, and you can tell that to the criminologists.'

Then came the expected lull and he started off again, 'And another thing while we're at it.' Another thing I like about this man is he runs true to form.

'Yes and while we're on the subject what the hell were you doing outside the Embassy at that time, anyway? Looking for a bit of limelight was that it possibly? News at ten with MacDonald the coon?'

And he thought, Christ perhaps I've gone too far this time, still he's asking for it, and has been for a long time.

Fizzer let 'the coon' settle, and said quietly, 'If you remember Chief, it was your idea that I should be on site, around the time when the siege was to be lifted?' and then tailed off. Manson was so fired up, that he was unlikely to listen to him. There's no point in getting into a row with the man; he was in bad shape. Let it go. Sweat it out.

So he took his time, and said 'Got you Chief.' He paused again, and thought, no I can't leave it like that and said, 'To be honest Chief I'm sorry about all this. I was out of order there and I accept your comments. We seem to be getting our lines of communication muddled here.'

If he believes that, he'll believe anything, and remembered that Manson wasn't listening. We never listen to each other, I suppose it's because we hear lies all the time, just like in Court. No one listens to anyone. They're not missing much.

'I reckon we all get pissed off about things when the pressure is on, maybe I got a bit wound up there for a minute, back in the mortuary too. I'm sorry about that,' he repeated, but he wasn't sorry about anything. Why should he be sorry? Anyway this wasn't a popularity contest. The reality was simply that this man, he's a nutter, he wants to do me over, and he's not going to let go. Thank Christ, Sylvie can't hear this lot. And while I'm at it why am I so afraid of her opinion, on, to be honest, just about everything?

And then he was aware that Manson was half smiling, and looking embarrassed, saying, 'Right, well I'm glad that we've cleared the air a bit. I really am. Does you good, like a good crap, in a way. Perhaps you should go off and think things out a bit. Perhaps we all should.'

And again Fizzer thought, what's the point, we're never going to get anywhere, why prolong the agony? One more minute and the thicko would be saying 'funny old world', and quoting the night thoughts of Margaret Thatcher, and so he came over all brisk and conciliatory, putting up a brisk show of efficient friendliness, 'Right Sir. Good idea. Will do. Good idea that.' Adding under his breath, my name's Hunt with a capital H.

'What was that?' asked Manson, 'I hope we're not getting funny. I wouldn't like that you know.'

'Nothing Chief, I just said, we Scousers talk a bit blunt like. You get me Sir?' Manson looked hard at him, 'I see, the Liverpool sense of humour, sort of thing and all. A bit that like us in London in a way. I like that in a junior colleague.' He's trying to pull rank, thought Fizzer. This man is more frightened than he admits.

And he thought, there's no point in holding back the latest news, he obviously hasn't heard it, and said 'What did you reckon to Abdullah then, bit of a turn up that?'

'Abdullah?' said Manson. 'Oh yes, Abdullah Right that's it, I've got you.' Manson was looking at him without a blind idea of what he was talking about, by the look of him. Jesus Christ, the man he hasn't heard a bloody thing, I can't believe it.

'Well, Sir, Abdullah, you know, the extra translator they brought in to help out in the Incident Room,' he paused.

'Yes of course, of course I know him.' Manson said, perhaps too hastily. Fizzer held on and said 'It came through on my way over. His body was picked up in Whitechapel. It's a full stop. One shot through the head. Plus he was stripped and they'd cut his bollocks off and shoved them in his mouth. Has to be an Arab job I suppose. They must have found something that they wanted, wouldn't you think? They didn't leave a stitch.'

Manson thought this one over,' Well they wouldn't would they?'

Nothing is as good as breakfast, but lunch is better than dinner. Everyone knows that. And in the glitzy restaurant it was quiet, comfortable and foody. There was an acceptable hubbub of talk coming from the chrome on the mirrored shiny bar, but nothing too noisy. In places like this, you expect a bit of peace and quiet. That's what the patrons pay for, and quite right too. There was the usual splattering of smartly dressed celebs with their pretty babes smiling goofily about, and screaming at their friends, the usual tables of well-scrubbed Showbiz punters, all talking in low serious voices about serious topics and looking at each other seriously.

At one of the better tables sat Sir Jocelyn Grant, Diplomat and connoisseur of fifteen year-old pubescent rent boys, 'No older dear, if you don't mind, they're not so pretty, poor loves.' He had quite enjoyed his *foie gras*, devilled kidneys and pilaff, followed by *creme brulee*. And the wines had been palatable, without being over ambitious. Under other, happier circumstances he would have felt relaxed and happy, permitting himself a few luxuriant fantasies concerning games involving oiled Moroccan boys, but not today. Inevitably there are crappy days in everyone's life, and this was one of them. His host, a well turned out gorilla from Manchester, was as urbane as anything, and said. 'And so you see Sir Jocelyn, you must realise I am sure, that basically it is important for everyone concerned with these sensitive areas, that your visit to Rome should be a total success in every respect. We are all depending on you to achieve a good result, as what I'm sure you know that. It will therefore, not be necessary for me to emphasise that our people looks for a successful outcome like, in this corporate endeavour, and we all look to you to further our interests and all.' He liked to come on a bit strong especially when he was putting the frighteners on someone, even if it did mean repeating himself, since he was proud of his turn of phrase. It showed a bit of class and, better still, it lowered the fear threshold, an important point that. Sir Jocelyn Grant kept up a pretence of interested concern, smiling in sickly appreciation, as he tried to look as if he was in command of the situation, as opposed to considering the alternative, namely the prospect of having a twelve pound hammer sledged into his forehead, whilst he was held down in a garage in Bermondsey, under a railway arch, later in the afternoon. A drop of sweat trickled down the middle of his back and slowly approached his unsuspecting anus. Several more followed in its wake. In an instant, his back discharged waterfalls of fearful sweat down the cleft between his buttocks; how he longed to pluck at his immaculate shirtings to relieve things a bit but, that would hardly do at lunch in the Caprice, now would it? He felt nauseated and faint but, nonetheless, tried to maintain his end of the conversation, and replied, 'Indeed, I'm sure that you know that you can rely on me,' knowing, only too well, that question marks hung over this confident statement and his ability to deliver anything, beyond the contents of his stomach over the tablecloth, given the way things were.

Oh Christ, how foolish he'd been. If he could be given the chance, he'd really like to explain to some understanding person, what had really happened. If only the boy hadn't died. It was vomit that he'd choked on, but he realised that no one would believe that, once they'd seen the photographs and, worst of all, heard the tape.

His host looked at him with total unconcern, 'Are you sure you wouldn't care for, say a nice drop of the old Armagnac? A digestif never hurt the old stomach, now did it, indeed I'm told it's good for you?' he said, belching softly.

'Oh no really,' he replied, 'what an enjoyable lunch it's been, I must say.' His host sipped his coffee, 'Hasn't it, and all, and I'm so glad that we've been able to iron out these problems. They just went away didn't they? I always find that, given time, one can talk these things through. I'm sure you'll agree that we wouldn't want anyone to think that you might be regarded as in any way, if you'll forgive the expression, thinking of shaking the fucking tree, or anything of that nature. You'll understand that this would be construed in a negative fashion by our people and you might end up with your aristocratic balls in a vice, you stinking old poofter.' And he smiled most affectionately. An observer might have thought that they had just settled an amicable deal over the marriage settlement of a favourite niece. In a way they had.

Sir Jocelyn smiled back, his parched mouth by now

approaching super-glue mode. His host said 'Well, that's settled. I do hope that you will find that everything is in order when you meet the people in Rome.' Jocelyn replied, 'Oh yes, I'm confident that matters will be brought to a successful conclusion, I don't have any problems with that particular scenario.' His host nodded, 'I fucking know that, dickhead. We wouldn't want to hear any bad news now would we?' He paused, 'And while we're on the subject, the Man thought that you ought to have some company on the trip, so we've arranged for two persons to go along with you. It's like insurance.'

Sir Jocelyn was horrified and tried to stand on his dignity, 'I don't see that it will be necessary.' His host said 'That's not how we see it.' And with that, he got up, and summoning the Head Waiter, signed the check and left, all in one movement, or so it appeared. Jocelyn watched him depart and was relieved to see him go, and even began to feel slightly better, until he noticed the small envelope that the Head Waiter had deposited on his plate. He opened it. The card inside said 'last chance – asshole'.

There was a discreet, slightly anguished and indistinct waiterish sound,

'Sir Jocelyn,' said the Head Waiter, 'your car is outside.'

As he drove through the West End on his journey home, he started to perk up a bit. He appreciated the comfort of his chauffeur-driven Roller as those dreadful Manchester people called it and he enjoyed the good things of life. His new Armani silk and wool suit felt just right. He stretched his toes in his slim Ferragamo loafers and yawned. He would really enjoy one of his manservant's 'pick-me-ups' as the wicked creature called them. But these Manchester people were, after all, nothing but a bunch of thuggy yobboes and, in his position, with his status as a Senior servant of HMG, he was entitled to above average protection, in times of danger. He was sure of that. It was written into a contract somewhere, he was sure of it, and he believed it. These people thought they could get away with all sorts of nasty things, and maybe sometimes they could, but not with him, thank you very much sweetie. And so by the time he was within sight of home, he had nearly convinced himself, until he remembered the note left on his table. In addition to this, perhaps fortunately, he failed to notice the followers, but then, they were paid not to be noticed. If he had noticed them, he would have been even more surprised to find that one of them was employed in the office beneath his suite.

As soon as he was inside the flat in Dolphin Square he felt better again as he looked at his two Hockneys on the pale blue walls, and all his chintzy bits. The recent redecoration really lifted one's spirits. The pale silken papers and the stark minimalist living room. He felt quite moist round the anus as he gazed fondly on his bits and pieces.

His manservant, Quinton, took one look at him, and thought, I know what the old queen needs, he looks a right mess, don't we sir, ran him a lovely hot foamy bath and fixed him a line of best Colombian and a glass of ice cold fizz, opened a box of chokkies, saying, 'After this little lot, Sir will stay in bed till your dinner date tonight and I'll get everything ready for the trip. Not a bloody word out of you till you're between the sheets. Well to be honest it's ready all ready now, and has been for yonks. Whoops.' Sometimes Quinton got ideas a shade above his station, but he did know how to pamper one. How would one cope without the likes of him, he wondered?

Sir Jocelyn dozed off after the initial rush. He was so knackered that it would have taken a ton of the stuff to raise his spirits, that it would.

After a refreshing nap, he felt so much better, just like Quinton had said he would, the soppy old thing. And so, after another bath and another line, he felt very much better.

The dinner party was in a modest house in Draycott Gardens. His host, an archivist at the British Museum, always entertained well, and this evening was such a change from the beastly lunch which, by now, he was beginning to forget. What a charming group of people they were, especially Francis X Sarno, of whom he'd heard much, but had never met before. A most interesting chap, clever and a real original by the sound of it. Something to do with the Foreign Office, he was told by one of the other guests who seemed to know everyone and was a charming, was it a Chief Steward in Canadian Airlines? Probably not, he'd misheard it, he was more like an administrator and a very cultured young man too. Mustn't get too interested or people will think I'm a gerontophile or something, horrid thought.

How lucky one was to have such wonderful friends, just like the man in the Sondheim thingy. By the end of the evening, he had enjoyed himself so much that, when he arrived home, he had practically forgotten the problems that had been nagging him earlier. Just before he fell asleep, after one of Quinton's special night caps, the phone rang, and a slightly butch voice said 'I hope you have a good kip tonight and enjoy your trip Joss.' And hung up. He tried dialling to check the origin of the caller, but got no answer. He hardly slept a wink all night.

CHAPTER SEVEN

PARTY TIME

There had never been any doubt about it; it was definitely going to be a great party. They had hired the Corporate Hospitality Suite in Flinters Hotel for the occasion. Flinters had just about everything one could wish for on offer for special occasions like this. Situated in Bloomsbury, 'the heart of literary and artistic London, famed haunt of well known writers and artists of yesteryear,' it offered, 'an atmosphere of tranquillity which reflected those quintessentially English and nostalgic echoes of the stimulating, yet relaxing atmosphere of the Bloomsbury era, still to be encountered in the downtown London of the Nineties; favoured to this day by the discriminating intellectual elite of the world's leading capital city, a true meeting ground and haunt for the literati and kindred free spirits,' as the brochure indicated. Wow!

It was something else, was Flinters. As you entered the palatial lobby, all columns and grand gilded pediments, you were belted in the eye by an explosion of interior decoration that encompassed a continuum that had started on the cover of *HELLO* and ended in Butlins. In front of you was the Cafe Strachey, a restaurant that remained open till two-thirty in the morning, and not only that, looked out over the street where real people could be seen walking to and from offices, art galleries and museums. On the opposite side of the lobby, also fronting the street, was the Middleton Murry coffee room, in which they served full English and Continental breakfasts, day and night. In the adjoining rooms there were many treats to be had, including hot roasty bits in the Charlston Carvery, Virginia Woolf beefburgers in the Trattoria on the Terrazzo, and Vladivar vodka in all the bars. Grub abounded.

In the courtyard and in the adjoining streets, around the clock stood an army of coaches waiting to take bewildered Japanese tourists to Windsor, also stretch limos to Heathrow or worse. You could even hire a bike. Inside the hotel the amenities included a casino, a pool, a health club, squash courts, Jacuzzis, a Turkish bath, a massage suite with facilities for colonic irrigation, dry-cleaning and a crèche; in short everything to keep you healthy and clean, inside and out. Unkind critics of the place had claimed that there was a Hotline to the Samaritans for those who were affected by undue proximity to the Tavistock Clinic, and the National Institute for Social Work, safe-house for stolen raincoats.

Quite a place too, was the Radcliffe Hall Corporate Hospitality suite, in which, as the brochure said, 'our aim is to provide an ambience of highest quality accommodations for an exclusive corporate clientele'. It had been specially decorated for tonight's party. It was large, subterranean, and low-ceilinged, and it might easily have doubled for an execution chamber in a Hammer movie. The off-white moulded ceiling, inset with duck-egg blue and gold, was studded interminably with sprinklers, smoke detectors and recessed spots, all of which were tested daily, and had never broken down. There were also air-conditioning vents, notices about fire precautions and dire warnings against loss of property left unguarded. It was an impatient unwelcoming group of rooms which urged its users to get on with things, and take measured doses of fun, but was against organised glee. Sage green curtains brushed the dark red carpeted floor. Along one wall there was a long table covered in drinks. One end of the room opened into a pay bar, while at the other end, there was a disco, complete with light show. A Country and Western Band called, 'Papa Doc and The Animals', was expected at midnight. The gilded chairs had seats that matched the carpet.

It could have been anywhere, or nowhere, depending on your point of view and blood alcohol level. The waiters wore short red jackets, to go with the curtains, red bow ties with matching cummerbunds, and they were assisted by an army of jokey, mini-skirted waitresses who dispensed drinks, parried jokes and deflected slithering hands, while hinting at the promise of sexual favours laid down by management in tightly defined policy schedules.

Despite this unpromising atmosphere, nothing mattered all that much, since this evening promised to be the mother of all parties, but would inevitably end up no better and no worse than any other. In this respect it was like most parties, and what could be wrong with that? The occasion called for a right old piss-up, and why not? Given the circumstances, it wasn't asking for much. And so, by ten o'clock, things were well on their way. Noise, alcohol, out-of-date house music, and a general air of relief would have made for frenetic celebration anywhere; the guests knew this well enough. They had few expectations beyond a red mist in front of the eyes, and the avoidance of eye contact with spouse or partner the next day. At least there wouldn't be a stripper or bagpipes. When Fizzer had taken a butchers at the *mise en scene* provided by Flinters in the full slap, so to speak, he looked around, and thought, Christ what a gaff, it's like a whorehouse in a Western, that's it. He felt defeated by lights that were too bright, the fussy carpeting in the lobby promising migraine, and the high noise level coming from the hospitality suite. No one spotted him as he came in, so he slipped into Vita's Cocktail Lounge and sat at a table. He called a waitress and ordered a Duncan Grant Wallbanger, wondering why the waitress was wearing a mini-toga and purple fishnets. Imperial Purple, of course, that was it. As he sipped the drink, he reflected that it was the familiar story; fun blunted by reality, he didn't want to be there, and at the same time, he wasn't sure where he wanted to be, never a good start to a social occasion.

66

Unable to face a second Wallbanger, he settled for a Bell Dingbat, after which he felt ready to face the party downstairs.

As Fizzer came into the suite, caught the music, and the punters enjoying themselves, he wondered why it was that they always ended up with something that never varied, irrespective of place or purpose, retirement or promotion. Such evenings usually ended amidst universal discontent. Groups of people split up as they exchanged glances of vague resentment, became miffed about fancied insults, went off huffily in search of clubs which promised crazy music and stronger wine, but delivered little beyond early onset hangovers, bad-tempered homecomings and out of sorts awakenings with a mouth like the inside of an all-in wrestler's jockstrap.

The frantic atmosphere was a ritualistic way of soothing the nerves of people lately released from levels of tension and apprehension that were higher than they would care to admit. When you have spent days and nights sitting, crouching or lying in uncomfortable rooms, not knowing what may happen to a group of terrified prisoners whose lives are in your hands, or watching a building from the street, circling in a helicopter, monitoring phone calls, totally involved in surveillance, you are entitled to feel exhausted.

Sitting on a time bomb, scrutinised by the world's media, telling you what you should be doing, entitles you to escape, and the relief provided by the undemanding banalities of traditional entertainment, even to have a major whoop-de-do. At its worst the whole thing could have ended in disaster. You've earned a harder dollar than the fat cats and smartarses who despise and mock you. Enjoy!

The noise level of the conversation was high, broken intermittently by waves of edgy laughter and the exchange of shrill, desperate jokes. Everyone knew that there was nothing all that cheery about the occasion. The triumphant jocularity of victory had left everyone relieved that terrorism and murder had once again been squelched, but, for Fizzer, there was this time, an element of personal disquiet about the affair. Six men had been shot to death by a corps d'elite that was not everyone's favourite, one that made its own rules, and that was reputed to like killing, more than it cared to let on. Also the dead terrorists had been protesting against a regime that had a dire record of despotism and torture. These things touched his conscience. Not that he was soft on terrorism. Like anyone involved with murder that masquerades as freedom's struggle, he knew the score, but this time he had some doubts. No more and no less. He knew that he would get a load of flak from Sylvie about it, when the evening was over and he was subjected to her debriefing; a prospect that didn't help greatly, in view of her impending involvement with a political group that was at best suspect and at worst, what?

Hell, what can you do? It was time to go in, and join the rest in the jollity have a few drinks and hang out.

He caught Dave Johnson's eye, but feeling uncertain, he made helpless gestures that were meant to say that he had been waylaid, so he turned and found himself confronted by gimlet-eyed canapé waiters, offering oysters in lukewarm tapioca, Lake Garda perch livers in diced quail's eggs, and similar muck, and was ready to panic until he caught Dave's eye again and started to make his way through the crush towards him.

Dave was talking to Jan, whom he knew to be a young woman who could fuel the fantasies of anyone with a penchant for dominant blonde women coppers in disciplined outfits of tight shiny black and a gold chain on the left ankle. He'd met her before, but he couldn't remember where. That was a lie. For the moment he chose not to remember. Perhaps it was as well that Sylvie had once again refused to come. And so Jan was probably worth a try, she looked as if she was up for it, no question about it. She pretended to look through him, and continued talking to Dave.

'What's he really like?' asked Jan, 'you hear all sorts of stories about him. Some people say he's stand-offish, and he's meant to have a funny wife isn't he? I'd heard. College girl.'

'Put it this way,' said Dave, 'He's what they call a copper's cop, with knobs on.'

'That's not particularly funny,' said Jan.

'It wasn't intended to be,' continued Dave, ignoring her, in traditional police fashion, 'Mr Edwards is a top man, or hadn't you heard?'

'You sound almost as if, you didn't like him all that much, don't you? Know what I mean?' and she realised that she had made a stupid remark too quickly, that she had been indiscreet. It was none of her business. Ordinarily, she wouldn't have said something like that, but she was already a little drunk. Not that it mattered too much, since Dave wasn't listening, and everyone else was drunk. At this point, there was a muffled cheer and a surge of welcoming laughter as Fizzer came slowly across the room towards them, exchanging banter. No one collects it.

Jan noticed that Dave didn't look at him, as he said, 'I wouldn't say that. It's just that he's my oldest friend and I know him better than most people.' And then he turned, with an opened bottle of champagne at the ready, and greeted him, urging him to come on over and get stuck in, saying, for Christ's sake, where had he been hiding himself all evening, to join them, have fun for once in your life you miserable old bugger, 'Here he is, the Wonderscouser, let's hear it for Fizzer,' he called out. Christ, I think perhaps, he really does dislike him, she thought. 'Hail the conquering hero comes,' shouted someone else. Jan noticed that Mr Manson hadn't shown up as yet. And the next thing, Dave was up and calling everyone to order, and Fizzer is thinking, Oh Christ, Dave is going to make a speech. I can tell by his mouth, it goes all tight, and to one side, and he can't smile properly and looks down.

Dave said 'Listen everyone, I want to ask you all to join me here in drinking a toast to Fizzer. OK, so he didn't raise the siege, single-handed, but all of us know that he kept those bastards on line, building up their hopes until the last moment and, I don't know about you, but I reckon that's bloody good, so let's hear it for Fizzer.'

Thank Christ, thought Fizzer, that could have been a lot worse, we got through it, and it was decent of old Dave, not a bad old sod, and smiled across at him, put his arm on his shoulder and said, 'That was good of you Dave, to say that. I appreciate that.' And Dave said 'Forget it mate. Come on me old son, let me get you a drink.' And smiled at him. 'Best mates, that's us. Right?' said Fizzer. 'You said it,' replied Dave. They must be then, thought Jan and giggled, wondering, what was that all about, male bonding I suppose, like they said in Cosmopolitan?

Just then, bloody Manson walked in, looking stony-faced, talk about good timing. He nodded briefly to Fizzer, as if to say, I'm here laughing boy so just watch it, you hear me? He accepted a glass of Scotch, and turned to some of his mates. And that was it, not a bloody word. He's trying to tell me something, thought Fizzer and was about to say something. Just then, Dave spotted what was coming down, and led him off saying 'Forget it my son, it's your evening remember. Sod Manson. Enjoy.'

Fizzer accepted a glass from Dave, smiling as he looked around as if nothing had happened, as indeed, in a sense nothing much had, beyond Manson's show of unnecessary pique. At that point the stripper came in, for once fulfilling a useful function by acting as a means of relieving the situation with tasteless diversion. Fizzer gazed appreciatively through the buttocks of the bored-looking young woman as she removed her nun's kit. She had hairy armpits and had cut herself when she'd shaved her bush.

He clapped politely and made tribal noises at the end of it.

He turned and then he saw Jan standing right there. She smiled back 'You remember me Sir. We was in the Range Rover together yesterday.' He looked at her again, noting her appearance and pretending to forget having met her.

Jan was not convinced, after all, had he not tried to cop a feel in the Range Rover? His affected indifference was unconvincing, the word was that this man was always planning to get into someone's pants, anyone's pants, her pants, no question, you could smell it. It was the way in which they thought that you didn't know, that was the bit that made you really laugh, as if they'd discovered this secret form of entertainment of which you'd obviously never heard. They were going to introduce you to the rare treasures provided by a semi-erect penis and beery breath. What a treat! You'll never guess what I've got in my trousers. Oh really, and what might that be? Gosh, I've never seen one of those before. What do you do with them then? It's my nodger, you see. Oh yes. Is that right? Is that what they call them? Who'd have thought it? What a funny name. Come over here darling and I'll show you! Show me what? And if you did say it just like that, half of them would believe you.

Fizzer said absently, feigning not having noticed her, 'Oh was I? Really? Oh yes, I remember, you're Jan that's it. Good to see you Jan. Nice party.' It was said too coolly, and a bit too casually.

'It's OK Sir I mean to...'

'What? How do you mean?'

'No need to call me sir. Fizzer will do.'

His hand brushed against her thigh, stopped and was pressed back, as she brushed the back of her hand over his balls in an appraising non-judgmental way as if she was selecting vegetables in the market in the Cut. For a moment he felt nostalgic for the days when such pressures inspired speculation instead of confirming a reservation on the Hairy Grotto Flyer. Rather like a travel agency. Sod it, he thought, why waste time? I'm in up to the eyebrows with Sylvie already anyway, and this one's as horny as a barrel of toads by the look of it.

'Jan, I was just wondering if you'd like to...'

Christ he doesn't hang around. She longed to tell the truth and say 'leave it out Guv. You're far too old,' But this wasn't in the script, so she said 'I was wondering if I'd like to, what had you in mind, because I haven't. Know what I mean?'

'Ruling passion strong in death Jan or hadn't you heard?' he said, almost defensively 'Anyway, one thing, I'm not too old if that's what you're thinking.' Not only is he too old, but he's a mind reader with it, she thought. 'No. I never heard that one about the ruling passion, Guv. Straight up.' And she laughed, head tossed back, just like in East Enders, 'I'll have a snowball.'

He smiled 'I got it from Jimmy Joyce.'

Dave intervened 'Why don't you tell him to pull his other one, it's got bells on it Jan – know what I mean?' If he says, tell her no it's got balls on it I'll scream, and she said, 'Not a clue Guv. Who's Jimmy Joyce? On the Met would he be?'

Fizzer ignored this lot, turned to the lads 'Sorry I'm late lads. Got held up. As usual.' Gales of laughter at that. Likes a laugh he does.

Dave said 'That's all right scouser. Tonight anything goes for you, our honoured guest' and thought but we aren't lads really, not any more are we?

'Thanks Dave. You're one of the favoured elite.'

'How's that?'

'Calling me scouser.' So then he turned abruptly and said to Jan 'You can call me Fizzer any old time, if that's what you want, like I said.' Jan smiled. She was, by now more than a little drunk and vaguely flattered by his interest, but she thought, I'm not that interested or am I?

So she said 'Must be nice. Perhaps I might join that club.'

Dave chipped in with 'More likely get in the club if you hang about too near Fizzer love. I've seen him in action.'

Why do men always have to be so bloody crass or is it that I'm just as crass and bloody drunk as they are. What does it matter?

So what did she say, for God's sake? ' I could take a chance on that one. Do I want to ?' It's like something out of Honey she thought.

Dave said to her 'I don't know about you but I fancy a dance.' Fizzer was immediately absorbed into another group of people, as Jan and Dave joined the dancers thumping, bumping and grinding. Popular guy, she thought, well he would be, hearing him chatting to a group nearby, as she tried to echo Dave's arrhythmic capering.

When they rejoined the group, he turned away, smiling to her, and offered her another drink. 'Right then what's happening next? I don't know about you but I'm beginning to get a bit tired with this lot. Do you fancy going somewhere else

Jan?' said Fizzer, as she joined him after the music had changed gear.

I don't believe it, is he trying to already? He bloody is, she knew that.

'What was that?' he said 'I can't hear with all this noise,' and laughed as she accepted the drink.

'You know,' he said 'I really fancy getting inside your pants,' but the noise level was by now so high that she thought he said, no thanks, and wondered why did he say that, he must be pissed, funny he doesn't look it. He tried again 'All I said was I think we might need a change of scene, I mean like maybe we should get something proper to eat, not this rubbish, all this booze and stuff it's not good for you, for your digestion. You should eat properly you know?'

She smiled. Yes he was. 'Well,what a good idea,' she said, 'but maybe we should hang on a bit longer, seems a bit off, you know, to go, just like that.' He laughed, 'OK have it your own way,' and thought, do I really want to get into bed with a young policewoman, yes I bloody do, perhaps I should rephrase that and ask, why do I?

She smiled and said 'Let's not make it too obvious shall we? Why don't we meet at my place after, say, at about one.' He said 'I don't know where you live.' She slipped a card into his pocket. 'Now you do. I wrote it down', she said. And then she moved on and said 'I'll go and talk to some of my mates. I wouldn't want to be seen trying to chat you up.'

Dave nudged him in the side and said 'Watch it Fizzer. I heard some of that. Don't drop yourself in it. Know what I mean?' Fizzer stayed silent and said 'Of course. Let's have a drink or something. After all it is a party, I'd nearly forgotten that, you see.' Dave is concerned about me, I'd never thought of that before. And so the party went on, people got drunk, nothing excessive, just too much, but no nastiness. The usual crop of stolen embraces, furtive regret, silly jokes and near quarrels. There was good food, plenty of good drink and much fun as it happened. Not a suicidal thought around, and no soul-searching chat. Jan's departure passed, more or less unnoticed, and as the evening proceeded, Fizzer settled down. No milk had been spilt, it was too early to cry. That would come later, no doubt.

When Jan opened the door of her flat he noticed that she had no clothes on.

'What kept you?' she said.

Later she said, 'Tell you what. You don't half come a lot, I mean in terms of actual quantity, just like some of the other girls said.' She also said 'A pity you couldn't have kept it in a bit longer,' but Fizzer preferred to forget that remark. Some things he felt, were probably better left unsaid.

CHAPTER EIGHT

WHEN SARNO MET SYLVIE

He's got the long-suffering, I am a loyal, badly paid, servant of HMG expression on his face, I bloody knew it, the air conditioning is on the blink. Serves him bloody right for arranging the bloody meeting in a crappy interview suite in personnel, home of the brain-dead, instead of his own gaff, putting on the frighteners at this stage, he's losing his grip isn't he? Air-conditioning malfunctioning, that's all he needs, and we'll be straight into his ruddy *sancta simplicitas* act. In no time at all, it'll be, here am I, a model of simplicity, see how I am put upon, even subjected to abuse, by a woman who purports to be reasonable, but who is, in reality, like something out of the French Revolution, all sweaty from *Carmagnole* rehearsals. I ask you what a bloody carry-on? Well let me tell you, Mr Cleverarse Sarno that you won't cut the mustard with this young woman. She's going to mark your card once and for all. This time, maestro, you may have met your match, Gott sei bloody dank.

Sarno was unaware of his colleague's mutinous thoughts as he looked peevishly across the barren desk at Sylvie. Nevertheless, he received Sylvie with a show of urbanity, oozing charm of an intensity that had made Blunger's eyes water, as he later said, after an all-night session of seven card stud, at the Twenty Nine Club, in the company of a person whom Sarno had described, somewhat petulantly as, 'one of old Ted Blunger's *poules de luxe de nos jours*,' adding 'who, they tell me, is no better than she ought to be,' with, at least one person commented, a note of envy. The *poule de luxe* was Sandra, a nubile blackjack dealer from St Louis Missouri; Blunger was her long-time 'gentleman caller', as Sarno might have described her, had he been in a less querulous mood.

It was two in the afternoon. Ordinarily, a time when Sarno would have been taking things easy, but this afternoon was important. He had invited Sylvie Edwards to come along and have a chat, as he unconvincingly described it to her, via his secretary who had telephoned her home at eight that morning, offering a barrage of bogus apologies from Sarno.

'I always like to make sure that these important people like Mrs Edwards are called as early as possible before an interview,' he had remarked smugly to Blunger on the previous evening, as sanctimonious as you like. Why does he need to tell me this, as if this was some arcane ritual that I'd never heard about? What does he mean 'these important people?' For Christ sake, he gave her husband an assignment a few minutes ago, now he makes it sound like he's only just found her name in the phone book. Everybody knows that this is his way of winding people up, 'You see then, they will have plenty of time to prepare replies to questions of which I know the answers anyway,' was his standard reply, delivered with, his, My-God-look-what-I-have-to-endure-in-the-search-for-truth, look.

'Well bugger me, who'd have thought of that Guvnor? You surprise me, you really do.'

But F X Sarno would never bother to answer such a comment.

'And Blunger, what would you suppose that our lawyerette of dusky hue, is up to? Innocent dupe? I think not. Devious and manipulative? Hard to say. Her course record suggests a degree of professional integrity that we will need to bear in mind. Any infractions on our part, might land both of us, well, to be honest, yourself, if you'll pardon me saying so, in very serious trouble, if we don't handle this properly. I'm told that she has friends.'

Sarno looked sympathetically at Sylvie, 'Thank you for coming, Mrs Edwards, and please to accept my apologies for any inconvenience that may have been caused. I will come to the point straight away. I know-well-know that you are an extremely busy person, as indeed are we all, but I felt it important to touch base with you, as I believe they call it nowadays,' he smiled at Blunger for support, as if he were asking for confirmation from a loyal junior partner in an old-established legal firm, called in, at short notice, to witness the fixing of an impost on liquid manure, and continued, 'I understand that you are under consideration for an important appointment, or rather a variety of political affiliation, if that is the correct term. Dangerous waters, some might think, but I'm sure that is not the case here. Still, one never knows does one? How very nice that must be, to be invited to lend one's name to a cause. It depends on how good the cause is, I suppose. What busy bees these young people are, are they not Blunger? Oh I'm so sorry, I forgot to introduce my colleague Mr Randolph Blunger, late of the Blues. What have you to say to that?' he said as he looked at Blunger who appeared to have inhaled something.

'Mr Blunger suffers from hay-fever.' he added. One day, he'll go too bloody far. If Sarno thinks that Mme Sylvie will be impressed by this sort of beginning, he'll need his eyes testing.

'It is correct that I have been invited to make a partial career change, but I don't see that it necessitates my attendance here, or that it is any concern of yours. This matter does not, in any sense, involve a breach of security, as far as I am aware,' she replied, adding, 'and I don't need to remind to you that I am not under caution and that there is one witness present.'

'That is something we'll need to look at, under the circum-stances,' he said unctuously, 'having regard to all the other factors involved, wouldn't you agree?' he paused, 'at the same time I feel I'd like to share with you certain concerns regarding your husband and the possible implications of all this for him, and I'm hoping that you'll be able to help me on that.'

She looked straight ahead, resolving to stay calm but wondering why she felt apprehensive. Fizzer always insists that felons are jailed on their own statements. It's police lore, I know that, and I've never believed it. He's a copper, he should know. I should know, but now, I'm not so sure. Christ, I believe I could end up being scared by this rubbish. This man's Chief will hear something about this from the Bar Council. But she knew very well that the Bar Council wouldn't give a toss. And she wished Fizzer was there. She did.

'You see, Mrs Edwards, I have reason to believe that your husband may have become a little over involved in certain matters during his last assignment. This has given rise for concerns. It seems he has made one or two odd remarks about the Head of the Terrorists, a Mr Ibrahim, now alas, gone to his fathers. Remarks indicating that perhaps, and I repeat, this is only a suspicion, that he might have become, shall we say, a shade emotionally involved with the late Mr Ibrahim. You know the sort of thing, I'm sure of that. We see this sort of thing happening now and again. I wondered if you had any ideas on this score?'

Blunger thought, I knew it, he's flipped. It had to happen sooner or later. I bet he's been doing speed or coke or something. I always thought it would end like this. What the hell was all that about? Thank God, my pension's safe. I can buy a tenth share in that nice little club in Manchester, put a deposit on it and forget about all this nonsense, once and for all. I never liked it all that much, anyway. And to think I've been a loyal colleague all these years. Sandra is right. I'm too good for this lot. Women know about these things.

Unlike Blunger, many people would have questioned Sandra's judgement. The word of a thirty-something year old blackjack dealer with a moderately expensive cocaine habit, is not necessarily the most reliable, but then, as FXS would have said 'Blunger always had a little too much *nostalgie de la boue* if you ask me, one of his more endearing traits, I sometimes think.'

'At all events Mrs Edwards, perhaps you could think it

over. It will be held in the strictest confidence as I'm sure Mr Blunger will confirm?'

He looked at Blunger who nodded. If she believes that, she will believe anything. I never thought I would ever think such a thing, let alone say it under my breath.

Sarno continued, 'As regards other matters, perhaps you could tell me what you know about the real purpose and intent of the Front for the Liberation of Kurdish Women,' Sarno continued, 'I understand that you have been invited to become its European president or something. How nice for you. Is that correct? I mean, look, what is all that about? I mean, I can't see why a person of your calibre would wish to be involved with that sort of thing and in particular with the likes of Mohammed Ahmed bin Sudairy *et hoc genus omne.*'

Wrong again, thought Blunger. Only F X would have the nerve to implicate a member of the House of Saud in the first five minutes. Plus he's on to the Latin. Lord give me strength.

'I've never heard of such a person,' she lied, 'Since you appear to know so much about it. There seems little point in my answering does there?'

That was a mistake, I don't think that I should have lied to this guy this early. He's too bloody sharp. And she smiled helplessly. That might divert him, but it won't. Stupid non-liberated chauvinist male, unable to come to terms with your own sexuality,what would you know? Also, he talks slightly past the point half the time, an old trick. Shit, how did he find out about Sudairy though? His name has never even been mentioned. I only heard about it myself the other day. Why did she suddenly feel shaky and uncertain?

'Come, Mrs Edwards, there is no point in being unnecessarily coy about things. I assure you that my questions and intent are motivated by a genuine concern. I wouldn't like to see you wandering into dangerous areas, especially since you are the wife of such a valued officer.' He smiled and looked at her with such innocence that Blunger ground his teeth.

'We know that you are thinking of taking up this appointment. What is the point in failing to take us into your confidence? All I ask for, is information about a matter which interests me. You are married to someone employed in areas which might have relevance to this organisation?'

... I like the way he's managing to make the words 'this organisation' sound like I'm a serial killer, she thought, but that's his job, and she smiled. She was becoming more apprehensive; about what, she wondered? Most people, given a chance to witness his questions, would say that he was a conscientious plodder doing his job; she was being over-sensitive. Uncertainty on her part, she supposed. How much did he know? He wasn't likely to tell.

'Surely you will agree that this must be an area of interest to us.' Still smiling. Jesus, thought Blunger, his smile is a turn off if ever I saw one. This way he'll end up with bloody lockjaw.

'I'm not sure that I share the notion that women who are trying to achieve justice in the face of torture and rape are anything other than what they purport to be, even if they are organised into a group for their own protection. And to claim that such a group poses a threat to security, is ridiculous. I regard your questions as offensive, inappropriate and intrusive. Be assured, that various groups concerned with Civil Liberties will be interested in this shabby business.'

Blunger thought, I like the way she sticks to the formula, answering his service without overheating. She's all right, is Madama Sylvie, and there's no doubt that what they said about her was right. I'm beginning to like her. She might get my vote one day. Well probably not, but it's a thought.

But Sarno who, by now, was reading Blunger's mind, said 'And you should be assured, Mrs Edwards that I am a fair minded person. My role here is to obtain answers to questions which I regard as perfectly reasonable.' He laughed in a, lets-all-be-sensible-about-all-this-bloody-nonsense-sort of way, and continued 'We're not a bunch of yokels from the FBI, we are not in the habit of falsifying evidence, shooting eccentric farmers in Idaho and the like. We are merely pursuing a legitimate line of enquiry. It's really a simple matter.'

'I can see that, but I still don't think that this a matter that merits such a high handed approach.'

Sarno wasn't going to buy that one, went straight past it, and said,' I'm merely interested in what you know about the organisation. What lies behind its cosy persona, that's all we want to know, you see.'

He spread his hands and did his, when did-you-last-see-your-father act.

'You appear to know about it, why do you ask me?'

'Mrs Edwards, I'm interested in what you know, not what I know, I promise you, that's all.'

'The Front is an organisation, founded in Europe, and dedicated to the support and rehabilitation of innocent Kurdish women, victims of torture and God knows what else, at the hands of the Iraqis. No more, no less.'

'Some have expressed another view, Mrs Edwards, which I do not necessarily share, but which I cannot entirely dismiss, namely that the Front has been dreamt up by a naive woman lawyer from, I believe Walthamstow, or is it Upminster, no matter? Neither area is entirely the sweet potato, in terms of one's point of origin Mrs Edwards. Yes a damp-knickered bleeding-hearts liberal, suffering from an overdose of Gertrude Bell, seemingly unable to spot the possibility of having been manipulated by a group of rather dubious people, and gone soft in the head from believing everything she hears, but no matter, what are you able to tell me? I do need some help. I ask only for your help, you see.'

'And if I decline?'

Christ he doesn't half go on.

'Had you thought that an uncooperative attitude might not be favourable as far as your husband is concerned, in terms of his career enhancement?'

'That's obvious, I'd have thought. But am surprised to hear you using bullshit and threats this early.'

'No threats Mrs Edwards. This interview is not being recorded. This is a normal enquiry which you are at liberty to terminate whenever you like, as you know.'

How much does she know about it anyway thought Blunger. She looks reasonable and I don't care what F X has in his briefing schedule which, God knows, looks like the eleventh edition of the Encyclopaedia Britannica. Where does he get all this stuff from? But she must realise that The Front is just the sort of group that interests us. After all, that's what we get paid for.

Sylvie was suddenly on her feet, angry but retaining control. She'd had enough. Enough of being patronised, enough of being let know that she was the inferior person here, the jumped-up clever nigger who didn't know her place in the world of real men and all that shit.

'I don't feel able to discuss this without legal representation, and that's final.'

Blunger thought, I'd give her a straight A, for cool.

F X Sarno continued, 'Mrs Edwards, it is all quite straightforward. The Front appears to myself and colleagues to have links with various organisations that interest us, please, there will be no need to become excited, I assure you. The links are obvious and undeniable. Surely you can see that this must be of interest to me and to my people. What can you tell us, can you help us with that? That is all I ask. We are simple people who want to find out the truth, as I'm sure all of us do, are we not?' Jesus, thought Blunger, he'll be asking her to remember her native country next.

'Understand, please that we are looking at the structure of an organisation and of its workings, that is all there is to it. We need to know how it operates. Its motivations are of no great concern. All ask is for an answer to my questions about these matters. How much do you know about them?'

Sylvie said 'Nothing, as it happens.'

'In that case Mrs Edwards, what would you say if I told you that your husband might, at some stage, conceivably be in danger from such an organisation as this, would that bother you?'

'I would say first that you are bluffing, and secondly, that it is no concern of mine.'

That's balls for a start thought Blunger, you lost some of my votes there. That was a stupid answer.

'Very good, Mrs Edwards, I can see that your mind is made

up for the moment. Obviously, you will have thought these matters over carefully. We need detain you no longer. You are free to leave. Mr Blunger, be so kind as to call a car, I am sure that Mrs Edwards would wish to go somewhere.'

And with that, Sarno got up and walked towards the door.

Would wish to go somewhere, she thought, what a way of putting things he has.

Sarno turned, 'A final question, Mrs Edwards. What did you think of the Suleimaneya Consortium in general, and of its recommendation as to materials management in particular? I'd be interested to hear your views some time. Feel free to call me, when you feel up to it, that is.'

And he walked out.

Sylvie knew then that she was probably going to be done over, that this man was the business. He didn't lose battles, she'd heard that. He was as good as they had said. It was a matter of time. Fizzer would have known what to say. That's his job.

'Are you unwell Mrs Edwards?' asked Blunger, knowing bloody well that she was fine.

'No,' she replied, 'But your colleague is.'

What, in the name of Christ, is Sarno on about this time. He bloody made it up, just like he did in Tokyo last year. He felt mildly amused at his chutzpah, and then he remembered that Sarno had predicted the Sarin attack in the Tokyo underground railway, five weeks before it had happened. Why had he conveniently forgotten that? The crafty sod, maybe I'll put the club in Manchester on hold for the moment.

Sylvia got up and walked out of the room, saying that it was all right, that she would make her own way home and that, as she knew that she was being followed, what did it matter? But it wasn't all right. Anyone could see that.

Blunger let her go. He picked up the papers that Sarno had left behind. Good luck, the silly bugger forgot them; a chance to look at his brief for once.

He opened the impressive tome.

It was a facsimile of the 1897 bound volume of the *Strand Magazine*.

CHAPTER NINE

RECRIMINATIONS

Fizzer walked home, he felt unhappy, dehydrated and nauseated. His prick hurt. A sharp strand of pubic hair stuck painfully to the end of it, cutting in like razor-edged wire into a plum. He felt bad. Maybe he should have stayed at Jan's and phoned to say that he was staying with Dave, or something. On second thoughts, that would not have done. So he had taken a cab from Jan's place, stopped it and walked the last half mile, trying vainly to rehearse acceptable explanations for his late return. All of them were equally ridiculous, so he gave up. He approached the block of Edwardian mansion flats where Sylvie and he lived, a solid group of red brick architecture with hydraulic lifts, high ceilings and mosaic-paved hallways.

It looked out over the piazza outside the front of Westminster Cathedral, the solemnly reproachful reminder of a Catholic boyhood. Not a rent boy in sight, he noted as he stumbled up the front steps of the building and was alerted by music cannonading into the early morning air. But it wasn't organ music from the Cathedral. It was from the flat. If only he had stayed sober, at least that would have lessened the impact of the confrontation waiting for him indoors. His failure to stay sober was only half the problem; inevitably Jan's name would come up. Names always surface. Still, with any luck, that could be postponed until later in the morning, after a deep and healing sleep. But, as soon as he came through the flat door, he realised that deep and healing sleeps were not on the agenda, no bloody way. A fanfare of loud music on return was a sure indication of trouble, but the chord sequences of Richard Wagner, turned up to maximum amplitude, were even worse.

Anything but Wagner. And to cap it all, it was bloody *Rheingold*. Jesus, that was the clincher; Richard Strauss, yes. Wagner, bloody no. Always a give-away on these occasions, sod it. Why had he stayed out so long? He knew perfectly well why; meantime there was the problem of getting the head clear enough to put up a response to the welcome-home-from-the-drunken-party reception committee. The sound level meant one of two things. Either Sylvie had taken a few more drinks than usual, something that occasionally happened lately, or else she was spoiling for a pointless fight; probably both. But it was even worse; when he came through the door, Holy Christ, there she stood in unaccustomed kit, the full Monty, and at this time of the morning too. She was wearing her *shagging kit*, as she derisively called it. Obviously she'd put it on to wind him up, a good way of thumbing her nose at him by means of a charade, dressing up like she was out of an Ann Summers ad, or a New Orleans cathouse, *Hey white trash, look at me, I'm a black whore, which, in case you didn't know it, I'm not.* Cop this and don't get too fresh, but if that's what you need to do, go ahead and treat me like one then, you white mother. A no-win situation. Not an easy one to handle, that. Despite the circumstances it didn't prevent her from being a traffic stopper though. Shit a large brick, you could hardly have missed it even in the aftermath of a Jumbo crashing on Number One runway at London Heathrow. He had looked at her as carefully and, given the way things were, with as much nonchalance as he could dredge up from his drink-thickened brain, and he had tried to say something, but was unable to as he was on the threshold of a truly spectacular exhibition of vomiting. This was going to be a bad one. It was hard to know which was the best way to start. Vomit first, or get into an argument? How had he let things get to this level? How would she start this time? Here goes, there was only one way to find out. 'I suppose a fuck would be out of the question?' he enquired, as jokily as he could manage. She doesn't horse around. But she ignored this feeble stab at jocularity and came straight back with an unexpected response, which given the time and circumstances, was pretty good. 'Did you really have to let it happen like that, all those people dead? Is that what you want? Where's this fair play that you're always on about?'

Not even a greeting, he thought lamely. She had asked the question angrily, looking coldly at him, as if he had been the perpetrator, without pausing, 'I thought that the boy wonder was the great hostage negotiator, who settles things without bloodshed, *always providing, that the terrorists are white, isn't that right?*' She spat the last few words out. He wanted to say *'Sylvie, it's not like that at all, and you know it.'* But this was not a Warner Bros movie, and he knew that she was angry, that he'd be wasting his time, that it probably didn't matter too much what he said, not even *somehow I feel that we seem to have lost the way, where did we go wrong hon?*, as if he would. No, she was in no mood for jokes. It was possible that she didn't care all that much, whatever he said. Did he care all that much himself, if it came to that? So he said, 'Hard to say. Listen Sylvie, I'm tired.' This was no use, and he knew it. There was no point in insulting someone's intelligence, even at this stage. She replied, sticking to her point with the zeal of a lawyer confronted by a guilty drunk, at two in the morning, 'Can't you see that we are talking about human rights here, like slaughtering people without due process?'

He'd half-glanced at her, 'I don't believe I'm hearing all this nonsense, Sylvie. I didn't notice concern for due process when they killed the two hostages, and in any case I didn't slaughter anyone, as you bloody well know, so don't talk balls. I'm not up for a lecture on civil liberties, and my failure to caution those who are about to be arrested for murdering some poor bastards in a siege, for Christ's sake. These people don't mind who they kill. Didn't you ever think of that? Didn't that cross your mind? You and your mates. Makes me fucking laugh.'

I've blown it, sod it. Going back never works. Tedious as bloody go over wasn't that it.

'Listen Sylvie Zealots kill you because they disagree with you, in case you didn't know. "It's a pity she wasn't pregnant, it would have been one less Brit," isn't that what the mick said? How are we meant to deal with people like that Sylvie? What are we supposed to do, hold their bloody hands and counsel them? Let them piss on us and drown us, is that what you want?'

She made no reply.

'Are you bloody crazy? Can't we let it go for now? Give me a chance to unwind a bit.'

I come in looking like a whore's ghost, and I'm walking into a political lecture. Leave it out Sylvie, still I suppose I could hardly expect her to unroll the red carpet, at two forty-five in the morning.

She had quietened unexpectedly, and said calmly, 'Is that what you said to your little *whitey slapper* then? *Give me a chance to unwind a bit.* To your little white whore, was that it?'

'Which little white whore? Or perhaps you'd prefer me to have a great big white whore, like big knockers Sharon, the upper-class *dripper* from Shepherd's Market.'

Sylvia looked at him. 'That's wonderful Fizz. That's right, just turn it all into one of your famous big jokes, and we'll all have a laugh, and you'll be off the hook once again.' She paused, 'You add a new dimension to copping out you really do. You're a contemptible person, not to say, bastard, when you talk like that.'

This could go on for hours, he thought. I come home for a bit of peace and quiet, and next thing I'm in a loony bin. And being cross-examined by a budding Q, bloody C with it. But he knew that it wasn't like that. For a start there was the little matter of Jan to explain. And that hadn't exactly been a howling success, now had it? *Do you always come as quick as that, half of it all over me stomach too,* that was one thing she had said, though he'd improved second time round. Jesus was it worth it? But now was hardly the time to start wondering. Pleading nausea, he had excused himself to go the lavatory and after copious puking, he'd looked at his tired grey face, as he dried its tripey stubbly surface. Not a good sight, that was a face with a low charisma count. What was going on here, he asked himself? He could hear her, sobbing, or was she laughing? Then silence. He went back into the bedroom. She looked forlorn and vulnerable. Now was the time to say something, anything. She said, 'Someone rang me and told me you'd been with this girl Jan tonight.' Fizzer paused and said, 'Is that right? All right, what if I was? You know what sort of a night it was; these things happen, people go to parties and get drunk and do stupid things, and let's not forget, you were asked to come, and refused, yet again.'

He felt that he'd skated past the truth.

She made no reply. 'You know Sylvie, it wouldn't hurt to make the effort and come to one of these affairs, just the once. After all it was a special occasion.' And then, he had remembered other special occasions, when she'd been with him, when they were first together; the looks, the smirks and lowered voices. OK, so that had stopped, but she was unlikely to forget that such things had occurred. She said, 'You don't understand Fizz, do you?' And he had thought, Jesus which cliché do I pull out of the bag next?

'Don't you have anything to say to me, beyond falling back on the bit about not wanting to come to a party given by policemen for policemen.' And he had remembered when she told him, for the first time, what it was like to be called, *black scum, dirty Nigger, coon* and stuff, and get shit pushed through the letterbox, and everything, and he knew that he didn't know, that he would, no way ever know, what that must be like. He realised now that she was not drunk, she was an angry, upset woman, and she continued, 'Don't you see Fizz, that sooner or later we have to sit down and talk seriously about things.' He stifled the urge to ask if it would be possible to stand up, and talk about things. But, frivolity was definitely not the answer.

He wondered who it was, this great and good friend, who had called her, and given her the good news about Jan and himself. It was amazing to think that anyone would bother to call someone up, at this time of night, and for such a reason.

Who, for God's sake? It didn't make any sense. 'Surely you can see Fizz that we are both being ruined by all this. I know that you don't mean to. OK so you're a good guy whom I love and respect and everything,' she thought, am I actually saying all this? '... but we're being ground down by the system. I mean all this suspicion that you spend your life in, it's bound to rub off on both of us. It's one of the things I don't like about being married to a copper. We live and work in it. How do we carry on? That's all I'm asking.'

Fizzer said nothing, thinking, She's right. But if we jack it in we prove everyone was right. *He married a paranoid smartarse black, and now they screwed up, I hear. Imagine that?* So what else can you expect? *I told you it would never work.* Q.E.D. We've to hang in. If we don't we're fucked.

'Feel better now Fizz?' she asked. He looked doubtful.

'I'm sorry I get too wound up.' He looked disconsolately around, burgeoning hangover oozing through his body, the sour taste of regurgitant vomit in the back of his throat, cutting into his gullet and making him gag. Oh the joys of alcohol, mouth like a blanket, the lot. It's times like this, he thought, when I almost wish I smoked, at least I could do something that didn't involve thinking. 'I don't know what to do Sylvie,' he said.

'Well you could get into bed.'

As he did so he had thought, but that's not good enough, that's what she'll say. She's right, I do need counselling.

'As good as Jan was it?'

Nice one. Thanks for the compliment.

'Now don't go funny on me Sylvie. Hold on a bit. What was that about Jan? What's she got to do with it?' now we're going round in circles again. But she wouldn't let go, 'Everyone said that you were dying to get into her pants. I didn't need a phone call for Christ's sake. After all it wouldn't be the first time. Are you real, I wonder? With your Turnbull & Asser suits.' He thought, why does she always have to get on to the subject of my clothes, and who does she mean everyone? But she followed up with, 'Sometimes you look more like an antique dealer than a copper.'

'Knock it off Sylvie.'

'No you knock it off. You've been after that little slag ever since she came on the squad. I shouldn't have said that Fizz. Should I?'

'You shouldn't. Well maybe you should, but it doesn't make too much difference. But then everyone says daft things, even lawyers.'

'Maybe you should get away for a bit.'

'Why is it everyone thinks going away solves everything? *A holiday will do you good.* It never does. It's like thinking that appearing on TV cures woe and solves life's problems. And telling all makes everything OK, especially if you're a serial killer, and say so to the world. Maybe I will go away. No I won't. I'm sure Manson would be pleased if I were out of the way for a week or so. Then he could really shit on me in my absence. That's what needles me. He'd have me back on the beat outside the University Bookshop if he got the chance, that is, if he hasn't already.'

What am I talking about?

'Well you'd better make sure you don't hand him the chance on a plate. Don't you see, with this playing around you're into, you set yourself up all the time. You dropped right in it, by going off in the Range Rover. Every time you do something like that, you give him the chance to say, "What did I tell you? He's a bloody chancer who's trying to get himself into *HELLO,*" that's all I'm saying.'

'How's that? Don't tell me you're on his side 'LEFT-WING LAWYER IN ALLIANCE WITH RACIST COP' She smiled at that, 'Can't you see, the man has a point. You're meant to be in the Incident Room doing what you do. Very well, that's what they pay you for, talking the guy along, but no, you have to get all greedy and want to be in the street, out where everyone can see you. It's not NYPD you know. You're a policeman, not an entertainer.'

Jesus, it's a conspiracy. What's happening here? This isn't Sylvie talking, it's someone else. We never used to talk like this, where did we go wrong? He thought, as he slid back into black and white movie mode. Possibly she has a point. But we didn't, we talked sense, even if we disagreed. Now we disagree, and instead, we talk balls a lot of the time, and it's getting worse. He turned to say something. But she had fallen asleep, as if nothing had happened.

He awoke methodically and opened his eyes with great care, eyelash by eyelash, eye by eye. Had anything changed all that much? He wondered about this, as best he could, allowing for the hammers that pounded his eardrums. Although he felt quite near to death, he could guess that nothing in his personal life had changed overnight. Was this good, or was it bad? It would be optimistic to hope for improvement, merely on the basis of a successful late night sexual arousal, triggered off by the inconclusive recession of a quarrel, and fuelled by alcohol. His dick was still sore too; the way it felt, passing urine might lead to collapse, even irreversible coma.

Sylvie was sleeping peacefully beside him and, as he looked at her he felt about as guilty as he knew how. The plain facts were, she was in the right, and he wasn't. Straightforward enough, when you thought about it. He winced as he remembered her first words. He might have felt better if she'd called Jan a slag, but a slapper, that was really below the belt. It was game set and match, and he knew it. For the moment the best thing to hope for was that she might remain asleep, for another hour, during which he would marshal some sense. Their sexual reunion was more of a truce than a cessation of hostilities. The moral questions raised by the outcome of the siege and his part in it, were unlikely to have been written down in the backwash of screwing, if past experience was anything to go by. It would be best to be practical, and make sure that the house phone was off the hook; there's nothing like an unwanted call for starting things up all over again. His dehydration was now so bad, that he could have drunk a bucket of ice-cold water, his breath would have stopped an African buffalo in its tracks. Also he was getting recurrent waves of nausea and dizziness and, worst of all, sudden jarring flashes in the head with loud noises in the ears reminding him that today must surely be national wet brain day, and that he was poisoned, but that given time and fluid replacement he might improve, provided the surges of vertigo stopped snapping and jumping inside his head. Usually, he was a temperate person, he'd never been one for boozing with the lads, another reason why Manson and his creepy Masonic friends had distrusted him. Manson in an apron, now, that must be a rare sight. And the bloody gloves, and all the downmarket, *I'll see you right, if you'll see me right*, kit. Back to main topics. Thank God Sylvie was a temperate person too, like himself, it was just that she had been going in for, what was it 'relief drinking', as he'd heard it called, and for that matter he'd been having a few extra most evenings. Maybe he should declare for Islam, in about half an hour's time, or call AA. He looked around hopelessly and was, as ever, amazed at the useless inventiveness of the hung-over brain.

She woke and said, 'It's not funny you know,' Christ, he thought, a mind reader, just what I bloody need, and then his eyes started watering.

She repeated 'Fizz, it's not funny, all this nonsense.'

He smiled and said, 'The Kraken wakes.' And she spoke again saying 'and that's not funny either,' and fell asleep again. Too bloody true, it's not funny, he thought, I never said it was. Nothing's funny, I'll have you know, and never will be. He got up and went to the bathroom where he managed to void without fainting. He looked in at her, and saw that she was still asleep so he went carefully into the kitchen, busying himself with the preparation of conciliatory juice and coffee. It was then that he realised that he really would feel better, possibly cured even, if he could eat eight slices of bacon and a six egg omelette. That was the answer, of course it was. How foolish of him to have overlooked that. He was hypoglycaemic, that was it, there'd been a piece about it in *The Guardian*... What did these so called experts know about anything? That's another thing, the pressure of thought crowding through the head, next thing it'll be a replay of key incidents from last evening. I'll be better when that dies down. And he heard her in the shower, and wondered why it was so noisy, the water in the shower, more like a hurricane. He downed a glass of orange juice, three paracetamol and one hundred milligrams of thiamine. He felt better already. He looked up as he heard her approach, and saw her in the doorway. It's not just some trick, some artifice, he thought, and it's not how she looks. It's that, she has the ability to stop me in my tracks and make me stop thinking. However, it would do little good to kick off with a thought for the day right now, nothing complicated, that will be best. 'Good morning Sylvie,' he said and smiled, 'I'm sorry I was such a shit.' He paused, 'I should say that I will try to do better, but I don't know how to do that, you see.' She looked straight at him and he continued 'so, if you can take that on board, I'd be grateful. I really would.' She looked at him and said nothing. He thought, sod it here goes.

'OK, now is not the time to discuss anything beyond my terminal state. I'm sorry I got so bloody drunk, I don't do so often, and once is enough and so on. Anyway...' and here he suddenly lost track and said 'We have to get the problem of The Front squared away sooner or later, and what you plan to do about it, this Kurdish shit. I mean are you going ahead with it, or not? We both know that we've ducked around it long enough Sylvie. I can't pretend that it's going to be all right if you do it, and you know that. For Christ's sake Sylv. I'm a dead man if you take it up.'

Nice one Fizz, he thought, you really know how to pick the best time to talk about key topics in a person's life. There she is looking fragile, and you want to talk about her new job. He knew how she would respond, but there was still enough alcohol in his bloodstream to make him incautious. That's why they breathalyse people the next morning when they collect their cars, he remembered. It made sense. If only it was a movie, and he could say, *Oh my darling what a fool I've been, please forgive me darling*, and it would be all right and she'd come to him, lips moist and slightly parted and give him one, tongue down to his boots, dissolve to bedroom, legs over the shoulders and all that caper, but we aren't playing that game. His dick really was sore. Christ, Jan couldn't have given him a dose, could she? And that was another thing, he had a dim recollection of having made various promises to Jan about future plans. Please Christ, don't let her phone. It's just the sort of thing they do 'Hello, remember last night when we were shagging, did you really mean what you said, I mean were you serious?' It would be important to find out. Even if she had felt disappointed in his performance in the sack, she could probably put up with that, if he had made promises that might smooth her career path in some way. Oh Christ, he couldn't have done anything that stupid. It's been known.

Sylvie said, 'I can't give up the Front. What's the matter with you Fizz? It's more than getting drunk and into bed with Jan, isn't it? What's going on?'

'Nothing's going on.'

'Something else has happened.'

'I don't know why you say that.'

'Sooner or later you're going to have to tell me what it is.'

'It's something to do with the siege. That's all I can say right now, because I can't explain it. I may be going away for a while, probably.' He lied as he was hardly listening to a word she was saying, all he could think of was how to get to Jan, as soon as possible, to find out how many pints of milk he had left to cry over at her place. If he didn't find out Jan would be sure to let him know, and Sylvie.

She said 'Since you asked about the Front, OK, perhaps now is as good a time as any. Why is it such a problem for you?'

'Sylvie,' he said, 'In case you'd forgotten, we're talking about you heading up the Front for the Liberation of Kurdish Women or whatever it bloody is, that's bloody what. They want to make you Mrs President Elect or did you forget? For Christ's sake. Not exactly first choice for the wife of a copper, making his way in the anti-terrorist squad, many might say. Plus I'm not impressed by the head woman, Helen Kershaw, the loony lawyer from Enfield, Forensic Crumpet of the Year.'

'I'll ignore your remarks about Helen for the moment. The Front is a legitimate organisation which is trying to obtain justice for a group of badly abused women, Fizz, that's all it is. And if it wasn't for women like Helen they would be denied even a hope of justice.' Woman like Helen, bloody pain in the arse. Sylvie's got a total blind spot about her. Anyone can see she's a right wet who'd believe any hard luck story she was given by the first wog off the aircraft. But he knew that the real reason that he disliked Helen was entirely different and, as usual, causally related to her repudiation of the proffered services of the bald- headed pilgrim. So he watered it down to a bland, 'Not everyone would agree. Helen may not be all that she purports, to be, that's all I'm saying. Also some of us think that the Front could be a cover for, I don't know, some shower of...'

'Go on, say it, ragheads. It'll be niggers next.'

'That's not right Sylvie.' In any case, he thought I'd never say niggers I'd say coons, and, that's it, it's true, I would say it, she's bloody right. I bloody would.

'There's no point in going on about this Fizz. This is something I can't make compromises with, it's too important.' He wondered really how important to her was the plight of women in villages on the dusty hills of Kurdistan, or was it that she was flattered by the attentions of Helen and the rest? What was it to him? Why should it be permitted to bugger up his career, this concern? And thinking, stuff this for a game of soldiers, asked, 'Even if it means me being landed back on the beat or Community Policing in Ealing?'

'Yes. Even if it meant that. Some things are more important.'

Jesus Christ, it'll be a lecture on community relations and good policing for today's society in a pluralistic world next. Lessons on non-sexist, helping old women across the road, to follow.

'I can't back off from this opportunity to make a

statement,' and Sylvie thought, the poor bugger, how pious I must sound.

He said, 'OK, then. Let's do it.'

She said 'Don't you think you should go now, and say your goodbyes, I mean your goodbye to Jan, before it's too late. And before I get quite astonishingly angry.'

Fizzer was out of the flat in under two minutes, hangover banished; faced with having to talk his way past another angry woman his symptoms were wiped clean away. Another medical breakthrough. Jesus what a bloody life.

As he was going out of the door she called out, 'And make sure you tie things up with her. I'm the one who's owed a few apologies, remember. And thought, I'm being hard on him and *I don't care too much*. That's the problem.

And he called back 'I'll remember,' adding, *I fucking will too*, under his breath.

As soon as she heard his car start Sylvie took up the phone and called Helen. She had a lot to tell her this morning.

CHAPTER TEN

GIRLIE TALK

'I thought that we ought to meet in a proactive, healthy environment you see. That's why I chose Thighs. Fundamentally, I see it as a cleansing process, a chance to mark this special day for The Front in a setting of healthy dedication. OK, so we're committed people, but even committed people need to be pampered, to have a celebration even. I don't wish to appear proleptic but my body tells me this is right. If my body is right, that means there's good Karma coming down, I know it. My body tells me.'

Helen Kershaw had a point. Who would argue with good Karma for Christ's sake?

Check out the vibes of Thighs SW3, cool workouterama and hip ashram for the tightest little asses in Town, as listed in Harper's and Queen, '100 Best Bums of the Year' issue. 'A Funfest of the *rectus abdomini* muscles of the beautiful people,' as one unkind critic had labelled it. But in a place where Perfect Health for All and New Hope for The Dead in the Millenium were on offer, who could resist?

The Atrium arched over your head like a mega pelvic girdle as it welcomed you to a better life style, 'a perfect setting in which to relax and play.' Awaiting you there were floral swinging ropes over the pool, piped music out of the walls, a rub down by babes with nipples like hazel nuts on the shell, and in the relaxation lounge, majestic Koi swam glooping languidly amidst the tropical plants. The gleaming steel and superchrome ambience of this Health Enhancement Facility was such that it had caused Anita Roddick to piss enviously in her Janet Reger Body, hurl her vitamin enriched non-alcoholic highball across the meditation suite of the Marie Stopes Memorial center and slide into an impenetrable sulk, relieved only by a one hundred point rise in the Footsie.

Yes, Thighs SW3 offered delights for every sense, the ultimate meeting place to nourish the self indulgence of the terminally useless, 'No bodily experience is left untouched, no feeling untapped' said the blurb, and by Christ they were right, as many a building worker would tell you after watching the clientele emerging on a summer's morning, fresh from the seaweed wraps, depilatory waxing and make-overs. Cool, lean, tanned, hard-muscled, an army of pelvic floor muscles that would squeeze your cock like a fucking blood orange on heat, as Blunger had said in a moment of voyeuristic abandon. Shit a brick, this was prime-time totty that would make you bloody weep. The place was double sexy. *Fraise des Bois* condoms in the Men's Cottages (as they were cheekily called) and kick start vibrators in the Ladies. There were starch-free bread rolls and kosher mineral water in the Refreshment Salon; get that, Salon! Not only that, but you could eat your face off in the *Ristorante Tropicana* where the menu ranged from organic vegetarian through electrolyte-stabilised products lovingly garnered in equal-opportunity regimes.

Most people were gobsmacked by this temple for the affluent loonies with their packages of goofy beliefs, *en route* from the Crop circles of Belgravia. There was even a visiting psychic complete with Tarot cards, ready to unlock the dysfunctional relationships of the seriously rich.

The bar provided an amazing range of non-alcoholic and organic alcoholic cocktails, the latter obtainable on production of a signed letter of medical referral. These beverages were made with triple-distilled Polish Organic Grain vodka, power-siphoned through filtered ice, with organic gin, imagine that! Some persons claimed that it was vodka flavoured with juniper juice. Who cared? What a powerhouse of physical, disciplined, healthy correctness it all was. People who tried to smoke disappeared like unsuccessful contestants in Fifteen to One.

There was only one disqualifying clause. Ugly people, the fat and warty didn't make the front door, let alone get past it. Go fuck yourself, monster. This is Muff City and don't you ever forget it. Why didn't they let fellas into the place for a piece of the action, for God's sake?

The rowing machines, stepmasters, and bikes had a military air, standing like F16's on a flight line. Day and night, they whined and hummed, hammering muscle groups, extending joint capsules and stretching anything on offer.

Helen Kershaw was a founder member of this club. It could have been created for her. Hold on, we're not dumping on Helen here. That would be impossible, since this remarkable young woman could have disarmed King Kong at a hundred yards. Whether you liked her or not was irrelevant. Helen was a talented polymath who always looked great. Also she knew how to behave, and you can't fault someone for starting off as well as that. Dysplasia and worldly success are uncomfortable partners. Why knock health and beauty? It beats its opposites by a raft. Let's all join the *Herren Volk* and go down the gym.

It was certainly one big occasion for Helen, as ever in pole position and togged out in the neatest gear in town. Helen Kershaw, charismatic legal wunderkind and drop-dead-gorgeous champion of all those who labour in deep shit. Once you had kissed the air round her head, *de rigueur*, after ten in the morning, you could do a lot worse than cop Helen's rig of the day.

As far as she was concerned, the right kit was totally heavy shit. This didn't mean that she was some narcissistic *klutz* who needed admission for intensive handbag therapy every time the clasp on her Gucci had an attack of the vapours. We're looking at serious total body care, starting with HiLo aerobics and twenty minutes Hatha at seven in the morning, right through the waking day to the correct dose of sleepers no later than eleven pm. Looking right, that was it. We're talking serious business here. Clothing? Leave it out. Perfection on every hanger.

The rest was a doddle for a woman who could gauge the value of detail down to the last perfectly coifed pubic hair. She had it all in spades, as she skilfully deployed her physical presence to black-glass the opposition before breakfast. This was a logical extension of the contemporary *zeitgeist*, for Helen was never one of your humourless Postmodern gits, she just took things a bit seriously at times. She looked so good and was so nice with it, it was bloody near impossible to dislike her, since she suffered from youth, the only disorder worth having. *In your face sunshine*, she waved it at you, reassuringly.

Frankly you felt sweaty and unhealthy in her presence. If she'd been a golfer her personal style would have affected the colour of her balls, let alone clubs. Take her gaff; straight out of ELLE DEC... In one month, minimalist chic had replaced art deco. Fantastic you say? Forget it, next month, you got decadent vampires in the moated grange. Camp, Kitsch or Postmodern, Helen delivered the goods. But in spite of all this, at times you sensed frissons of unexpected, appealing vulnerability. Who looked after her when the shit hit the fan? Deep down, Helen could never be superficial. She was as multilayered as the next person. Barring head bangers, who isn't? Nobody's perfect.

The Club Director, Denise Cherry, was totally uncreased, even in a blue linen suit on the hottest day of the year. Nothing wobbled. Walk behind her, cop the two Galea melons in a bag, and forget your dry cleaning bill. In Lycra, great balls of fire, she'd make your bollocks fall off. Every time the insides of her thighs rubbed together, they emitted susurrations of unashamed rut. Bloody hell. Forget that she was Tracy Jackson who had learnt her trade in the Romany Club de Danse in Beckenham after elocution lessons, a course in advanced *fellatio* in Hamburg and graduation to The Monkey House in Dagenham where Frankie 'Crusher' Davis changed her career direction after giving her one in the back of his BMW. With credentials like that, how should she fail?

The cachet of Thighs was the first reason why Helen had

picked it for the meeting with Sylvie Edwards, her most prestigious addition to the ranks of those who could advance the cause of The Front. Which leads to the second, uncomfortable reason for her having chosen Thighs SW3 for Sylvie. It was simply that Samira al-Harfi had politely told Helen to move her arse and do so when she called her from the Front's safe house in Winchmore Hill.

'Find out where this Edwards is going and why,' she had said as she put the phone down, adding, 'His wife will tell you.'

She owed Samira some, did Helen.

But now, did she not look totally bloody stunning, as she lay beside Sylvie? Thigh to thigh. Tight buttocks glancing with oiled body-shine. Shudderama. Today was one big mother of a day, for Sylvie was Helen's discovery, and things were going well. Sylvie was exactly the person needed to sharpen certain slightly hazy, even dodgy, aspects of the Front, imagewise. The right person was required to stand up and say 'I'm backing the Front.' Sylvie was that person, no sweat. She possessed a style and dignity that could silence a roomful of malcontents, bringing them round to the correct way of looking at anything from crypto-racism in the kitchen, (BLACK PUDDING – RACIST SLUR), to unfair labour practices, (MENS WC LESBIANS BARRED PROTEST.) Best of all she was a cast-iron professional, invaluable in the continuing fight against injustice. Features that might embarrass The Front would be diminished. Not that there was anything to be embarrassed about, but it pays to be careful. Sylvie's other attributes were merely coincidental. Any Front member could tell you that, and get you to believe it.

When Sylvie first met Helen, she had been dazzled by her intellectual curiosity. Helen needed to know what was happening, her diversity of interest was boundless, whether it was the state of the equities market, female circumcision in Somalia, the national disgrace of deficiencies in alternative therapy (INTELLECTUALLY CHALLENGED DENIED AROMATHERAPY LOCAL COUNCIL SHAME) no matter, Helen had to know. In a word, she needed to know the brains of every dog's asshole. Sylvie was flattered by her understanding and ability to empathise. Everyone else was flattered by it, for Christ's sake. Helen knew so much about one without having to ask. She personified so many attributes to which Sylvie aspired, although she might have gone on the defensive about the need to make occasional compromises.

Places like Thighs SW3 were not usually on Sylvie's visiting list, but Helen had fixed Sylvie's critical duff once and for all. Helen exemplified unattainable things for the likes of Sylvie. Chill out child. Being white does make a difference, no matter what the brothers and sisters might say about the morality or otherwise of it. Helen possessed all these things, plus the capacity to fascinate, and Sylvie was bewitched to the extent of wanting to wear the same clothes as Helen. She even asked her advice about clothing while ignoring certain inconsistencies in Helen's persona.

But Fizzer, ever the wary copper, was on to all this crap in a flash. He didn't reckon window-dressing, and said so. That didn't help their increasingly friable relationship one bit. Fizzer's reaction was ill-considered, as were his snide comments about The Kershaw Synchronised Swimmers, as he called Helen's circle. Hostile sentiments of the sort you could expect from a bigoted copper, snorted the captivated Sylvie, as she uncovered more about Helen. Fizzer grew resentful and thought, *if she goes on like this I'll...*, but he didn't know what he'd do, so he stopped and fell back on coarse comment, hinting at Sapphic leanings in one breath, wanting to get into her pants in the next. Who wouldn't?

'Well, he would wouldn't he darling,' said Helen when this was relayed to her. Then the silly bugger made a complete dickhead of himself (Sylvie's words), by assigning Helen stereotypes, ranging from power-dressed, whore-mistress-from-hell, to Superdyke-Nympho. But Helen couldn't be categorised that easily. Worse, he had tried vainly to illuminate her sexual life with the magical powers of his livening stick, the Arcadian Kidney wiper, only to be handed the frozen mitt. *Once you've had some real cock, you'll be all right love.* The universal panacea that stops supposedly intelligent women talking bollocks, that's all they really understand, as laid down in the Senior Police Officers' Manual. Cop this lot darling.

'What else could you expect from someone who functions at mid-brain level?' asked Helen, who had read snippets about the Neurosciences in *The Guardian*, Science Section.

And now here was Helen, diamond-bright in silver Lycra, smiling at her new possession. Wow! That was the trouble. When Helen took you on, she possessed you. An attractive incubus, certain nasty-minded enemies had said. Oh yes, Helen was an extremely attractive person.

But she would never have described it as anything so simplistic as that. She would have called it 'the experiential experience of the presentation of the self in its interaction on role-playing-capability and personal-empowerment,' and, depending on who you were, you might be given the Helen Look. Fizzer had come well unstuck when he reacted to the Look, uninvited and sulky at a Front *Soiree*, when he took a fit of pique, and hinted that she could do herself a double-favour darling, if she came across.

An impressive person was Helen. To be honest, she was probably as full of shit as the next person, but then who isn't? In any case, once you had defined shit, Helen would agree with you. What else could you expect darling, the way things were in a corrupt society? Life was never dull when she was around.

She eased herself off the sun bed, uncrossing her legs a shade slowly. She looked at herself fondly in the mirror. Who knew, perhaps there was a camera behind it? She permitted herself a languorous flash of her perfectly moulded undercarriage. Quite balletic.

'What I can never understand is, how that husband of yours got himself involved in all this sort of thing, really? I mean, I'd have thought that just sticking to being a copper, catching villains and things, would have done? Tell me. I'm interested. I need to know if I'm wrong.' This should start the ball rolling. The tiresome black cow would deliver the goods sooner or later. She looked keenly at Sylvie's brown skinned body. She knew damn well that she was wrong, but she was tactically interested. 'You're not feeling tired are you? I mean, maybe we've started you off too high up on the DynoThrust Fasttrack Walker?' She glanced at their reflections in the mirror, 'Tell me more about him. He fascinates me. All that domination. Pathetic isn't it. Aren't men?' Dreamily said.

Sylvie smiled and said, 'Tired? Not at all,' as she eased her painful lumbar spine. God. How her arse hurt,' It's a long story, I suppose it was all an accident based on his own experience, you see.'

And she thought, Christ, I'm talking like Helen now. Fizzer would say that, and laugh. Then he'd say, next thing you'll be calling me darling and using your Harrods accent.

'I'm not sure that I do,' said Helen, 'Would you like to try the heavy lifter with the biceps pads? Improve the spread on your *latissimus dorsi*, love, or you'll get all saggy round the rear end.' It was reassuring to discover that Helen could be a bitch. Sylvie smiled. Frankly, she was shagged out, but it didn't show and it certainly wouldn't do to let on. Christ knows what other bloody pointless tortures the place had in the pipeline. She was sure that she looked better than Helen, and Helen wouldn't reckon that. That was for sure.

Sylvie thought of saying that Fizzer's story began with hostage taking rendered banal by a public that didn't give a toss. Competition from stories about IVF and football is hard to cap. Hijacked aircraft rate few paragraphs. End of story, so what's new? Forget the lefty devotees of terrorist chic in N1, go fuck your collective mothers, but what can you say? She might have said something like that, but frankly her ass was too chewed up by the exercise machines.

So she settled for, 'It's a long story,' wishing to Christ that she could take it easy for a few minutes as Helen jumped on the bloody treadmill for the fourth session. And she didn't even have a sodding bead of sweat, nor a slight moistening around her perfectly formed mons. Didn't seem fair somehow.

'Tell me,' said Helen, 'I have to know,' in her therapy voice. Helen had been doing pelvic thrusts for twenty five minutes and could have picked up a fifty P piece with her World Series style Singapore Grip, and cracked a Brazil nut between her glutei for an encore. And what was all that about therapy you might ask? Oh yes, Helen was definitely into therapy, as long as it didn't get out of hand.

Sylvie could have come back with an explanation of anti-terrorist tactics – wearing-the-buggers-down, and establishing a relationship, with no deals struck. Sylvie could have said all this, and a lot more, but she was a shade out of breath, and to Helen's annoyance, the black bitch was undoubtedly a traffic stopper.

'What's the matter?' asked Helen 'Not too heavy for you is it? as she looked over Sylvie's smooth, unspotted brown skin. Fizzer had a name for that, but Helen didn't know that, just as well, since she would have disapproved.

'Would you like me to massage you, I can get some Tea Tree Oil.' She tried to sound casual, but Sylvie's smooth thighs were not renowned for inducing calm. Creamy brown, it was too much. Helen tried tightening her anus but even that didn't help. If this went on much longer God knows what might happen. She smiled caringly, her voice as steady as possible, 'You must have whatever you wish. It's all the same to me.' And looked admiringly at her own reflection. Christ, was that a wrinkle on the angle of her jaw? Hold on, just a lighting error. Twenty minutes in front of the mirror to tighten the sterno mastoids, just making sure, that's all.

Sylvie could have said that the police invented negotiating techniques, and sorry, but bollocks to that, it's all done by shrinks or worse, whose well known skills heal all. Yawn. People hear what they want to hear.

'I'm thinking, I'm not sure what I want,' she replied, and that was all she could say, thinking, it's funny the things that happen, like that dumb Swedish cow who got laid by her captor.

Helen was looking at her, massaging the insides of her thighs, trying to look calm. She said 'I find this very relaxing you know. It relieves tension. Would you like me to page Martica?'

Sylvie thought, sometimes common sense goes out the window, that's what Fizz had said, at the time. He met the requirements; someone who could bargain for people's lives and hold the line at the same time. And all for no extra pay. A small price. She didn't say that either but concentrated on avoiding eye contact until she felt less knackered.

'Thanks,' said Sylvie, 'I'd like to try the parallel bars. I used to do that in Liverpool in the Union.'

'Good heavens. Of course,' said Helen, 'Liverpool, I'd forgotten. How grim that must have been for you. The one that got away, that's you.'

'It wasn't as bad as all that, I was born there.'

'I'd never have known it. Not a trace of the accent.'

'It was great really.'

She still said great with a touch of scouse, 'grayth'. Christ, now I'm feeling horny, perhaps it's the vitamin enriched water.

'I don't know about you, but I'm going to relax the rules and rest for a few minutes. I think a mineral water might hit the spot.' She as near as damn said the G spot, but hardly liked to. It was all too much.

'You were saying about Liverpool. That's where you met him, you told me. Amazing things relationships aren't they? So capricious.' I wonder what she'd say if I asked her to go down on me.

'Under what circumstances? I'm not sure I follow you there.' I don't want to get a funny head half-way through this sodding workout. I feel fit enough. What's her problem. And in any case, what is she on about life in Liverpool for? Probably trying to make things easy. I suppose I must look a bit, no I won't say it, stressed out. Fizzer always laughs if I say that, sod him. I wish he hadn't done it with Jan though. Anyone but her. Looks like a nymphet-turned-concentration-camp guard. And I don't mean anyone else but her, I wish he hadn't done it with. It's with anyone but anyone, that's what I mean. Sod it.

'Relationships. Well, the way things are at the moment, I think we should leave that on hold.'

'Do you fancy the saline douche or the Colonic irrigation? It's great for removing impurities. I know. Must be difficult. I'd heard he he'd been known to display an interest in seeking

106

fresh sheets, someone must have said something,' she laughed. This bloody woman is beginning to get up my wick.

'Good, here come the drinks. I'd forgotten, I ordered us a surprise celebration. Champagne non-alcoholic cocktails. Yummy.'

Fuck that, I could use a real drink. Thank Christ Fizzer can't see this; he'd really do his nut. Fresh sheets. Who's fooling who here? She must know, that I know about Fizzer and how he tried to give her one. He told me as much, after the party at the Embassy. We laughed. He said he wouldn't mind getting into her pants OK? But he didn't reckon the medical exam, let alone the questionnaires. He does make you laugh. Bastard. I wonder where he is now.

'I hear he's going away. You did say that didn't you?' She sipped her drink,

'Wonderful, sometimes I think one can overdo the booze, don't you?' and smiled, 'On holiday is it, he's going, that it, is it?' Getting a bit eager now, that wouldn't do.

'I'm not sure,' said Sylvie, and thought, that little blonde cow and her tight ass, 'To Rome, on business.' Black knickers, I'll bet, and Impulse sprayed inside her thighs. How infantile can one get, I wonder? This isn't me talking is it? Thank Christ Fizzer can't hear me. I bet she does though. Spray herself.

'Yes, you know how it is, in the Force. You never know what's coming up next.'

'I can imagine. Poor you.'

So it was Rome after all. Samira was right.

'Oh, not at all. Things have been a bit difficult lately. We both need a change.' I wonder where he is at the moment. I've half a mind to ring the little cow up. That wouldn't do though.

'I think I'm ready to have go on the mortifier, as I believe they call it. How about you? You decided on the *Cotoletta al Fungi*, wasn't that it?'

They sipped their drinks. 'Anyway, enough about the policeman's travel arrangements. We've more important things to talk of. I'm hoping you'll address the Plenary session at the meeting in Paris. Excuse me for a minute or two. I have a call to make.'

CHAPTER ELEVEN

SQUARING THINGS AWAY

And so he had called her as soon as he'd finished with Sarno; told her he would have some news for her when he got home that night, and that it was important for both of them, and had immediately hung up, going silent and white with sudden anger. Sylvie knew that it was never good news if he hung up. He had spent another desultory day with yet another debriefing, more paperwork and talk. After the high of the siege it all seemed even more tedious than ever and it hadn't helped when he looked through the post mortem reports and saw the bodies again, cold, bloodily steaming and gaping in the cold mortuary air. Which one had been Ibrahim? Foot and eye should not... did it matter, had it ever? Whose foot? Whose eye? Better not to ask. As if anyone knew anyway. In any case who would you ask? Too late to ask him, Ibrahim. What was that he'd said 'You're a dead man Mr Fizzer', like he was putting me down? What did he mean by that? A man with soul so dead. But he was a dead man, how would he know anything? Get off.

Waiting for his return she was looking out of the window, unsure now, whether she wanted to see him, but knowing that she did, for all that. She knew that when he came through the door, she'd still be unsure whether she wanted to see him at all, for the moment, perhaps longer, or did she dare to think about that? Perhaps everyone had been right, her family, her friends, his family, the lot. It would never work, no one seemed able to stop saying that; at least that would please his mother, what a tiresome, superstitious old cow she was, no wonder Fizzer couldn't handle her. Like he said one time, 'Listen Sylvie, when it comes to mothers, it's even Steven whether they're Jewish or Irish, except that the Irish are the worst variety.'

Always the funny man.

A few streets' distance away, she heard police car sirens erupt, and she started, a sudden flash of fear inside her, like a blow really, in the pit of the stomach, the books are right. That's where you feel it. This is another thing that I don't like about this life. Frights, always frights, and always, they bloody come when you don't expect them, I suppose I did know. I'm not stupid, that's what he always says. You're not stupid, like we coppers Sylvie, what are you complaining about? Got a good education, didn't you? And laugh.

He came in lively enough, all unconvincing and cool, but it lost itself there, as soon as he started in with, 'Here's where we're at Sylvie,' he said, and stopped dead in the water. He's more tired than I've ever seen him, even for a copper. Pale and grey, stubbly ghost face, just a tired copper. And it's not just the drink and bloody Jan, it's more than that. She thought, I don't like the way he looks, and I don't like it when he tries to talk like Harrison Ford, it means he's worried, and he's nobody's worrier. He's not kidding around here.

She said, 'Manson must have said something really heavy. What's happening? Got fired did you? That it?'

And checked before she almost said, 'at last.' And hated the thought.

He stood, looking awkwardly at her, all stiff and on the defensive. Not himself now, was he? He'd spilt something on his jacket, and where was the handkerchief from his top pocket? When she first knew him, she used to say to him sometimes, 'You do know, one day I could go right off you?' Could she? People did go off each other. The shallow waters of affection.

'Who said anything about Manson?' he said, too quickly. She thought, I can read his mind. He looked at her 'You see, something came up earlier. I meant to tell you before but... Sylvie, I'll be going away for a while, out of the country on a job, just a few days. You know. It's a special secondment, just a temporary thing you see?' But she didn't see.

He had approached the door of Jan's flat feeling apprehensive, foolish and indecisive. It was on the first floor of a terraced house in Pimlico next door to a greengrocer. On the corner there was an Irish pub with all-day food, Sky sports TV and pool tables. Somehow, her door didn't seem as inviting as it had appeared the night before. Also it looked different. On the previous night it had given him the horn, the smell of her body spray on the stairway had indicated that her pants were up for grabs, but in the morning he could smell hot bacon fat, and it made him feel queasy. The night before he'd heard pleasant low music as he came up the stairs. In the morning it was Chris Evans and Prodigy. It was an unfair world, what with a hangover and all, and now, who knew whether there could be waiting for him a woman who wanted all sorts of rubbish, of which the best to be hoped for was promotion, a problem easily solved. He had the feeling that it might not be as uncomplicated as all that. She was a calculating little scrubber, wasn't that the most likely thing? Bloody whore. Open your legs to the Guvnor and here comes promotion, right up to the moustache if you want it.

Most important was the fact that he didn't want to be there at all, as simple as that, and wished that last night had never happened. Immediately he became aware of the significance of the words of the song that he had been humming all through the day at work, his old man used to sing it, and it had always got right up his throat, to be honest, 'Eyes of blue, five foot two, she is my little kootchy koo, has anybody seen my gal?' or, had he got the words wrong, and did 'five foot two' come first? Had anybody seen last night's balls up, would be nearer the mark. Being on the brink of a total professional and personal cock up is never a good way to start anyone's day, and may lead to the unremitting fuzzy reiteration of the words of other people's half-forgotten songs. Maybe there is such a thing as the unconscious, how hidden conflict drives you down strange pathways when you don't know it, like Oliver James in the *Sunday Times* Colour Section. I definitely will never get into this sort of thing again, definitely. But he probably would, that was the trouble.

Jan had smiled as she opened the door. Not exactly a welcoming smile, more of a let's get this over for God's sake, you tiresome wanker, I knew you'd bloody turn up, what's the matter, got a sore dick have we, sort of smile. She looked about as welcoming as Camilla Parker Bowles greeting a delegation from Gay Pride.

'Well and about time. What held you up? Wouldn't be cold feet, by any chance or did your wife give you a smacked hand?' she said, smiling not at all sweetly, tits well up though by Christ, and nipples that would poke your eyes out, you had to acknowledge that. He had sweated and had felt his sperm count rising. Then he remembered that she probably knew more than she let on, about something, it had to be. Even the fog of booze permitted recollections of certain unexpected knowing remarks she'd come out with.

'What was all that about this bloke Ibrahim? Is that a problem for you or something?' she'd asked after they'd done it the first time. How much did she know?

Then she'd said 'What's this foot and eye you were on about? You kinky or what?' You wouldn't believe it. You can't bloody win can you? Either of them or both. They've got your balls on a plate from the off. In any case what's meant to be so wrong about being afraid of getting your bollocks sawn off? Seems normal enough.

So Fizzer had said 'It's not that simple. Listen Jan, about last night, hey, maybe we got a bit adrift there, but it was not to be.' Holy shit, this sounds like an ancient Associated British Pictures movie, as shown in the early hours of the morning, he thought. Maybe I should add, *we did our thing but forget it, it's a one way ticket to nowhere kid. We had our thing. It was fun though.*

Jan replied, as deadpan as you like, 'What's on your mind? Last night, you had a lot to say as I recall. I know, you probably feel unable to remember it, but you will.' A pause, 'You mean you don't remember. Big changes coming and all that. What was all that about? Or don't you care to remember? You forgotten? And when you nearly cried. You forgotten all that?' She made a choking sound, soft and inviting. Hoarse orgasmic chuckle.

'I don't know what you're saying.' Christ, but no question, she was a horny little thing even after a heavy night. I'm bloody sure I will remember what ever it is, that's the trouble, you cheeky little cow, he'd thought. What's going on here?

'And, OK so it was another one night stand after all. That it? Perhaps you should think about one night stands. I mean, how do you really know this was one? I mean is that what your idea was? You should think about it one of these days.' Yes, and one of these days you're going to miss me honey, you bet your sweet ass. They never let up do they? What a bloody stupid question. Is she expecting me to call marriages births and deaths in The Times for Christ's sake. Jesus, what a nerve some people have.

'You gave me a strong impression of a man who was having a hard time with his wife, the way you went on. I'm not just a walking shag you know, I'm me, and I think you need to realise that and think about it.'

Jesus, he thought, I really need this. It'll be counselling next. In any case, what's wrong with being a walking shag? You could have fooled me, straight up you could. She's been rehearsing this old shit.

She wasn't going to let up however, and continued,' and so I thought that even allowing for all that, possibly there was a little more going on for both of us there, at least that's how it seemed to me.'

She'd smiled and said 'Why don't you come in and have a sit down or something?' Jesus, he thought, sit down, yes that's about all we're looking at Miss Bloody Whiplash, you can forget about the 'or something,' from where I'm standing. At least she didn't commit the worst offence and say something daft like 'fancy a coffee then,' so maybe, there is some hope for her yet. Whether or not she read his mind, remained an open question, but she had replied, 'When someone starts talking the way you are, he's going to tell you that we should forget about what was said last night, and that we'd had a few drinks too many, and sometimes we all get a bit excited, and it was let's face it a special occasion, we're adults, both of us, and so I'm sorry, sod off OK, but don't think you can just play with your own feelings like that. Right?' I love the understanding, don't be-afraid-to-look-at-your feelings, bit. Where do they get this shit from? Calculating bitch. Jesus who wrote this script for her?

'It's no good Jan love, don't give me that old crap. I don't talk like that and you bloody know it,' he laughed, 'I think you're getting a bit ahead of the game here Jan. It's not a question of saying, sod off, Jan. It's just that I thought we should put things on hold for the moment?' And thinking, why is it when you say, it's not a question of anything, you really mean, it is a question of, and nothing else? She doesn't know what I'm talking about.

'If that's what you want. All I need to know is what it is you really want from me, from yourself, maybe you don't know.' She's bloody right there. Perhaps it would help if she told me what it is she thinks I want, or better still, whatever I might have said to make her think that I wanted anything. Beyond wanting to get out of here about an hour ago preferably. This is all getting out of hand. Where are you *New Zealand Woman's Weekly?*

'I don't think you understand what I'm saying. Just because you've got sort of a biggish cock, you don't have the right to do anything much purely on the basis of having one you know.'

Funny the way they always go on about your cock sooner or later. What else do they think about?

'I'd heard about that.'

'And it doesn't give you the right to come in here and set terms and conditions.'

'Who said anything abut terms and conditions.' She's doing her nut, that's it, straight off. A few drinks and I'm landed with a nutter now.

'Let's leave thing as they are for the moment. OK?' It's just that I'm not sure how they are.

'Whatever you say, maybe you should go home now Fizz, and we can talk about it when you come back. You should look at your feelings a bit more.'

That's it, that's the clincher. He'd walked to the door and turned, deciding not to commit himself, he said 'Fat chance.' and started walking away. Why were women so bloody unreasonable? Hormones? PMT? He turned, 'And you know something Jan. Sylvie was bloody right. You are a little slapper. Tell that to your girlie pals.' He paused, And while we're at it, please don't call me Fizz. Just bloody don't do it, ever. Got it? Only my wife is allowed that privilege.'

Odd thing that, he thought, that she had known that he was going anywhere, let alone somewhere. What was all that about? Maybe Dave had told her something at the party. That must be it. Has to be. Why would he do that though?

And now leaving aside the question, I ask myself, of where anyone in the world dug up someone like Mr F X Sarno and put him where he is, Jesus where did he get a suit like that? Tommy Nutter's estate I suppose, where else? Leaving that aside, there's now the matter of explaining to Sylvie what is going on. Where does F X Sarno come into all this? She'll want to know who he is, what the hell am I doing swanning off somewhere, for no reason that I can give her? To myself, if it comes to that. It's no good pretending that his explanation makes any sense. She'll need answers to these questions, legal mind and all, and, the way things right now, I don't have any, that is, if there are any. Mainly because I don't know, and she's not likely to believe that anyway, which will leave unexplained, the unanswered questions surrounding Ms Jan and all who sail in her. And another thing, who does Sarno think he's fooling? All this shit about him not being sure whether we end up in Athens or Rome. Mr Sarno is not a front runner in the straight answers handicap. As soon as I've told Sylvie, I'll need to talk to Dave, at least he knows how things stand with Manson.

'You're not listening to me are you Sylvie?'

Christ, she thought, perhaps I'm not listening. Hard to with the lies and all. And maybe I don't see and what's more, I'm not going to see. I can tell that by the smile. Who does he think I am? I don't know, that's the trouble. Who does he think he is, for that matter?

'There's nothing new in that. What's it this time or shouldn't I ask?' she paused, 'Frank answers haven't been the strongest point on your agenda lately.'

He looked as if he didn't want to hear that question, let alone answer, but said.

'Sylvie, it's one I can't talk about easily, first, because I'm not meant to, and secondly because I'm unsure about what the assignment really is, not that I expect you to believe that. OK, so I don't have the right to look for favours from you at the moment, but I need a favour or two, just for a few days. That's all I'm asking. I'd like you to do that, if you could watch my back for me, whatever way you can. Watch my back. Until this is over, that's all I'm saying. After that we can...'

She interrupted, 'Just go on as usual, is that it?'

It's a bad sign too, when he starts off by calling me Sylvie, and then carries on, as if that was how he always started a sentence. But he wasn't going to accept any ball that she threw to him. He just looked as if he was going to continue talking, he looked so bad though, she thought. Jesus, this is worse than I thought.

'The first thing is that you should assume that there's a tap on the phone, probably has been for days. Next, believe me, you'll have pavement artists round you, all the time when I'm away. Obviously, you'll not let on that you know anything. I hate this shit Sylvie, Christ knows I do. Keep your ears open for Dave, you know you can trust him. He'll be listening out, and he'll be in touch. I know it.'

Thinking, as things stand, I don't know it, for certain as

yet, but there's no need to go into that. I'm not sure who I can trust. Maybe it was him and her in the movie. Jesus, what's wrong with me here. It's just another crazy trip, yes that's it. The police do this all the time. But it wasn't like that. Not the way he looked. But it isn't. It isn't right.

'If Manson should want to see you, you'll need to go along with him but I doubt that it'll happen. And yes, if a man called Francis Sarno should call you, play as dumb as you can.'

Watch his back, how would I do that? So she said 'There's no point in asking what's going on, I can see that.'

'That's it Sylvie.' He looked relieved that she wasn't pressing him, that she was just looking at things, preferring to see nothing, just pointing his head in the right direction for him, possibly. She said 'All this sounds like the SIS or something to me. Am I right?

'How can I answer that one. Just assume that I'm not sure myself at the moment. On the face of it, I'm just off to carry out a simple assignment. But it smells bad, and I don't know where the smell is coming from, except that I don't recognise it. I've said enough. Somebody is playing games with me. I can handle that, as long as I know why. Doesn't seem much to ask. It's a whole crock of shit Sylvie.'

Sylvie said, 'I'll do like you ask, as best I can, but whatever I do or don't do Fizz, you know that somehow you've to be honest with yourself about Ibrahim sooner or later.' Fizzer said 'And, what the fuck is that supposed to mean? Are you crazy? What's that to do with anything? Why bring that up now?'

She's right, I suppose, but why now, when I'm asking a favour. I'm running around, getting ready for amateur hour with a bunch of spooks from the Box, and she wants me to sort my head out. And she brings in Ibrahim, as if I'd got his name written on my forehead. What's it all about?

'Great, Sylvie, one more time, I'm sorry if I'm such a bore. But I'm off on the bloody ocean wave, and Lil's in the family way, don't you get it? We're all on the wrong train. Christ, the phone's tapped, they've got a tail on you, Christ knows what else, and now, you want me to confront my feelings and all that

116

shit. Is that it for Christ's sake? All you can come up with? Sylvie, it's getting my balls shot away, I'm talking about, and it isn't how to make a fucking American quilt time and look at relationships, or didn't you know? Someone wants my arsehole and all you want is a load of chat. Is that what you want?'

It was no good. Her presence banished anger too, he knew that. How did she do that? It worked.

She said 'Are you thick or something? I'm trying to do my best to get you to look at what's happening to you, to us, and all you do is make smartarse remarks. Right? Fizz, I've never seen you like this. It's not just this trip that's the problem, or the Front. You can handle anything, you know that. It's more. I'm looking for reasons, that's all.'

And he knew that she was right; there was more to it.

Sylvie asked, 'I have to know more about this trip Fizz. Can't you give me some idea?'

'You know I can't do that,' he replied, and weakening, said, 'All I can say is that I'm going to Rome. And that's all I can tell you.'

And as he left the room he said, 'Foot and eye should not lie,' but she didn't want to listen to him as she looked straight ahead, not smiling.

She had picked up the phone and was saying 'Hello, Helen, is that you? I need to talk to you soon.' As she put the phone down she was suddenly impatient with it all exclaiming, 'Foot and eye. Is he going soft or what? No he'd not do that.' She didn't hear him going, but he'd heard her.

CHAPTER TWELVE

SHAKING THE BAG

It had all started off pleasantly enough, though Sylvie had felt annoyed when she was summoned, out of the blue, to 'have a little informal chat' with Sarno. On her way there she'd felt apprehensive and angry, but by the time that she arrived, these feelings had worn off, to be replaced by a dull sense of weary resignation. She realised that, in all probability, he was only doing his job, and that perhaps her best course would be to go through the motions and not get too steamed up about things. What was the point really? Indeed she was quite pleasantly surprised when she was greeted, almost apologetically, by a rather Sloaney young woman of the sort that Sylvie instinctively would have loathed, but who seemed friendly enough. She realised that the young woman, a fresh-complexioned, mildly gawky ingenue, who stalked about as if she was walking the course at Badminton, was someone who had probably been groomed for the job since schooldays at Heathfield or a similar finishing school for retardate aristos. She had possessed a Hermes scarf, Shires appearance and big hair, from birth you could say. Big knickers too, probably. Plus the mandatory immobile upper lip and jaw. And a smile that flashed on and off, like the light outside a minicab office, and too many teeth, by a raft. What else could one expect? But she

118

couldn't have been more polite actually; what a bore all this must be for you, I'm really maste frightfully sorry, you poor thing, you must be famished, here, let me get you a cup of coffee, did you have a frightful time finding us? Poor you. Which latter Sylvie enjoyed no end, as it happened, and thought, mindless little sod, she's a victim of an oppressive caste system which churns out young women like her by the battalion, ever ready to service the needs of upper class male dominance until the day that she dies. Well, she would see it like that.

'What a ridiculous how d'you do, it all is, wouldn't you say? I mean, I say, I really am sorry about all this. You see, it's just that there are one or two loose ends that seem to need tying up, so if you'll kindly bear with me for a while, I'm sure it won't take too long Mrs Edwards.' Sarno had stood there, looking out of the window, as she came in, and he had hardly turned round to greet her, didn't even give her a look. Not one. He let the words trickle over the tip of his shoulder as she sat down. And then he turned and smiled at her in quite a friendly fashion. Again she was pleasantly surprised, after their previous meeting, half wondering if this was some special manoeuvre from the spooks' manual, the chapter about how to conduct an interview with a black person who is likely to be uncooperative; that was how she interpreted it, but then, as he still seemed to want to be more polite and friendly, she dismissed the notion from her mind, remembering that anyone can feel touchy, oversensitive, even paranoid, under these circumstances. She resolved to make the best of it, to give it her best shot.

In any case there's no point in getting annoyed about this pointless intrusion into my personal space until the matter has been dealt with, she thought, they probably mean well, in a way, and I'm damn sure that Helen would deliver the goods to the bastards, if they abused their position in any way. The situation was ideal for Helen to deal with, and she didn't see Helen letting it go by default. No way. That's all it was, a game as far as this lot were concerned. But it was odd about her having failed to get hold of Dave, like Fizzer had suggested. He'd probably gone away for the weekend or something, that was it, Fizzer always reckoned that Dave had a bit on the side. How she loathed that expression. Fizzer had them, bits on the side. Why was that? Did he know? Do any of them?

'Please to sit down and make yourself comfortable Mrs Edwards.' It's Liberty Hall here, that's what we call it, as I'm sure Mr Blunger would confirm, if he were here.'

I'd always heard that the upper class people like him were arrogant insensitive bullies, but he seems to be better than at first sight. But, be fair, I'd never really believed it, as I'd never mixed with them. Maybe it's because they don't actually have to do anything much, except go to galleries in Bruton Street and parties and stuff. Why has he asked me along for another interview? Not that I'm worried. And these, and all her other little doubts and fears were safely laid to rest, in no time. Just like that. This was going to be, if not a doddle, nothing much to get bothered about.

'Good enough, but before we start the ball rolling, I thought it might be rather jolly if we had a look at this movie.' Just like that again. Out of the blue, a movie. She was astonished. Who wouldn't be?

The lights dimmed and Sylvie was shown a movie of herself entering the offices of the Front in London, entering an office and being handed papers and a package that could have been a handgun, but could equally well have been a book. And somehow then it all became mixed up with a Tom and Jerry cartoon where Tom falls through a television set into a swimming pool full of ice cream and then gets a bang on the head, and is found wandering around with loss of memory and a bandage round his face after Jerry squashed him in a door, and he is flattened like a postcard and poured into a jug and over Jerry's breakfast cereal, and the huge dog with big teeth tries to eat him, and then it was Sylvie with some woman. Couldn't make out what they were doing. Oh No.

'Very good' she said, as calmly as she could, 'we've just seen a movie of someone who looks like me entering the offices of the Front and stuff. So what?' Sarno's face seemed to change for a second, she checked, no it was just a trick of the light. Why had they shown her that stupid film? It was all a bit of a muddle in a way.

Nevertheless, she felt she should maintain the semblance of a position of strength, and she asked, a little sharply, 'Is this interview to be conducted without witnesses?' adding, 'I say that, because, if it is the case, then I must request that I am legally represented. I feel that I should protest against the manner in which I've been obliged to come here. I would have thought that with my husband, at present employed by you, as far as I can make out, without the knowledge of his superiors, that you might have wondered if you might be getting more than a little out of line, by subjecting me to, what any Court would regard as a form of harassment with that stupid movie. Inspector Edward's superiors aren't going to like this. Had that not occurred to you? It's a form of harassment too loudly in my opinion.'

Sarno smiled at this and replied 'I don't think I quite follow you Mrs Edwards. Do you think that you could clarify what you just said, again, if you please.'

'Is this interview to be conducted without witless?' she asked, 'I say that, because, if it is, I must request that I am legally reported. I protest strongly against the mannerisms in which I've been obliged to come hero. I would have thought that with my Husbandry, at presently employed by you to pry on people, as far as I can see, without the knowledge of his superiority, that you might have wondered if you might be getting out of linen, by subjecting me to, what any Cunt would regard as a form of harassment. Fizzer's superiors aren't going to like this. Hadn't that occurred to you Horse? It's a form of horsemanship you see. It's the boh you understand.'

'I see,' said Sarno, and smiled across the desk to Blunger, and said 'Well that certainly makes things a good deal clearer, wouldn't you agree with that Blunger?'

He smiled back in agreement, and nodded encouragingly at Sylvie, saying softly 'Yes it certainly does. Wouldn't you agree Mrs Edwards?'

'I thought that he wasn't here and now you say he is. And is this interview to be conducted without marked waitresses?' she asked, 'I say that, because, if it is, I must say that I am sorry that I am illegally repellent. I protest strongly against the manneritsic in which I've obliged to become here now this were it? You knew what I meant too? Into it again I got it. And would have thought that with my husband, at present employed grainfully, as far as I can understand, without laboratory coats knowledge of Hershey bars, that wondered if I bargle getting of line, by subjecting me to, what any memorandum would regard as a form of harassment of a state. Fizzer's superiors aren't going to larger lager, sorry, I mean lager this. Hadn't that occurred to you? It's a form of harassment you see always, it's so hard.'

'Why do you keep repeating yourself Mrs Edwards?' said Sarno. 'Blunger I wonder, have you noticed, Mrs Edwards keeps repeating herself?'

Sylvie said 'Why are you talking likely thatly?'

'I'm sorry Mrs Edwards, I don't think that I quite follow you. Is something the matter?'

'Waht did you sayner yan?' almost shouting now, said Sylvie as she started to shake and her eyes angry wet with tears. And she shook more violently and her mouth was dry; her heart pounded. What was happening here? To her? Her thoughts? Hot urine spurted into her pants.

Sarno said only, 'I think the time has come for you to cut out the crap, Mrs Edwards. What have you to say to that? Oh, and please, you shouldn't bother to talk of not coming here to be insulted, or any such nonsense. Let's be clear about one or two things here, Mrs Edwards. Be assured that Inspector Edward's superiors will do exactly what is required.'

All she could do now was to stare ahead. What was happening?

'You are not impressing me Mrs Edwards, by trying to pretend that you don't know what you're saying if that's what you think you are doing. This does not impress anyone here.' He smiled, and then seemed to change, 'I'm sure, Mrs Edwards,

122

that we could work something out, if you could first of all, help me to resolve my difficulties with The Front. Or do I mean doubts and uncertainties about an organisation that appears to be tainted? I feel that I don' t understand its purpose and so on. That's all I am asking you see.'

'I don't know what it is you want me to say. All I know is that the Front is a bona fide organisation.'

'In any case Mrs Edwards,' if he says Mrs Edwards one more time I might just freak out or something, she thought, that's what he wants, of course, so I won't. I'm not really worried by all this nonsense.'

'As I was saying, Mrs Edwards, until I appeared to lose your attention a few moments ago, this interview is not being conducted without witnesses, since you have brought the subject up. Legal representation is another matter. Perhaps you had failed to notice the presence of my colleague, Mr Blunger, who is sitting over there.'

Sylvie looked in the direction to which where he was pointing, pointed or whatever he had done. Odd thing that. Blunger was there, on the opposite side of the table, sitting beside him. She hadn't noticed him before, or had she? He hadn't been in the room when she came in, and hadn't Sarno said as much? It was odd, she couldn't remember. Feelings of panic lurked and mounted. Fear without content. What was happening? Blunger certainly was sitting on the other side of the desk. He was right. No, the tablet it was. She had failed to notice him when she came in, that was it. Simple really. Heat of the moment. Sarno droned on, 'Mrs Edwards, we have been inner here for an hour now, and I think it really is time we achieved a modicum of progress.' He smiled patiently and exchanged glances with Blunger, or was it Blungert? He was saying such odd things, perhaps he wasn't a wall person. Did I think 'wall' there? What did I meaner when I thought that?

'Non nonsense,' she protested, why did I repeat myself?' Sorry did I say that before? I've only been in here ten minutes at the mostery.' She looked at her watch. An hour and a half had elapsed since she had come into the room; perhaps her watch had gone wrong, or was it fifteen minutes. She couldn't remember and the watch face looked unfamiliar. Was it a new one? She didn't recognise it. She didn't recognise the suit she was wearing. When did she put it on? It wasn't hers. Why was she wearing the wrong clothes? They weren't hers at all. She looked at Sarno for encouragement, and at Blunger. They smiled, but nothing came through. And they smiled at each other and then back at her. They didn't seem to be themselves. It had never gone wrong before had it, that thing on her wrist, what was it called? Anyhow, what was the maltter with her worlds, they seemed to went wring, no wrong. I wondered only what was that world. Hold on a minutely. She sounded fenny, no finny, not find to the words the inside her head. What was happening? She looked at that thing on the wall too, it was to tell the time, what it is called to tell it. It was no longer there. Oh yes it was, what is, what is called the name that tells the what it tells. What? Why wouldn't the words come out, when she thought them as she scrolled them through her mind? Funny, it seemed that it was better now, they were all right now, I must have been a bit dizzy for a moment there. It's a hot afternoon, that's it. What is his name? And also the other man's name it?

'Excuse me but, I have to ask you, I can't remember your namely is a namely and is it? Could I have something to drink, my mouth is a bit dry, you see that? Oh my God, I am sorry that I...I am what, are am I? Where I can't. Oh Christ.'

'Mrs Edwards,' said Sarno, 'Is anything the matter? You seem abstracted, yes that's it, isn't it Blunger? Abstracted, that's it.' He smiled.

'Perhaps Mrs Edwards would like a cup of tea, Blunger. She's abstracted you see, perhaps she's unwell. Would you like us to call a member of the Medical Profession? No Please Blunger, do see if you can find a cup of tea for Mrs Edwards, there's a good fellow.'

I'm not a bloody tea boy, he'll never realise that, but I'll oblige him this time as things are beginning to get interesting. She should start coughing any minute. You have to hand it to Sarno, no doubt about it; it's as if he's been up for a crash course in the Dept of Pharmacology in Cambridge. 'Always use the best information source Blunger. One or two biggish doses of Chlormethiazole, and a few hundred milligrams of a serotonin re-uptake inhibitor to spice it up, and her memory will be down the tubes in no time at all, Blunger, and it's immediate short term memory loss, on a fucking plate. And why will she cough? I'll bloody tell you why she'll cough, Ted. She'll have been scared shitless after the memory disturbance, and not getting her words right, that's the one that really pisses them off. To the point that she'd sell her dear old granny down in Alabammy, right down the river, you mark my words. They say the worst thing is, not being able to remember what you thought you'd done five minutes ago. Some of them shit themselves, you know.'

I always thought he had racist undertones, Alabammy indeed. She doesn't even remember having, was it tea in Reception they gave her? Cheap too. Fuck Amnesty International.

'You were saying Mrs Edwards? About The Front?' Sarno was now efficient and brisk and beginning to look unfriendly.

'Yes, well you see, as far as I understand it the Front is a perfectly legitimate organisation with a real interest in the promotion of justice on behalf of persecuted people.' She spoke more clearly now and felt better.

'Come off it and don't, please don't come at me with any of your infantile political sloganising, this isn't some bloody activist group in Brixton Mrs E. amongst the all brothers under the skin brigade, thank you very much. This is bloody life, and it's telling the bloody truth time, you black cow, and don't you forget it. Don't you think it's time you started giving us the full SP if you catch my fucking drift.' He paused and smiled innocently.

'Not exactly undertones are they?' said Blunger, to anyone one that cared to listen or answer. 'So let's hear from you, you bloody jumped up barrack room lawyer. Bleeding hearts bloody do-gooders and people like you make me laugh, in case you don't know. Had it not occurred to you that The Front is exactly the sort of organisation which might be the subject of misuse, a cover for other activities.' He smiled.

'I've no reason to think so.' She was struggling not to lose her temper, she knew where that would lead.

'And Ms Kershaw, just exactly what is her function in the Front?' he continued, as if he'd said nothing that was in the least out of order, once again smiling, 'It would be helpful.'

'She is the National Co-ordinator.'

'I see. Mrs Edwards. My information is different, we don't seem to be getting very far do we?'

'It would be. Your information, I mean.'

'I am told that The Front is a cover for a group which has well established links with an active terrorist group, and my information is that Ms Kershaw is well aware of these matters. What have you to say to that?' He wasn't going to give up.

'I am sure that you are incorrectly informed. All you people are paranoid fascists. Everyone knows that.' She was trying to remain calm here, but he was getting to her. What would he come up with next?

'*Bordelles de merde*, Mrs Edwards, if you believe that you will believe anything, and I may add, I ain't just whistlin' Dixie.'

Blimey, the Chief is getting a tiny bit wound up here. Sometimes he lets the French go to his head.

And then, quite suddenly, Sylvie started talking. Just like FX had said she would. And told them all she knew about the direct links with Hizbollah and Hamas. Not a great deal, but enough.

'You realise that I have strong grounds for seeking redress over this irregular interrogation,' said Sylvie some minutes later, none too confidently.

'You must do whatever you choose Mrs Edwards,' said Sarno, 'of course you must. But I must caution you that there is now the matter of your husband and his immediate future to consider. You have a narrow, almost non existent range of options Mrs Edwards. And, I might add, your professional future is far from a bloody rose garden. The Bar Council won't take kindly to direct links with organisations that employ murder, intimidation and kidnapping. And, no pious crap about Freedom Fighters, if you please. Mrs Edwards. Your feet won't bloody touch, by the time we're done with you.'

'Don't say you're dragging Fizzer in as well. What is this, some sort of blackmail, you're trying to intimidate me?' But it was no use. She realised that she was beginning to sound like a line from one of Fizzer's favourite movies. But, Oh Dear, he wasn't going to come through the door, like Warner Baxter, cordovans and an open neck shirt, and say, *Honey, guess what? I just built the Great Boulder Dam.*

Sarno ignored her question, he had her, cold as a dead mullet.' You tiresome woman, I'm talking about Inspector Edwards. You don't seem to understand, or perhaps you hadn't heard. His plane has been hijacked you see, and we wondered if you might feel able to assist us in getting him off the hook, now that you've blown the whistle on your raghead chums. You got him into it, so to speak.'

He's putting me on. No he isn't. He isn't, he's telling the truth. She stared ahead. 'If what you say is true. How could I possibly help? It's nothing to do with me.'

'Mrs Edwards. Don't fuck with me please. Your husband is in a hijacked aircraft and if you don't, or can't help us to help him, anything that happens will be your responsibility and no one else's. Do you understand? It's down to you Mrs Edwards, you see. Now, in a few moments I propose to call Ms Kershaw. You will persuade her to do what is appropriate. If you cannot do that, then your husband will not see you again. I hope that you understand.'

He'd said that Fizzer would not see her and he was right, she did understand. That was the worst thing of all. Game, set and match to Mr Sarno.

CHAPTER THIRTEEN

TRAVELLING MAN

The inside of the Airbus 300 was cool and up to a point, it afforded you a guarded, carefully-measured welcome. Rotors whined quietly. The air-conditioning hissed, the interior of the aircraft was new and unworn, giving false comfort to those fearful travellers who were likely to be impressed. If it's that new inside, it must be in good nick, or would it be better if it had evidence of just a little more use? Even the sick bags suggested that vomiting might be a life enhancing experience. Some passengers were reassured by the illuminated route maps displayed on video monitors. Therapeutic party games designed to bolster the confidence of the nervous passenger, or are they customers? Everything was blandly reassuring, given the suspension of disbelief that is needed to encompass the outrageous notion that several hundred tonnes of metal, assorted plastic, avionics and machinery, all full of flammable liquid can be anything less than a fireball waiting for a match.

As long as the fly-by-wire kit was up and running, and the computerised systems remained virus free, frankly, Fizzer wasn't all that bothered. He'd never relished the prospect of receiving the attentions of International Rescue Services, that euphemistically named company of quietly-mannered body snatchers, who assemble bits of people and their effects after the latest disaster has happened, but you never knew. No doubt the cabin staff bore all this sort of stuff in mind as they welcomed you aboard with glacial smiles. Why is it the Virgin Airlines women all have beautiful bums, and the British Airways ones always look as if they want to check the regularity of your bowel movements? Better than the worst days of Pan Am, en route for fiscal collapse, when the cabin staff sometimes appeared to be manned by not-so-young women who behaved like concentration camp guards.

As Fizzer settled into his seat, he scanned the passengers as they came by. Sir Jocelyn and his minders were safely in the first class, on the same side as himself, and well within sight, apart from the curtain to be pulled impatiently across the gangway during mealtimes, lest steerage passengers become enraged by the sight of the fat cats in First Class stuffing their greedy faces with airline muck. So far, so nearly quite good.

As he looked at Sir Jocelyn, it was difficult for Fizzer to see what was meant to be such a major big deal about the poor bugger, though he did look a bit more pompous than he'd expected. That went with the job and its status, and would mean that he wouldn't be an easy sod to pull in; he'd make a fuss until the last bloody minute. OK, so the man was a toff who used the privileges of the diplomatic bag to run a business, dabbled in Middle-Eastern politics to inflate his feelings of self importance and was about to overdose on hubris. Hardly novel. He was unsure of the minders though, he wasn't expecting them; second-raters by the look of them in their Boss suits, button down Ben Shermans and crappy shades. Jesus. They had not been on Sarno's agenda, but from what he'd picked up about him, that was no surprise. Sarno, now there was an odd guy for you, not your typical spook, gridlocked well down in memory lane, yearning for the good old days. At least he hadn't banged on at him giving him a load of cobblers about tradecraft, drops, dead-drops, safe houses, dry cleaning and all the bloody rubbish that the SIS arseholes got into, when they'd have been better employed reading the papers and listening to the radio, where all the real heavy shit was.

What a bloody shower of craphead amateurs they were, for Christ's sake, leave it out. All the stuff comes from punters who sell it doesn't it? But they just couldn't see it, with all their party games on the go, bloody shower of big-girls blouses. Most of them wouldn't last three months in the average nick. No need to get steamed up though. All he had to do was keep an eye on chummy and lose him, full stop. Goodbye promotion, me old son. Cop this. At least the sod hadn't done a runner, and so maybe it was as well that he was tucked up with the gorillas, whoever they might be. The poor bastard looked about as cheerful as someone who had just signed up for voluntary euthanasia on a wet November evening in Amsterdam, gulping down the fizz like a man with no arms. And, after all, what were they going to do in Rome? He didn't see himself trailing Sir J. around the city around the clock, hanging around gay bars. There would have to be a simpler way of arranging things. You could always enjoy Italy, but Rome was not favourite. Now, if it had been Florence, and he thought of the River Club, its baroque, fire-in-a-whore-house furnishings, and pretty maids all in a row. He'd enjoyed the more traditional side too. Be fair, you have to get out a bit, to break the soporific boredom of an International Conference on Terrorism, even in Florence.

More passengers came aboard as the muzak played 'The way we were.' He noted that Barbra Streisand's whinings were as awful as ever. Thank God some things are sacred.

A dozen walking-dead package-tour dickheads came on line, shuffling along in cheesy trainers, shell suits, baseball caps and anoraks. Already some of them were rehearsing complaints about fancied fears of an unexpected run on the duty frees, wishing that they were back home in Nuneaton eating buns. Yellow tour labels fluttered about as they struggled with their in-flight baggage. Next, a few Japanese, body-odourless and vomiting continuous psychotic smiles, a quartet of surly, whiffy backpackers brandishing their baggage, paradigms of obnoxious awareness. Then a few assorted Middle-Easterners. As usual, the Jet set hadn't booked in on this flight. Where

130

exactly did they travel? In their own Lear jets, he remembered, that was it. Had to be. Also there were no nuns, stretcher cases or groups of veterans in berets off to the scene of another World War two cock-up, poor buggers.

Fizzer bore in mind the presence of our Middle-Eastern friends. Or perhaps he was a bit suspicious. Right, at least Lord Snooty and his pals are in the three seats three rows ahead to the right. He wondered if a brief wander into the first class, and a better look at him might be useful. Perhaps not. Looks green, right enough. Wouldn't blame him. Hang on, now I'm getting twitchy. He thought of pretending to recognise him and then apologising, but thought better of the idea. I'm a copper, not a Butlin's redcoat. Hello Sir Jocelyn, fancy meeting you, do you remember me from Lancaster House? Reception for the Brazilian Secret Police Chief, remember and you tried to cop a feel with his son in the carsey? No point really.

Next thing he was interrupted by the arrival of a youngish geezer who looked a shade more interesting than the average passenger. A bit flash there mind you, but a mover right enough, always sniffing around for a piece of the action, judging by the way he looked around, slightly jerkily, side to side with the odd shrug, but when you looked at him more closely there was more to it than that. The man was a watcher and a noter, no doubt about that, he looked handier than most and that included the cabin staff, tight bums, bossy mouths and all, not to say the Chief Steward, your typical airline nancy boy. Yes, the newcomer was tasty with it, when you took his gear on board. Prada jeans, black silk shirt, off-white jacket, big gold Rolex that you wouldn't pull off his wrist if you valued your ass, somehow that came across; gold I.D and alligator boots. Looked as if he'd had the odd run in with the law in his time, didn't care who knew either. He might be a good to better travelling companion, if he didn't over-do the chat.

'Excuse me. This seat isn't taken is it?' he said smiling at Fizzer, as if he knew him, now there was a point. Why would he do that? Now, who's paranoid? Fizzer wondered about this, as he shook his head. 'No, of course it isn't.'

'Well hark at me, how stupid. I've got my boarding pass, look at that, amazing isn't it?' And he laughed.

Fizzer wondered why anyone should be amazed at the possession of a boarding pass, but the guy looked like someone who might go through life in a state of amazement. Some people like being amazed and it probably does them good. Perhaps the man had spent too much time in the Middle East or something. He might turn out to be a bore, that should be borne in mind. Some people lose their brains once they're on board an aircraft, and next thing they're telling you about their brother-in-law winning at darts last week, or the pub quiz, South East London Region. Or what they'd do if they won the lottery. But he said politely enough, 'Go ahead,' not being naff enough to say 'be my guest.'

His new companion laughed as he sat down, 'That's handy then,' he sighed, 'for a minute there I thought that you might object to me sitting next to you. People are funny. I thought, fuck it, that could be double iffy for me what with sitting next door to a copper, know what I mean?'

Fizzer wasn't going to buy this straight up, no way was he, and replied 'How did you mean, sitting next to a copper then?'

'That's all right, anyone can see you're one of the boys in blue. Nothing personal, if you catch my drift?' and he looked at Fizzer dead straight in the eye, slightly mockingly but friendly with it. I bloody know who you are chum, but you don't know me, sort of look. Again Fizzer had the feeling that there might be more to this guy than just another Jack-the-lad with too much lip, but thought, wait and see. Something said, don't mess with this man. Look beyond his flash appearance, there's more edge to him than that. The man was not easy to slot. There was something a bit contrived about his gear, however, he was harder than his beach bum exterior suggested, no sweat, by a bloody mile. Big neck on him, for his height, for a start.

And so Fizzer made a few friendly noises and looked at his paper. A lay preacher arrested, grave charges. A fourteen year old crack dealer had won a scholarship to Merton. Male problems. Adult videos. How I beat Cancer. What's new?

The aircraft was nearly full by now. In the row behind two women settled in. One was giving the other a hard time, because as soon as she sat down she'd asked when the drinks were coming. The hard-time giver was sharp-faced and cerebral, hair pulled back and a tight unsmiling face. *Guardian* held like a passport. The persecuted drinker was one of the damp knickers brigade, all ankle-length denim, navy tights and pointy shoes that turned up. Also a helpless expression, archaic lipstick and beads. Fizzer smiled. A little light relief would be welcome. The prospect of the routine pulling-in of Sir Jocelyn Fancyarse did not appeal and frankly, now that he'd had a better look at the man, he was beginning to wonder what all the fuss was about, but realised that this might be a reminder to be careful. That smarmy ponce back there at the Box was no fool, and who knew, there might be more to it than just pulling in this fellow, and anyway what the hell was it all about really? Why bring in the heavy mob to cover the glorified drug bust of a toff who fancied under-age rent boys? Got to be more to it. Jesus, I am getting paranoid. I wonder what Sylvie's doing right now? Not Jan. Probably talking to Helen. I don't know. What do they talk about? Me sometimes.

'I really can't understand Liza why you insist on demanding alcoholic beverages as soon as you enter an aircraft.' said the insistent voice behind. Liza replied subdued, but determined, 'But you see Mary, surely you remember that I travel badly and get these awful feelings in my tummy whenever I fly. It's fear of flying, I know that, but I find just one small drink seems to help and in any case,' she added, becoming forlorn, 'it is meant to be a holiday isn't it?' This was not good enough for Mary, who sailed in with, 'Holidays are not meant to be exercises in self indulgence my dear. If you are unable to see that alcohol is merely a crutch to avoid problems, then I hardly know what will become of you. You should use this holiday to look at things, perhaps more closely, a time for self-examination and the like. You should read something. That might help.' If Liza agreed with this statement, which Mary handed out, like a life sentence, she gave no sign. Mary now changed tack, having disposed of the potential evils of strong drink and turned to higher things, 'There's a good piece in *The Guardian* about the new production at the Almeida. You should look at it and take your mind off silly fears and their relief by alcohol.' Mary said 'Well I just thought that maybe one drink wouldn't hurt, that was all.' At this point Fizzer's companion looked over the back of the seat and said 'Too right darling. Go on, let her have a bloody drink. I'm going to have one as soon as they unchain the booze any way.' And he winked at them fondly, adding for Mary's benefit, 'Go on darling, why don't you go for it too, you look as if you need one too.' Mary didn't reckon that and looked frostily through him, as he turned to Fizzer and said, 'Do you reckon she's a member of the shag-in-the-sky-club?' Jesus, perhaps this guy will turn out to be a pain after all and here I was thinking we might have a laugh and what does he do? Look at me folks, I'm a right arsehole. Who knows? Who cares?

Undaunted, the young man said, 'My name's Leo Jackson, most of the punters call me Jacko, you'll understand that they're an original lot, my friends.' He laughed. 'I'm on my way to Rome for a movie I'm involved with, working on, know what I mean? Sound engineer. Mixing with the VIP's one day, recording a blockbuster a few weeks later. That's what I do. It pays the rent.' Fizzer was more uncertain about him. A rush to judgement possibly. Well, at least we've got a Joker on board. Perhaps I'll call him that. But when he looked at him, he saw that it wouldn't do. I'm not a Battery Sergeant in the US Marine Corps, and this isn't Parris Island. He was a lot more than a sound-recordist in the movie industry, he was sure of that. Still he's a change from the yellow skin club and the backpackers.

So he said, 'OK Jacko. Just one thing, I mean look, I'm a good travelling companion and OK, so maybe I am on the Force. A word however, I don't need to advertise that, I'm sure you'll understand. So let's enjoy the trip. Incidentally, how did you get the shooter on the plane? I didn't know sound men used shooters, or is that something new?'

'What shooter?' said Jacko all surprised and innocent, 'Shooter, my life. You joking. I swear it. You crazy. Me with a shooter on?' Fizzer said 'The one in the left crotch holster. A nine millimetre Makarov; definitely not kosher. Got friends at Court, have we my son?' This is what we call establishing verbal authority, I should tell him that. Jacko adopted a mocking tone, and said 'Clever with it aren't we? OK, so I have a piece. Not a hanging offence is it? I work in some bloody funny places on certain news features, and sometimes, it can get real heavy, know what I mean?' 'It depends who has the hardware and who gets shot.' replied Fizzer.

'Here come the drinks.'

FOURTEEN

LUCKY FIFTEEN

Ted Blunger had been a member of Brinks for quite a few years. He always referred to it as 'The Lucky Fifteen' because it was Number Fifteen, a four storied Regency house in one of those streets in the area around W1, the sort of area where you never know which end of the street you are in, and where the front entrance of the building and the rear end seem to be exactly the same, on the identical side, you could say, but they aren't. It was a pleasant handsome building which had escaped the Office development strategists of the area and managed to retain its identity but had let go of its original dignity. Like many of its upper class patrons, it had gone down in the world. Some said that the place had formerly been the home of a Duke, others said that it had been a knocking shop. Neither story was correct. It had been the property of a Hungarian whose family had, since the sixteenth century, held the sole right to import feathers from their native land. They had fallen on hard times at the turn of this century, after the decline of the hat, and sold the place to a bankrupt hotelier who hanged himself on his braces in a bedroom in the Ritz. Nevertheless it still looked like a family home, from the outside, a down-at-heel hotel, possibly, but unmistakably upper crust. You entered through a dark hallway that smelt of gravy and wine bottles. It could have been the entrance to an inn in a seedy market town in Hampshire. Then you walked up the stairs, past prints and photographs of the Russian Royal family before the visit to the cellar, to a bar where people talked in loud voices, greeted you in a friendly way but would probably knock you down if you didn't like foxhunting or claret. They smoked without guilt, ate meat all day, and they didn't fuck around with white wine and mineral water. They would screw your wife, as soon as look at you, if they fancied her. No sweat. And they didn't wear shades or any crap like that. They drank astonishingly large quantities of Scotch and Champagne before, during and after partially edible meals. Cocktails were available for the timorous. The cuisine was, let's face it, a coronary on a plate, cooking on the fatty side. In the bar there were photographs of past members, an Almanac de Gotha of the nastier dregs of the aristocracy, certain racing car drivers of the thirties and a catalogue of effete psychopaths whose spiritual home was Kenya, or as they called it, 'Bwitish East.' There was also a photograph of a fascist Duke and his American whore. The bar furniture was a mixture of leather and chintz, and there was also a club fender and newspapers that no one ever read. Its detractors spoke snootily of Brinks as being an ongoing AGM of the living dead from the Shires, slavering after the jam roly poly, while they eyed the lubricious waitresses in their fifties who were reputed to give certain older members smacked bottoms and blow jobs now and again.

In the anteroom, Blunger sat at a table with Helen Kershaw. 'Yes, I've been a member here for a few years, more than I care to mention, my father put me up for it when I was at school.' It's no good, he knew well, I'm too old for all this. Sometimes I long to be an old fart, and then I wouldn't have to go through all this nonsense. Just go to the Twenty Nine and play a few games of Waitomo Jack when I got tired of Seven card Stud. Can't be bad. Sandra could do the cooking.

FXS had said, 'Don't forget, make it sound like you're getting on a bit, and while you're at it, refer to the place in

Wiltshire, that never fails, and remember, these things count Blunger. You can tell her that your brother is Joint Master of the Beaufort, anything; she'll be so bloody angry, she'll believe anything you tell her, there's nothing like anger to suspend disbelief, and she'll cough. I'm not asking you to marry her you know.'

Bloody great. Thanks a bunch Chief. Some times I get the impression that he thinks I don't know what I'm doing.

Sarno's introduction to the idea of how Blunger should spend the evening hadn't impressed either, 'Now that grumpy Mr Plod is on his way to the foreign, we must busy ourselves, Blunger. Knowing of your penchant for the society of interesting women, I have decided that you are to be awarded the plum assignment of the month, a social divertissement that will call for a range of tact and sensibility, available only from a person of your degree of *gravitas* and style. It will be an experience that is certain to be regarded as the most coveted *desideratum* of the intelligence world. I know that you'll dote on it.'

A Senior Civil Servant might well be found bludgeoned to death in the Vauxhall spookhouse, thought Ted. Why does he have to talk like that? It's the schools they send the poor buggers to; spending your formative years getting your arse felt by teachers, plus the toffee-nosed bastards you're with. Daddy's Roller. What he's got lined up this time? Steaming romps in the House Training School, after a call from The News of The World, as like as not. Or the Chief Nursing Officer of the staff health service, advocating the legalisation of dope. If only it were. Frowning, he had ventured, *'Is that right? I'll look forward to the briefing, in about a week, if it's all right with you.'*

'Come along, Blunger, many a young fellow half your age would leap at this one.' That's another of his acts that gets right up my nose; hearty housemaster at a second-rate public school. I hear you've got your Colt's cap and there will be walnut cake for tea. My lady wife would wish to have parley with you with you fellows, anent the disco for the Midsummer Ball. Please God, don't let him do his Sherlock Holmes, I couldn't bear it.

'And what would that be?'

'Don't be such a crosspatch. I want you to get to know *La Belle Helene, la fille du regiment*, you know who I mean, Ms Kershaw, one of the rising stars in the legal firmament, and a possible Lord Chancellor one day, if the Gianni Versace Foundation ever gets its way, or so I'm told. Benenden and King's, the best start one could ask for amongst our legal brothers and sisters Blunger. Need I say more? I'm told that she wears an OE tie in rare moments of intimate disclosure. I feel that we don't know her as well as we should. I don't have to remind you that she is the woman who recruited, if that is the correct term, Mrs Sylvie Edwards for The Front. We need to know much more about all this fucking nonsense than we do so far, and before it's too late Blunger. Don't bother me with her file. It tells us nothing, that's why we have it. You know that too. Take her out to dinner or something. I'm told she's the best of company, and knows everything that needs to be known about various matters of interest. Better still, she is, by all accounts, quite a gossipy little piece. Now, I bet you wouldn't have thought that, would you Ted? I did hear one tiny word that might be of use, however.'

And that was that. Sod that for a game of soldiers, he wasn't to be had for the chance of spending an evening in the company of the Medusa of The Middle Temple. So he came back with 'From what I've heard, that sort of thing is about as likely to succeed as taking The Rev Ian Paisley to the Annual General Meeting of *Opus Dei*,' he paused, short of the right answer. 'They say she's not the sociable type, or so I'd heard.' The way things are, I'm surprised he didn't say he wanted me to find out what makes her tick or something. Jesus.

'You have been doing your homework, I can see that. I need the information for tomorrow morning Blunger, so you'd better get on to it, now. I have arranged dinner *a deux* for the two of you at your own club. When I told them that I was your uncle, they were *absolument bouleversee*. This saves you the trouble of arranging it yourself. Who said that your best interests are not constantly guarded? I notice you didn't ask me what I knew about her, that might be of use. How remiss of you. Sometimes I wonder if you listen to a bloody word I say.'

Helen Kershaw? Jaws, you mean? Serves writs like Kleenex; she's not going to fall for a heap of crap like this.

'Hold it Chief. This chick pisses barbed wire and razor blades, according to Sandra.'

'And how, Blunger, would Mme Sandra, if that is how she is addressed, how would she know?' He's right. Hang on, how would Sandra know anything about Helen?' Look Guv, Sandra's all right, do you have an attitudinal problem here?'

Sarno didn't even bother to answer that one. Sarno was right, Sandra, isn't exactly the sort that Helen's likely to have met. Where for Christ's sake? I mean Helen and Sandra, not exactly soul mates. It's the fishnets I suppose.

'If I could summon your attention, Blunger, I asked you a question.'

'Well, isn't that amazing Guv, I'd got something else planned for this evening. As it happens I have a heavy night at the British Avionics Society in the pipeline tonight at the Royal Institution.' I don't think he'll believe that one somehow; Jesus he means it, this maniac, he expects me to meet this bloody woman this evening and discover all, just like that. And buy her dinner, when I could have been playing blackjack at the Twenty Nine. It's not only not fair, it's a one way ticket to Manchester. How would Sandra know her for Christ's sake?

'You haven't been to a professional meeting for three years Blunger.'

'Point taken,' replied Blunger, 'In any case, how can we expect Helen K, to meet me out of the blue, just like that?' Blunger drew breath, 'Surely you can't be so bloody soft as to think that she's going to come along, and it's, hello, how do you do, Mr Blunger, I've heard so much about you. Oh yes, how very interesting, I've always wanted to meet someone from the SIS; very interesting work it must be too, preserving the security of our dear country, I mean. Yes, of course I'll take my knickers off, will this doorway do? Let me help you. Ted Dear, you seem to be having difficulty getting your dick out. Well one would, wouldn't one, with someone waiting for it, with a two foot length of cheesewire at the ready?'

'I really don't think, Blunger, that you need to descend to puerile pornography,' said Sarno loftily.

Helen looked intently at Blunger, as they sat in the bar and sipped the Club famed single malt. 'Frankly, I don't know what I'm doing here, but you see, I don't often get the chance to come to places like this, you understand, Mr, I'm so sorry, forgive me, I'm hopeless at names, you see I've forgotten it already?' I don't believe it. This could be good for a laugh. She's doing the helpless act. Why bother? She's bloody taking the piss. I like that. That gets you a few votes, Helen. For a start she knows who I am, and second, she knows heaps of places all over London, they're life support systems for the likes of *la Belle Helene*.

Maybe Sarno had been right after all. 'Wear that dreadful striped suit of yours, and do your gambling-man act, start off at Brinks and get her over to the Twenty Nine. Horrify her by introducing her to your louche gambling friends. It'll set her off and induce indiscretion on her part. Remember Ted, anger clouds the mind. Moralising superbitches often yearn for a bit of rough, Blunger, and it may be your chance to provide her with it. She'll be so affronted by your decadent ways that you never know what she might come up with and you can get into your right-darling, drop 'em and quick-about-it act, in a manner of speaking that is.'

He's at his most bloody crass when he tries to be coarse, it's foreign to his nature, as he would probably not say. What's wrong with the suit anyway. I got it at Cecil Gee, didn't I? Mind you, she might be amused to meet Eddie the Greek and Barking Mad Robbo from Dagenham.

'I don't know what you're talking about Guv.'

'It can work like a dream with the most unlikely women, or so I'm told,' he said, and raised his eyebrows, dripping with virtuous disapproval of the sinful ways of the *canaille*. Make you sick.

'Look Ted, here is the pitch, as I believe it's called,' That was bloody rich that was, next thing he'll be saying, follow that cab, 'actually you're interested in the Front, a well meaning wealthy philanthropist or something, a friend of the Arab, pissing in the faces of the Israeli lobby, I don't mind. And are prepared to put up money to the tune of one hundred K. You'll be amazed how many doors that will open. Especially when she sees you arriving in your chauffeur driven Roller, to collect her, Blunger, are you listening?'

Imagine it. He hadn't told him that he, Sarno was going to be the chauffeur. Not only that, but when he dropped them off, he'd said 'And Cinderella did go the ball after all. And by the way, the word is that you might have something in common. Someone told me at lunch, don't forget it.'

Helen continued to gaze at him with concern and interest as he said, 'Yes, I was interested to hear from Al-Gossairi about you. He's very impressed with all that you're doing with the Front. A real contribution to Arab unity.'

That is, providing you've never seen the smelly buggers, eight deep, waving their boarding passes in the transit lounge in Jeddah and scratching their dicks.

He certainly moves in influential circles by Christ, how the hell did an old tosser like this get in with that crowd I wonder? Sounds as if it might just about be interesting. Has to be.

'Al-Gossairi, Oh really, I've never met Mansour, but I'm told he's one hell of a sharp person. I find the well-educated, westernised Arabs, such fascinating people. It's the interplay of cultures I suppose. A challenge and a statement, all at once, is how I conceptualise it. Wouldn't you agree? Writes very interesting verse I'm told. Didn't someone review some of his stuff in the TLS? How lucky you are to have access to such interesting people.'

People like her actually believe all the crap they talk. They'd have to, wouldn't they? Jesus, she's practically fluttering her eyelashes. Interesting verse, my arse and parsley. Bloody Pam Ayres more likely. I didn't think she'd fall for the educated Arab bit though. For Christ's sake, he probably stands on the lavatory seat to piss. No doubt about it, the most unlikely women wet themselves over Arab money.

'Oh yes, well of course, my Middle East days are ancient history by now, but I spent some time in that neck of the woods, some time ago, I'm afraid.'

I prefer to hold off the Middle East for the moment actually, dogbreath, it really doesn't do to sound too interested just yet. Time enough.

'I know. Fascinating. I hear what you're saying. We must talk about it some time. I'm just so impressed to be in this place. It's really surprisingly atmospheric, in spite of everything. Oh Dear, have I said the wrong thing? You must think I'm an absolute yokel or something, I'm afraid.'

'Not at all Helen, I hope you don't mind me calling you Helen, my dear,' Something tells me I'm not going to like this young woman. She's far more creepy than I'd realised. Too narcissistic? No, it goes beyond that. Watch her Ted, you'll be calling her, Darling next, and Sandra wouldn't like that.

'Not in the least,' she laughed. OK turdface, what happens now?

At least she has the air of someone who never plumbs the depths of asking what one does. That's a point. You never know.

Here bloody goes. 'I wonder if you'd be interested in coming to another club I tend to visit. I play cards there.' She'll assume it's a bridge club. And it'll be interesting to see what she makes of it. The Blunger test.

'We can have a little something here first. The Steak and Kidney is pretty good and of course, in the Thirties they invented, their own special drinks here.'

'Oh, really. I think I'd heard that somewhere.' Get the furniture, will you somebody. I suppose I could always throw up over the chintzy sofa in the bar. 'It's amazing how real class always shines through, isn't it?'

Who does this bloody woman think she's fooling? He nodded 'That's what I always say. There's not many of us left.'

143

There has to be an afterlife, to reward me for all this. It's not asking much. It wouldn't do to run into Sandra at the Twenty Nine Thank God it's her night off. I suppose I could have got round it. Oh yes, Helen, darling, this is Sandra, she's helping me with a study on splitting tens against tens, and the risk factors involved in doubling down on split pairs. But it wasn't Sandra's evening off, as it turned out. Just as bloody well; Sarno remarked later.

As they got out of the cab outside the Twenty-Nine, Blunger sniffed the showy affluence of W1, big silent cars, not a doler in sight, hints of perfume, unwrinkled, unsmelly clothes and thought, how atmospheric it all was, on the whole and wondered if Helen was noticing it and marking it down for early demolition by the fluffy-haired prat in No 10. She'd been talking about the Front for the past hour, and Blunger was dead weary of it, give you a pain, who gave a toss about the Front for Christ's sake? The past hour, all the bloody way through the Club special Mixed Grill, with a side order of Black Pudding, bubble and squeak and a pint of Black Velvet in a Club silver goblet. Even that didn't silence her. Never bloody drew breath, moving from grievance to grievance. And all that booze and fodder went down her neck, as the rarely astonished Blunger, later remarked, without touching the ruddy sides, make you bloody puke. No question the woman was full of surprises. The cab rounded the corner of Lower Hay Street and there lurked the entrance to the Twenty Nine, tucked between a Travel Agent and a bent gallery that sold the best cocaine in Town, the doorway flanked by two small velvet lined windows, each of which displayed a solitaire Champagne bottle, a dangerous break with tradition this, deplored by the more conservative Club members.

Inside the doorway stood Shiner, two hundred and fifty pounds of controlled contempt, dark blue gabardine and wrap around shades. His white shirts were dangerously so and his feet Ferragamo shod. Tasty.

'Turk's in, Mr Blunger.' he said, 'Team handed.' That was enough. If he said nothing, then was the time to start worrying.

They passed through the lobby, all welcoming and dark red-flocked expensive paper, gold candelabra, smiling hostesses, the full shmear. All perfectly executed down to the last tax deductible penny by people, whose business it was to remove as much money from you as possible in the shortest possible time. The only give away was the presence of watchful men. The lobby reassured you with good lighting, nothing too bright, but a contrived, comforting sub-brilliance. At the end of the lobby, you caught glimpses of the rooms, where the bright lights were confined to those which shone on the table tops. Glimpses of the usual mix of punters, real gamblers, crazies and the plain desperate, all of them wound up, and in deep shit from birth. Plenty of body language in there. The shaky hand, dead giveaway of the punter, ace high, waiting for the flop.

'Turk's waiting for you in the bar Mr Blunger,' said a dealer who wore an ID saying 'Gilda'. It rounded off her dealer's kit very well, and already Helen was ready to go apeshit. Was she ever?

Turk was big, and wore wrap round shades. Black tie. Not a drop of sweat on his body. It was generally agreed that he had been lucky to obtain a work permit. It was supposed that he must have friends in some Government department. Little was known about him except that he had started life in Dothan, Alabama, had served for a time in the US military, and had then been employed as a weaponry expert by the Vinnell Corporation, an American-based company that taught emergent countries how to kill each other with anything ranging from cheesewire to tactical nuclear weaponry. He was reputed to have a butterfly tattooed on the end of his penis. Most people didn't bother to say much about Turk beyond, 'Don't mess with Turk.' And they didn't enquire about the butterfly. Strange company for Blunger, whose friends, particularly those who didn't know him well enough, and those who knew nothing of the *arcana* of gambling, never understood this abiding interest, at variance with everything else about him. Their notions of gambling were reinforced by popular myth, nourished by the Aspinalls and Goldsmiths of this world who tell less about gambling but more about rich obnoxiousness. But then, wealthy assholes with big mouths are two-a-penny in any walk of life. The Five Million Dollar men, the World Series operators of gambling, the guys who made fools of the Nevada gambling Commission, are sharp cookies, steeped in probability theory, who spent their time in Vegas beating the system, where there was little time to do much else. Being Jewish helps; Jews are more intelligent than Gentiles. Also gambling is a Jewish vice. Gentiles drink too much, Jewish people don't. Ted Blunger could easily have been a professional gambler; he had the conceptual simplicity of the expert gambler and knew instinctively, that Poker stops being a game of chance, once the deal has started, that the six rules of blackjack can be learnt in ten minutes, and that people who say 'I never back a horse these days, the odds are so bad,' are bloody fools and not worth talking to. That was why Sarno had picked him.

Turk nodded at Blunger and said, 'Who's the brass then?' Helen's gaze would have stopped a Chieftain tank, but Turk meant no harm, he was genuinely interested. 'Looks as if she gives good head,' he remarked appreciatively, 'Listen, Mr Blunger there's a problem. There's a counter on twelve and we thought you'd help out. Thanks.'

And he turned and walked away to his legions. The incandescent Helen drew breath. 'I think that I'd better leave right now,' said Helen. 'That was barbaric.'

'I wouldn't take too much notice of Turk,' said Blunger, 'He's all right when you get to know him. In any case, you should stay and see the fun.' For the first and possibly the only time in her life, Helen had been near enough wrong-footed. 'You see, Helen, it's important,' said Blunger, 'Always play in your own league.' Curiosity weakened her, as she heard herself asking, 'What did you mean a minute ago, fun?'

Well done Turk, thought Blunger, you've been a real help, honest you have, more than you'll ever know. And he said, 'This is it, Helen. Turk has just said there's someone in the house counting cards at one of the Blackjack tables. He's asked me to check it out, that's all. Stay and watch.' Helen's sense of outrage fogged when she heard this; there was more to this old fart than she'd thought.

So she said 'OK, if you say so.'

Blunger continued, as tolerant as you like, the Kindly Uncle to a Young Niece out on the Town for the first time, 'You see my dear, card-counting is a grey area. Why shouldn't people count the cards, I heard you ask? After all, clubs encourage addicted gamblers and head bangers; quite right, they do. That's one way of looking at it. The other is, why open your flank to the enemy?'

Like a rapier, Helen replied, 'But this cuts across the percentages, I mean doesn't it?'

Nice one, thought Blunger, Helen, you know more about gambling than you let on. I wonder what that's all about.

He smiled, 'Shall we go to the tables my Dear.' He had her on ice now, and he bloody knew it. As he let Helen go in ahead of them, Sandra just happened to be there, that's all, and said to him softly 'You dirty old bugger. How ever did you get to know Susan Kippax? You'd better tell me later, hadn't you?'

There goes the bloody Club in Manchester. Ted Blunger was lost for words.

CHAPTER FIFTEEN

FLOOR SHOW ON THE FLIGHT DECK

The in-flight movie had fizzled to a stop; 'We hope that you will enjoy our in-flight offering, selected for your continued travelling pleasure,' a family story of unrelenting banality which recounted in winsome detail the adventures of a family of intellectually challenged Swedish Americans, complete with inane smiles, two rows of teeth per person, a dog, a cat and a trio of steely-eyed children of resolute hygienic vileness. And now it was inertia time. Drinks had been served yet again, and not much was going on. Sleepers woke up, scratched their genitals, broke wind and fell asleep. There was not a trolley of Duty Frees to be seen. Not too long to go now, and in no time they would begin the descent to Rome. From the galley, a man who had been asking the cabin staff for more coffee, turned around and called for everyone's attention like a Master of Ceremonies at a wedding. As it happened he was certain to gain everyone's attention, since he was wearing a balaclava and held a hand gun which was big and nasty, like a sewer rat. Big and shiny. Funny thing that, he'd never liked guns in *any way, shape or form*. It was the dull metallic bit that was the turn off. Dave always said you soft bugger, you're more like one of those Doctors who faints at the sight of blood, you are, call yourself a copper. Could do with Dave here now, we could. I really hope he isn't getting his leg over with Sylvie. He couldn't be could he? Oh Holy Christ, it's the floor show, and Fizzer looked at Jacko. It's a practical joke, staged by the squad, sort of a joke, like a farewell present from the lads, have a good trip Fizz me old son, we miss you. No stripper though. Funny that. Best to keep the voice down. I don't think they'll want us to converse somehow. Excuse me gents, could I solicit your opinions on the proposed new translation of *A la Recherche du Temps Perdu*, scheduled I understand, for two thousand and two and a fair old treat for those of a literary bent if you catch my drift?

'See the balaclava-wearing terrorist appears, plus, where's his chums, I'm asking?' said out of the corner of the mouth by Jacko smiling, as calm as you please. And then, as if on cue, three more punters appeared at the rear of the cabin; you wouldn't believe it if you saw it in a movie.

'Cop this,' said Fizzer, 'one of this lot's a bird by the look of it, what d'you reckon to that then?'

'That's funny,' said Jacko, 'Why isn't she wearing an *abiya*? Islamic Womens' Liberation Front? That's got to be it.' And smiled, looking over his shoulder at Mary and Liza. Fizzer was now aware of the stirrings of fear. 'I don't think I can handle jokes at the moment, Jacko. This man isn't the Prince of Peace.' The Arab bird, that's got to be weird. The *mutawa* isn't going to like that one. I'm whistling in the dark aren't I? Never fancied Arab women did I? Shaven gearboxes and no clits. Takes away the fun and keeps them in line. Who showed you how to enjoy it? They reckon that's what the husbands ask them, before they cut their throats. That's what Dave reckons. He'd know. Reckons they like it up the back. How'd he know that? *A radio playing Capital FM in an office somewhere; the smell of Dettol and Nescafe Gold Blend. Strip lights and big operating room lights on the ceiling.* Her face looks a bit familiar. Hang about, the next thing, I'll start losing my bottle if I go on like this at this stage.

The first man spoke quickly and calmly, darting watchful glances around him like a conjuror looking out for tiresome children in the audience who might interrupt and spoil his tricks; he was saying, 'Now I want everyone to listen carefully, and please we will have no sudden movements. My colleagues and I are people of a freedom loving group which will restore peace and the justice to our oppressed peoples. You are now our hostages. We will execute anyone who steps out of the line. So you should do as you are told. Listen to your Captain.'

The Captain's voice came over the intercom, strained and edgy, 'This is the Captain. It appears that we are the subjects of an attack. I ask all passengers and crew to cooperate with these people so that the safety of all may be preserved. Our captors have requested that we re-route. I am in touch with Damascus in the hope that they will give us permission to land.'

Passenger reaction was instant and at first, near chaotic. Most people were dumbfounded, a few screamed and carried on in fearful protest, but were silenced by the weapons waved in their faces. One passenger tried taking a swing at a terrorist; no luck sunshine, he was cut down with the muzzle of a hand gun across the face, blood streaming out of his crushed and splattered nose. It all happened so quickly that within seconds the terrorists had established authority with confidence and precision. These lads are major league. Eyes down for a full house.

And Jacko whispered, 'These guys have been on the advanced course you reckon?'

'Keep whispering my son,' said Fizzer. 'As if I wouldn't.' replied Jacko, still as cool as you like.

The head man went on, like he was as bored as a bingo caller in Peckham on a wet afternoon in February, 'I am Nasser. Perhaps you will all be calm and it will be the best. You are lucky. My friends and I could have blown this aircraft to pieces half an hour ago.' He looked around, quite pleased with himself. I'm your friendly neighbourhood terrorist.' No heroics please. Our course is peaceful. When we get to Damascus, terms will be negotiated for your release. You will realise that everything therefore depends on your co-operation. Until then you should stay calm and do as you are told. *Allah Akhbar.*'

When he'd finished, he signed to the woman terrorist and together they walked the length of the cabin looking at each passenger in turn. As they passed by Fizzer, the man turned to the woman and said, 'That is the man.'

She replied, 'I know it.' A slender, dark-eyed woman, severe and handsome, black hair *en brosse,* brown lips and dark brown nail varnish, in punk contrast to her henna-dyed palms. Fizzer noted too, a gold chain around her ankle. This is definitely going to be a time when silence is golden. Who did she remind him of? Well she wasn't the one who always plays a copper and gets her kit off, that was for sure. Foot and eye. *Hey white trash, look at me, I'm a black whore, which, in case you didn't know it, I'm not. Cop this and don't get too fresh, but if that's what you need to do, go ahead and treat me like one then, you white mother.* She can't be all that liberated. She looked at Fizzer and, smiling, she said, '*Tal Umarak,* Mr Edwards,' and half smiled.

'Watch it,' said Jacko 'Could be that you lucked out. I reckon she fancies you.' I doubt that, I seriously do... *come on Edwards... you wonder which of these two... heaps of shit was formerly the late chummy on the blower to us then, the one you were so chatty with. That's what you wonder. What was it then? Fancy him did you? Was that it you dirty bugger?* No he never said that.

Fizzer froze, 'Hold it right there Jacko, no jokes, for Christ's sake.' My best course is find myself the lowest profile of anyone here, well of anyone in the world, that would sum it up. That woman has my card marked, for some reason. What's all that about I wonder? He had a fair idea what it was about but now wasn't the time, now was it? Christ, I hope Sylvie's all right. Why did I say that? She always is. I wonder what that raghead bitch would look like with her kit off, bollock naked. They shave their muffs, Dave says.

... Abdomens open, rib cages neatly sawn like unrolled crown roasts. Running water sounds and the farty smell of dead guts. Wet hair hanging down over dead faces. The Professor dictated, 'Body one is that of a young well nourished middle-eastern female of about twenty seven... I mean male. '

Jacko kept looking straight ahead, 'Does this sort of thing happen to you often, then?' Fizzer replied 'He's damn right you know. He bloody would do it, too. They're doing it right by the manual. We're all in the bag, as from this moment. These buggers are no amateurs.' Bloody load of mad bigots. Are they any worse than Arsenal fans? Or Man United? Be reasonable.

Jacko said 'What d'you say?'

'Silence is what we do now chum. Shtoom. Keep your shooter out of sight. If they search you, you're fucked. I just thought I'd mention it. Chances are they're as scared as we are. For the moment that is.' *We stay with them for now for as long as we can until they start to get tired. They're at their most dangerous now because they don't know us yet. Cuts both ways.*

'I hear what you're saying.' Why do people say that, I hear what you're saying?

Fizzer glanced at him. This man is too cool. There is more to him than just your flash Jack the Lad with a shooter. I've got one man in the team, maybe.... *body is that of a... well nourished middle-eastern male... twenty seven. There... fifty gunshot wounds commencing in the maxillo-facial region on the right side... proceeding in linear oblique descending order through the neck, anterior thoracic wall, abdominal wall and left...* Jacko said 'Cop this. I don't like the look of the toff up front, the one you've been chatting up, your mate. Big problems there. Moves his head like he's in West Side Story. Christ, he's getting ready to address us. Who's he when he's at home?' Fizzer took a flyer, 'You know bloody well who he is.' *...in the majority of instances the projectiles have caused extensive soft tissue damage...*

Jacko smiled, 'I'd heard a bit. Just testing. Nothing personal.' The Arab woman looked at Fizzer contemptuously and said, 'I am Zeinab, Mr Edwards.'

I'm bloody sure you are darling. I bet you'd fuck like ten men if you got the chance. *What was that Ibrahim had said, on the phone, about foot and eye should not lie? What foot? What eye? What the fuck was the bloody man on about? He knew what he was on about, well enough. Was this him, Ibrahim, on the table? Yes it was, it had to be. What was this one here, was this his foot, his eye?*

And now, the bloody prat is up on his fat feet and running, giving the Arabs the old chat, I don't believe it. And about as full of old shit as you could wish, or fear, depending on how you look at it. Jesus, would the man ever shut his mouth and give his arse a chance. Just what we need this is, some clown getting all shirty with a trio that would blow him away, without a thought, I mean without a bloody thought. This lot would blow Liverpool Football Club away, if they felt it was on the agenda. And he was up for a big deal promotion in the Ministry was that it? Strait jacket more likely. Didn't they teach them anything in the Foreign Office, or the Treasury? *Wet hair hanging over dead faces.* Bowls a good off-break and all that stuff, at the interview and holds his knife properly, not like a bloody drummer. Protesting like buggery of course; there was panic there, just the thing to unsettle an adrenalin laden terr and make him squeeze the tit on his Beretta and blow his fat ass out; they might even have grenades for that matter. Reveal self to him or chill him out, that was the question?

By now it was like an old Ealing comedy or early Hitchcock with this poofy old fart, in his Airey and Hall lightweight, declaring his non-existent hand to anyone who had enough bottle left to listen, and banging on in his fruity pompous voice, you wouldn't believe it, 'I demand to be heard. This intrusion is intolerable. As a British subject and an official of Her Majesty's Government, I must insist that I be permitted the use of the radio and speak to the nearest Control Tower.' Jesus at this rate he'll be calling up room service for smoked salmon sandwiches. The bloody man had to be silenced. One mouthful from this pompous windbag could jeopardise everyone.'

Should he enlist Jacko, that was the next one. Too many questions, no answers. From the moment that he entered the aircraft Jacko had looked like a guy that could handle himself. No sweat, he looked handy, even though he was probably a villain, but he had a shooter, and seemed to know more than he let on. No time to wonder about that before the fucking aristo blew the whole thing. Best to wade in and trust Jacko to pick up the cue. He looked round at him and Jacko responded with a half wink. That did it. The guy was definitely on. We're team handed.

Perhaps he should try the facetious approach, better forget that, just bloody do it, so it was straight into his, this is a Metropolitan Police warrant card, may I see your driving licence, voice 'I don't think that you'll get far this way. We may call our souls our own Guv, but these people have our arses; they might nail them to the wall.' Fizzer thought, well that's it, let's see what the man comes back with. *We loved the Saturday night pissheads best of all. Everyone got a bloody good whacking. We still had the six foot rule in those days, and we could break all the heads we wanted and we bloody did. Blood on the walls, round the clock. No tapes and no briefs sniffing around. That's what I call thief taking like it ought to be.* Without pausing to draw breath, the bloody man shifted into the gear used when dealing with the nearest prole. 'Who the devil are you, may I ask? When I require your assistance I'll ask.' The Terrorist looked at him and then at Fizzer. He couldn't have cared less what anyone said. He had the Beretta, and, worse still, it didn't even shake in his hand. Fizzer took that on board. This man knew his stuff. So he said quietly, 'Just belt up you stupid sod or I'll whack you myself and save the ragheads a job. Now cool it; live long and die happy.' Fattycake looked at him in disbelief. No one had ever addressed him thus, he swelled with anger, 'You insolent yobbo, I've met your sort before.' Jacko said 'Do what he says. He has a point here.' One of the minders then interrupted, 'Get off this man's back mate or I'll...' Fizzer said, 'You'll what?'

'Just leave it out,you're out of your depth here,' said Jacko quietly. If we don't cut the chat friend Nasser's going to get impatient. I wouldn't blame him. When you've just hijacked an aircraft the last thing you want is a deputation from the Consumers' Association.

'I'm losing patience. Do what the man says. None of us calls any shots with this lot.' Sir Jocelyn began to deflate. 'Well I realise that perhaps. Oh Christ. What should I do?' It was looking as if he was beginning to understand what was happening, and that his being Her Majesty's anything counted for nothing any more. Hard lesson. How he longed for a young man, any young man, to comfort him.

And still the head terrorist said nothing. Fizzer thought, it's like an examination, as long as the examiner says nothing you're scoring points, that's what they told us at the Defence College. At this point he decided to make the next move and start talking to the Terr. but, just when things seemed to be easing up a bit, another joker appeared in the pack, as a man stood up and called for attention. He had a beard and a University of Middle England accent. He looked as if he was addressing the local council. Wankerama. Funny, the way in which we react to scary things, some of us shit our pants, others can't stop talking, this bloke has probably never said a word to anyone in his life about anything, now he looks like he's going to make a speech and drop us all in it. Jesus where do they come from? Fifteen minutes of fame was it the man said? Now what? Who was this bloody man? Everyone's getting into the act. It's amateur night.

'Friends I'd like to share a few thoughts about our situation here. I work with troubled young people and have an awareness of violence.' Yes, and you'll have a bloody sight more if you don't cut this crap out sonny. Where do they come from? Watch too much telly that's it. Disaster movies. Well there's no Shelley Winters to swim her way out of it here, sunshine.

'I feel it is up to us all to cooperate with these people in their struggle against oppression in any way, shape or form.' At this the head Terrorist lost patience, nodded to his pal Zohair who immediately decked him with his Beretta, after which Zeinab gave him a well placed kick in the balls. Thanks ragheads. You did us all a favour there. And bloody Zeinab just kept on looking. Give you the creeps. *I suppose a fuck would be out of the question?* Not really. No sense of humour there, somehow. *That's wonderful Fizz. That's right, just turn it all into one of your famous big jokes, and we'll all have a laugh, and you'll be off the hook once again.*

'Keep your voice down, I heard that.' said Jacko. 'I'm keeping everything down all the way to Damascus,' said Fizzer. 'Any plans then?' said Jacko 'I'm working on it,' said Fizzer as he closed his eyes and tried to pretend he was dozing. Who would that fool?

Jacko said to no one in particular, 'We'd better keep close to Mr Edwards, hadn't we?' I'm not asleep yet, Fizzer thought, I wonder who he's talking to, but let it go, he was bushed, but he wouldn't be sleeping, somehow he knew that. *Funny thing about Ibrahim though, he seemed, well different from your average toerag. Educated chap, what was it he said, Baghdad University? Keeps going on about it. Still some of the Provies were educated when you came down to it. Yes, in a way, he had quite got to like the guy, no doubt about it.*

There was nothing to do now but wait till arrival, he thought, as he picked up a paper. How long, he wondered, will it be before someone has a heart attack, starts over-breathing, or gets the squits. Still it's the sort of diversion we need to unsettle maestro Nasser, who at the moment, looks as calm as anything. Jesus, the bloody Arab bird looks like something out of the Addams family. On second thoughts I don't fancy her. It's the no clits side of things that does it. No way.

CHAPTER SIXTEEN

WHEN SYLVIE MET MANSON

Was there any point in walking straight into an *impasse*? Sylvie had wondered about this as she walked the corridor towards Manson's office, passing through his outer domain, a large open-plan area full of VDU's and people she didn't care to look at as, coldly, they watched her passing. Knowing who she was and contemptuously scanning her smartly dressed cool. Here's the Black Brief come to see the Chief, looks tasty, I don't care what they say. Listen, a bloke in F division told me, straight up, he reckons like once you've had a bit of black grumble you never want anything else, like sticking your dick in a bag of mad worms. She was overcome by feelings of unrelenting desperation that drove hard inside her head, churning her brain into porridge. Imagine this happening. I'm on my way to beg this man for his help, any help, in saving my husband's life. Even Fizzer would find it hard to laugh at that one. So that's it then. I go in to see him and I should say, *please help me Mr Manson, do anything you can to save my husband's life,* and he'll say. *Oh yes and why should I do anything for a pushy black brief then? Do me a favour, pull the other one, its got bells on it?* And he'll think, listen to the black bitch, hey maybe I might just think about helping her if she sucks my dick for a few minutes. I suppose he wouldn't last all that long, if that's any consolation. And I would, if it helped, wouldn't I?

Manson was unsmiling and about as welcoming as the Pope meeting the Chief Rabbi; cruel slab-faced Slavic smile, *Ah yes, Our Jewish Friends, where did they go? They all seem to have left.* Why should I bother with this man? He's not going to do anything anyway. Unsmiling, he said, 'And what can I do for you Mrs Edwards?' At least he didn't say, *I'm a very busy man, what with all that's been happening lately, know what I mean?*

'If you don't mind me asking, why is it you hate my husband so much Mr Manson? What has he done to you? OK, I can handle the fact that you hate me and people like me or whatever, but not him. He's on your side, he's your sort, a whitey copper or had you forgotten that? Like his being on the Unit, is that it? Is that so bad? Is it so much of a threat to you, is that what it is?'

'Listen Mrs Edwards, if you can give me one good reason why I should like your husband, well and good, then I might even think about giving you an answer to a bloody offensive question. Whether I like him or not doesn't affect our professional relationship. We're there to do a job, not hold hands and tell each other how much we love each other. And you can cut out the holier-than-thou amateur social worker act with me. I don't give a shit about that sort of stuff, as it happens. Another thing, Mrs Edwards, the way things are, I reckon that you'd do your cause a lot more good if you learnt some proper manners. It's what we call doing good by stealth, but you probably never heard of that. Also, don't come in here giving me the I'm the clever brief act. He'd no business to be on the bloody aircraft had he? Had that not occurred to you? It's none of my doing, none of this. If he wants to line himself up with a load of bloody spooks, that's his problem. If they're so bloody clever, let them get it sorted. What he did has been well out of order, and normally would be subject to disciplinary procedures as laid down in Metropolitan Police guidelines, as per the official documentation.'

He makes it sound as if Fizzer's failed to use the right

parking space in the Yard yet again, in defiance of established policies and procedures. And if I want to get it sorted, I should go through channels via personnel. This man is unbelievable. He's a thousand times worse than I thought. Suck his dick? Suck a dead maggot, more like. Forget it; there's no way I'd suck his dick and that's definite. You can suck your own dick, buster. Jesus, I feel better already. Fizzer would like that. Now that I've seen this guy in action, I'm beginning to see what he meant. But Manson continued, 'You see, I believe in straight talk Mrs Edwards, something your lot isn't much interested in all that much, in my experience. You want me to get your husband off the hook. That it? Being another sanctimonious do-gooder who reckons the likes of me are a right load of old shit, it must come a bit hard for you, coming to ask a favour of a thicko Mr Plod like me.' He's got a point there.

He looked at her. What would you to say to that smart arse?

'I thought the police looked after each other. I thought that's what they were meant for.' She was very cool now.

'Who said anything about not looking after him? But that's not it, is it Mrs Edwards? You're looking for someone to ease your conscience, isn't that what you're doing?'

'I don't know what you mean.' But she did.

'Come off it. You dropped him in the shit, isn't that what you did? Calling up your friends in the Front and telling them where he was going. What was all that about Mrs Edwards? Travel news? I just saw this offer in Ceefax? Knock it off Mrs Edwards. Let them help you. You bloody Dykes are all the same. Stick together like shit to a blanket, isn't that what it's all about?'

'Another police homophobe, I see,' she laughed, 'only what you'd expect I suppose.'

Manson wasn't giving an inch, 'Suppose we let that one pass shall we?' Nan had said, *You'll see, Len, it'll be lovely for you in the country, this is no place for you with your Mum gone away.* Try finding out what it's like being a ten year old boy a million miles from nowhere in an orphanage in bloody Lincoln, Mrs

Edwards, and the vicar tries to bugger you, and who gives a toss about you except the sanctimonious poofter who wants to fuck your little arse. And see how you bloody like it. And see how far that gets you, you supercilious cow, but I'll not give her the satisfaction of telling her that just yet.

'You see, Mrs Edwards, I think, you and your sort have a lot to learn. You don' t know so much.'

Why is he so angry all of a sudden? Fizzer had been right. They'd had a tap on the phone from day one.

'And in any case, what am I supposed to do?'

'It had occurred to me that you might be involved in negotiating a deal with these people, that's all.'

'That's bloody marvellous, Mrs Edwards. You're in the pocket of a load of right old scum like this lot and you're asking me to get your husband off the hook. Shouldn't you be asking them?'

He has another point there. Maybe I should have asked Helen.

'Had it not occurred to you Mrs Edwards, that getting yourself involved with people like this was not just a bit of your bleeding hearts liberal Hampstead crap, running after bloody Wogs and wiping their arses, Mrs Edwards? Don't you people ever look at what goes on in the real bloody world Mrs Edwards?'

He doesn't let up, does he? 'Like I said, I just thought that maybe you might feel some obligation to assist a colleague, that's all.'

'Your husband never had much use for people like me Mrs Edwards. Clapped out old fart, something like that, I bet. Over the hill, not in touch with contemporary Police practice. Burn out, that's what's wrong with Manson. Wasn't that the sort of thing he said, Mrs Edwards?'

The words were familiar enough. 'But it's not just that. I can understand him having different views on things. Chalk and cheese Mrs Edwards. No he's not my problem. It's you Mrs Edwards and your sort and the things you do that worry me. And I'm not talking about the colour of your skin. I'm talking about a woman who sells her husband down the river and I'm not referring to just letting them know about the flight, though that was bad enough. I'm talking about the Suleimeneya Consortium. That was something else, wasn't it Mrs Edwards? I can handle you getting in a rage with your husband and wanting to get back at him, but this is rather different wouldn't you say?'

...A final question, Mrs Edwards. What did you think of the Suleimaneya Consortium in general, and of its recommendation as to materials management in particular? I'd be interested to hear your views some time. Feel free to call me, when you feel up to it, that is...

'What's Materials Management Mrs Edwards? Isn't that what Mr Sarno called it? Quite a man for the words by all accounts. I think you know what I'm saying here. It's all right, I'll spare you the details.' He paused, 'Perhaps you might want to say something a bit more specific, off the record. It might help.' Would he really say that? Who does he think he's fooling?' This man wears crassness like a designer label. How much of it is a put-on?

And so she caved in and coughed everything that she knew about the Consortium, but she didn't feel any better. I've betrayed everyone now.

'Thank you Mrs Edwards. It helps to clear the air, that's what I always tell the younger officers. It's always best in the long run.' He didn't add that he knew all that she had told him anyway. That Sarno was an odd bugger and no mistake. What sort of a name was that supposed to be for Christ's sake? Sylvie was looking at him, 'I can't say any more at this point Mrs Edwards, as I'm off to Damascus in about an hour or two.' Funny the way Margaret had said to him, at breakfast it was, 'I see your Mr Edwards is in hot water then Len? Such a nice young man. Do look after him if you can.'

They really knew about finding things out, did women when you thought about it.

CHAPTER SEVENTEEN

NATURAL BREAK

Nasser had been just a bit too calm when he looked at Fizzer and said 'I think you should speak to the Tower now.' What was all that about? Fizzer picked up the phone that the Syrians had run in through the flight deck entrance ...*No alcohol or psychoactive substances should be permitted to any persons directly involved in a hostage type situation. Only simple pain relieving medications such as small doses of paracetamol should be administered... Remember that Diarrhoea and vomiting can be useful allies for the hostage negotiating team...* They had brought bottles of Sohat water and juice. The water was warm from standing on the tarmac. Through the window he felt the dusty air of Damascus airport, hot on his face even at six in the morning; smelt the woodsmoke from the perimeter, saw a string of goats wandering along, heard a car changing down, picked up floating fragments of local rock'n roll and a few shouts. ...*That's the real world there, not all this shit on the flight deck with Nasser and the crazy ragheads and all the poor terrified buggers in the aircraft wondering if they'll ever see anyone ever again, or get their guts spilt in the sand just because some nutter wants his cousin out of Parkhurst...* So what do we do to get us out of this lot? Remember what they always said, think of it like you're taking an exam. As long as they're doing the talking, you're scoring the points. When you're doing the talking, you're wasting your time

162

and all you're doing is losing points, sitting in a cab with the meter running. Your job is to get them to do the talking and keep them at it. That way, they get tired and think you're dumb but co-operative. So he accepted the phone. I don't believe it. It was your actual Manson on the other end. Who else would you expect when you thought about it? Surprise, surprise. Manson, our man in bloody Damascus, crappy lightweight suit, smelly and knackered like a sweaty bingo-caller in Southend. God, I bet he must be enjoying this one. Dramatic irony, you'd call it, except that he wouldn't know what it meant, which, I suppose makes it even more so, in a way. I'd like to have heard him at the press conference at Heathrow with his mates; three woollies looking straight into the tube, all of them, elbows touching, jammed behind a table with a green cloth on the top of it and a grey screen behind, looking pale, like they all needed a bloody good shit. 'At this time I am not at liberty to say anything, beyond that we are informed that one of our valued officers is involved in negotiating a hostage type situation with persons whose identity I am not as yet in a position to disclose, beyond saying that they are of a terrorist nature and armed. This will call for delicate handling of the sort to which we are not unaccustomed. My role and that of my colleagues is to find out what we can do to unravel this difficult situation at this point in time, and I'd like to say a personal word here to his wife, if I may. Don't worry Sylvie, love, we 're doing our best for your man, who is, as you know a valued friend and colleague of all here. He's a good lad is Edwards.' *They dial nine-nine-bloody-nine for someone to wipe their arses half the bloody time.*

Be fair, it was a likely event with Manson being here, given his track record, but it did make your guts turn over a bit. Who's setting who up here that's what I want to know? When Nasser had come back from the flight deck he'd looked at Fizzer, straight in the mush. He pretended to be all surprised as if he'd just woken up, heavens where am I sort of thing? But he knew it immediately. Nasser had him sussed, you could tell, really. It was like being caught without a ticket on the train. They can see you haven't got a ticket from the other end of the carriage. He'd rumbled him from the first minute probably; hang on, no need to get too paranoid. His cover was gone. From now on it was faeces in the air-conditioning. Nasser smiled politely, lit a cigarette and said, 'Mr Edwards. I think it that you are in the deep shit, as you would say.' That's better, for a minute there, I thought he was going to say that he had us in his power, it is useless to try and escape English pig. But it wasn't better, he knew it wasn't. Why is this creepy woman looking at me like all the bloody time if it comes to that? You'll know me next time you see me then darling. Foot and eye. Why should I keep thinking about that? Anyone would think I'd cut a deal with one of his mates or something, unless you count Abdullah. That's ridiculous. Not exactly a deal, more of an arrangement. *We make no deals. It's a matter of policy, you know that, no member of the Anti-terrorist makes deals with the likes of your people, call yourselves Freedom Fighters.*

'My friend Zohair has an armed device with which we can blow this aircraft and all of us away to pieces.' Sounds as if he's trying to sell us one. Wouldn't you like to buy this bomb? Colonel Gadaffi bought it from one of your countrymen in Watford or was it Pinner, at the arms fair? It's worth toughing it out, I suppose. He's a funny looking bugger when you come down to it, looked better with his balaclava if you ask me. No one's asking, try Sylvie's, dumbshit nigger act. That's what she calls it. 'Hey Man, what you saying man, who you callin' Edwards? Hold it bro, you got the wrong dude mister. My name's...' And while you're at it give him the high five. Perhaps not. Yo.

Nasser said only, 'Don't play the games with me. I know your face, your name, your voice. You are Inspector Edwards, we know that. I will make you an offer and you will accept it. I don't incline to waste time. It will be better.' Fizzer was now thinking, hold on, this is a new one. What's coming up now I wonder? And he said, 'Offer. What offer was that you were talking about then squire?' Jesus, I can do better than that, surely.

'For you to make a deal with us, to do what we say and make the things easier for your people here.'

'I don't make deals. Since you appear to know, OK, so you know that part of my activities involves negotiating with the likes of yourself for the lives of innocent people.' Nasser laughed at this, 'Ah yes. The negotiator. Like the deal you made at the Embassy in London, Mr Fizzer. We have heard of that one.' Jesus, he really does know the score, well he fucking would, wouldn't he? He might have told me. Save us all a bit of time it would. 'We heard all about it on the tape,' Jesus Henry Christ, he must be, yes he's talking the tape that Abdullah nicked and got shot for. Thank you Abdullah wherever you are. I know where you are Abdullah. Fizzer looked hard at Nasser and said, 'Tape? What tape's that then squire?'

'The tape that recorded your conversations at the embassy. It is all there. It is written.'

'Look, I don't know about any tape and say again, I make no deals. Everyone knows that.' That should hold him for a nanosecond.

'You made a deal with our freedom fighters and broke your word.' he looked angrily at Fizzer now. Here, wait a minute, calm down sunshine, the last thing we want is you to freak out as soon as we start talking. *Wellahi Mr Edwards I think that Ibrahim will be pleased about that message you sent him. I don't know what you're talking about Abdullah do I? Oh yes you do, Oh no I don't.* It's like a bloody pantomime. That's what Abdullah came up with. He had to go after he said that. Stands to reason, and Manson and the rest were never on to it. Funny that. That is if it really happened.

'Bloody nonsense, what do you mean?'

'We heard that tape many times, Ibrahim trusted you, until he was killed by your assassins.' *I thought that the boy wonder was the great hostage negotiator, who settled things without bloodshed, always providing, that the terrorists are white, isn't that right?*

'Right, you can cut out the amateur dramatics Mr Nasser. He was part of a group that was holding innocents hostage, or hadn't you heard? He took a risk and he lost.'

Or did I mean holding innocence hostage? Foot and eye.

'You let him believe otherwise. You lie to yourself I think.

You lie to me, no matter. To yourself, that is *haram*!' Now I'm getting a sermon from a murdering git. Nice one. 'Assassins. That's handy. What's your lot supposed to be then, stress counsellors?' *Did you really have to let it happen like that, all those people dead? Is that what you want? Where's this fair play that you're always on about?*

'There is no time for the convenient western ideology, Mr Edwards. You must decide what you want to do. You go with us to a place of safety or we all go to heaven or to the hell. Mr Fizzer, we believe in things above football and the sinful women. You are of the walking dead, those with no souls, even while you are alive I think. Money, Sun Newspaper and telly. I think you must make up your mind, Mr Edwards.'

Funny the way he said all that, like a bloody sermon and him with a shooter in his hand. It's almost as if Sylvie had written the script for him, more of a libretto really. She's always banging on about choice and accepting responsibility for our actions, bearing the consequences. Typical bloody lawyer. She's had more time than me, for choices maybe and talking crap. And that bloody Zeinab stood behind Nasser all the time he'd been speaking, straining to pick up every word and all the time staring at me. Funny the way she keeps appearing from bloody nowhere. *He looked up as he heard her approach, and saw her in the doorway. It's not just some trick, some artifice, he thought, and it's not how she looks... she can stop me in my tracks and make me stop thinking.*

Spooky cow. It's rude to stare. *Funny thing that, one of those two punters, the one... you know... well, I... reminded me a bit of your good self, no offence.*

Didn't they teach you that when you were burying your lunch in the school playground? Too busy learning the Book by heart, I suppose, no hang on, they don't allow women to read it, or do they I can't remember? Anyway I wish she'd lay off. She even feels familiar somehow. I'm losing my bottle, this is a load of rubbish. Just ignore the bloody cow. *She had asked the question angrily, looking coldly at him, as if he had been the perpetrator, without pausing,* 'Yes, well in that case, I'll need to

166

speak to Control won't I? Yes and while you're at it why don't you get Minnie Mouse here to lay off and stop staring at me all the time. Frankly she gives me the creeps.'

Nasser ignoring the last bit, was thinking this one over, 'This will be possible, but no coded messages. No tricks. You must ask what they want and discuss the answers with me as you go.' The usual Arab six levels of meaning, that's what they told us on the course. *Six levels of meaning and none of them mean bugger all. That's what you'll find. Words as a substitute for action, that's the only real weakness you can hope to exploit with this shower of shit.*

'I'm familiar with normal procedures.' Normal, that was good, that was, with this lot. Remember where your Arab is concerned, the normal is abnormal and the abnormal is normal, and whatever they say to you, never forget that you are a bloody infidel and they can say anything they fucking like, it doesn't count, because they don't waste words on infidels. Thank you very much, that's a real help, I'll remember that in future.

Nasser ignored the remark and called Zohair, who obeyed his instructions, almost before he'd given them. That was it, he bloody knew them didn't he? Forward planning. Had to be. Perhaps it was Zohair who called the shots. And he looked, and met Jacko's eye. And catching it, exchanged a shared recognition. It was obvious when you thought about it. Zohair was the head man. Nice one Zohair. Or was it Zeinab? Time to talk to Manson. Can't hold back any longer. Where does this hard-eyed cow fit in? Who are you anyway? Maybe I should ask, well not just yet. She sort of turns you on in a way, apart from the absent clit.

'Hello Mr Manson,' There didn't seem much point in saying anything else. Manson replied 'Well Edwards, and what have you to tell me? Let me guess, they want a deal. Well, you know what to tell them.' *A College educated prat. Your Edwards and all his lot if you ask me. One of your wet-behind-the-ears coppers, that's your bloody Edwards and the like.*

He might have said how are you, or something, but why should he? I didn't ask him how he was.

'Mr Manson I'll make it as quick as I can. These people are

Premier League by the look of them. I'll play the long ball game as far as I can, problem is they want a safe passage to Libya with me as a side order.' Did Manson chuckle or was it crackle? 'You know the answer.' They can't bloody have you and you know it. 'There's no use in going on, time isn't on our side, what the fuck's going on now? Next thing Sir Jocelyn barges in, grabs the phone and starts coming on strong, straight to microphone, if you please. 'Whoever you are at the other end, I have a duty to protest, as an accredited Senior Representative of Her Majesty's Government. And as such I claim the right...' Even Nasser looked nonplussed, exclaiming 'What is wrong with this man he is mad?' as Zohair laid him out.

Nasser got angry now 'We do not play the games. Perhaps you people will understand – we will not tolerate any interference. The next one to behave like this will be shot dead.'

When Fizzer sat down again Jacko said quietly 'I'm not looking at you, but I'm talking right?'

'I'd noticed.' *Associated British Pictures nineteen fifty-four, after the ban was well in force; movie, black and white, two guys rob a factory, one has his foot in plaster, low budget, of course, they kill the guard and get hanged, demo outside the prison doors. Society is to blame, they hanged my Trev.*

'I could hear all that stuff between you and Nasser. What was all that about then?'

'It's none of your business and I'd be wasting time if I explained.'

'Who were you on the phone to?' Fizzer replied 'Look, I'm not answerable to you Jacko.'

Jacko replied, 'Stuff that. It's not a case of being answerable, it's like you need anyone you can get on your team, in case you'd forgotten.'

'Got you. It's Manson; he's my chief, you could say. He's out here handling the negotiating with these people.'

Jacko said 'That's a bit previous isn't it? Someone got him out here pretty quick, know what I mean? Makes you wonder who knows what, and what do they know sort of thing.'

This remark seemed best left in the air. How did he come

up with all this stuff? 'You could say that.' So Jacko said 'OK, what about Nasser earlier then. He's got you well stitched up.'

'You said that already. Any case how did you hear what we were talking about?'

'It's called lip reading. From my days in a machine shop.'

Fizzer laughed and said 'Of course. Lip reading; who'd have thought that, just fancy? I'd never have guessed.' Lip reading my arse. This man knows a bloody sight more than he's letting on. Go along with it. Don't ask, he'll tell me soon enough anyway.

Jacko said 'OK, maybe I should ask a few questions. You're the top man aren't you. That's the way I'm seeing it?'

Maybe I should level with him a bit, 'You can say that if you like. Listen, this is it. I don't know what the hell you're on, Jacko. I'm in no position to choose, so I'm taking a chance. These buggers want my arse.'

'I'd picked up on that.'

'Right, in which case you could do me a favour here. Keep your eyes on the V.I.P. for me.'

'OK but,what's his problem? I know the old nonce deals. You can't open a copy of Hello, but he's there in fancy dress or his dinner suit in some flash gaff in Belgravia, eyes and nose running, showing out to the aristos.'

'You know a lot Jacko, and now isn't the time. Let's say I want to know which way he's going.'

'You're not going to tell me?'

'Listen, I'm taking a chance here. OK. It's not just dealing It's a bit more than that.'

'Could we be looking at a matter of security, like they say?' asked Jacko softly.

'You could say that, I didn't. What's the difference? We can't go much further in. My concern is to get us out.'

Zeinab stood by listening to everything and smiling to herself, not saying a bloody word. Maybe she's just a nutter from the local bin and they couldn't get rid of her. His sister. *No tricks please. Don't try to fool me You forget my friend I am Ibrahim, a man of education, unlike I think, yourself. Remember Mr Fizzer I*

169

*am a graduate of University of Baghdad unlike yourself, who, I
suspect went to a poor school in your Liverpool where you learnt
nothing except to drink and to shout at your Anfield isn't it? I don't
want the Christian lies.*

No time for jokes. Chill out for Christ's sake, don't let them
get to you. As if he didn't care, and make it clear that there was
no way around anything. No deals, no nothing, straight, gift
wrapped, bugger all, just hand me over to Mr Nasser, or we get
our balls shot off. If I hear 'no deals' one more time I'll do my
nut, I swear it. I wonder what Sylvie's doing. He picked up the
phone, and all of a sudden he wanted to hurl it as far away as
possible. Spend all my time being the great big deal negotiator,
and now it's my arse on the line, my life, my future, and I'm in
Manson's hands more than Nasser's, maybe.

So I should tell him like, *Here's the full SP Guv. The
passengers are holding out but these people are a new breed Mr
Manson. Usually I can pick up a hint within a few minutes, but not
this lot. It's a bit personal you see.* He has his reasons. Foot and
eye. Anyway, like I said, they want a free flight out of here with
me as their hand luggage. What do you say to that? What could
he say?

He'd love that, would Manson. Why bother to ask when I
know exactly what he's going to say. After all, it's not as if he's
never had to before. All I'm doing is asking him to do
something which he won't do anyway. Manson, as smooth as
you like, in the driving seat, all he has to do, is say quite
comfortably, and he'd be in the right, that's the best of it. *You
know the answer Edwards. We don't make deals with these people.*
That's what he'd bloody say. Surprise surprise, guess who's
come to tea Mabel. Put the kettle on, it's a soap, remember. You
could try and sound less delighted about it you wanker. He's
just doing his job, obeying orders. And he's right.

So he held back and said to Nasser 'Give me five minutes,
I need to think.'

Nasser said, 'As you please, but no fooling, Mr Edwards.'

As he walked back to his seat he caught Jacko's eye. 'Have
a decadent western Coke' said Jacko 'everyone else is, what's

going down? I watched your face when you were talking there, don't tell me it's a change of plans.' Fizzer said, 'OK here's how it is. They want out of here with me as their safety. I can see their point. Our man won't hear of any deal; fair enough, that's policy, but Jacko, there's more to it. I think he wants me out.'

'I'd wondered. You don't half pick your colleagues well don't you? You must have upset him.'

'You know a lot. Who the hell are you, if it isn't a rude question?'   ·

'I wouldn't say that. I have an interest in our VIP chum too, as it happens. He deals with a group that has upset people. That's it. He sells or persuades people to sell dodgy hardware.' Fizzer thought, all he's saying is that Sir Jocelyn sells tanks and stuff to people we don't like. Good Lord who'd have thought it? Are you sure? We let him do it, absorb the profit, and drop him in the shit with the people he's selling to, who are meant to be our friends anyway. Nothing new in that either.

So he said 'Get on.' Jacko laughed and said, 'In a manner of speaking.' This bugger Jacko, maybe he's setting me up too. Not the best time to ask him.

'Anyway,' said Jacko 'the way I see it is, time flies when you're having fun. Hold on, I said I'd keep an eye on Mary for Liza, she's worried about her. I'll need to chat her up a bit.' And he's on his feet, looking over the back of the seat. Fizzer thought this guy never misses a bloody trick. Keep an eye. Jesus.

In the Control Tower, Manson and Col. Saad of the third most important secret police force in Damascus were not hitting it entirely off. Manson was deeply unimpressed with the place. Not exactly the nerve centre of international air traffic control, he noticed. Half the VDU's were on, but displayed nothing but snow. The place was dusty and smelt of weary, shoulder shrugging Arab incompetence and stale farts. The crusty smell of the unwashed Arab arsehole. Paper cups of tea choked with condensed milk seemed to be everywhere. And Col. Saad was being as politely uncooperative as only a Syrian confronted by a Westerner knows how. Colonel my arsehole, he's no more a bloody Colonel than your bloody legover Scotch git with the beard who's the Foreign Secretary.

'You see Colonel, from what Mr Edwards is saying, it seems that this group is much harder to deal with than we are used to. Mr Edwards is an experienced man, one of our best, and if he says so, I have to listen, if you follow me.' He smiled, I wonder what the bloody raghead will make of that, Mr Mustafa crap, the heap in the desert. The old jokes are the best, no doubt about it.

Accursed infidel, you smell of the alcohol on your dirty Saxon breath, 'I don't think you understand Mr Manson. I think that we cannot continue to talk with these people too long. You understand, our Nation is not so patient maybe as you, a matter of National honour. We have to fight with these people. We are not weaklings. We cannot be dictated to by the gangsters.' Unbeliever, may you die with your mouth full of pigshit.

You stupid fucking Charlie, Christ give me patience, 'I take your point Colonel, but we have a delicate situation here. You realise that a Senior British Diplomat is one of the passengers, travelling incognito, all above board, you'll understand, and we are convinced that the terrorists don't know this – it could be embarrassing to all parties.' Taxpayers' money going down the drain for some old nonce. Put that in your hookah and puff on it you little smelly ponce and try wiping your arse for once in a while, the rat inside it died six months ago.

This pig eating bladder of Christian filth must be silenced, *Inshallah*. 'I understand that Mr Manson but I urge you to see our position. I am confident that our forces could overcome the terrorists. We have the right on our side, you see. Allah will punish the evil doer.' He smiled confidently. Even Manson, astonished by the man's stupidity, was unsure what to say beyond, 'I suggest we hold off as long as possible... but I take your point,' and hope for the best. Holy Christ, roll on my five. 'Listen Colonel, I think I should speak to Mr Edwards before any decisions are taken.' I wonder what laughing boy will have to say this time round, he picked up the phone, 'OK Edwards it's Manson. How far down the line are we?'

Fizzer replied, 'Fair enough. Here's the full SP. Right, we've been here for long enough. The passengers are holding out, just about, but these people are a new breed Mr Manson. I don't see them being amenable to negotiation. The head man doesn't want to listen. It's a bit personal you see, I mean he doesn't like me. He has his reasons. Anyway, like I said, our hosts want a free flight out of here with me as hand luggage. What do you say?'

'You know the answer Edwards. We don't make any deals with these people.' He thinks I don't know, I don't believe it. And he put down the phone. No point in wasting valuable emotional energy, whatever that might be.

'Listen Nasser, give me five minutes please. I ask you that one favour *habibi*.'

'As you please, but no more Mr Edwards.' Nasser is beginning to look tired. That's a point in our favour. They tire too, I'd forgotten that. The shits die too.

'Look Jacko here's how it is. They want out of here, with me to go. Our man won't hear of any deal; fair enough, that's policy, but there's more to it is time. I think he wants me out, my Chief, I mean dead out.'

'I'd wondered. I got the message.'

'You know a lot don't you.'

'I wondered if they'll bring the Limo when they come to pick us up.'

'For Christ sake Jacko, don't make jokes.'

If Fizzer had been able to see from the rear of the aircraft, he would have spotted a Syrian assault group approaching ready to enter and he would have had a major coronary infarct on the spot.

Fortunately, even Fizzer couldn't see it, as he said, 'We're in it enough as it is.' 'You will do well to remain silent. Mr Edwards – call the Control Tower and tell your Mr Manson we start shooting the people one every half hour until our demands are met.'

'You mean it don't you? It's a bit early in the day to start shooting.' But he knew he was wasting his breath. Nasser didn't like the West. A hard lesson to learn, that you're not liked.

Fizzer picked up the phone without being asked. He was amazed that events had moved so quickly. There had been a chance. Now there was none.

'OK Mr Manson, here's the final deal. They start shooting passengers or whoever every half hour until their demands are met.'

'You know the answer Edwards, but you can keep him talking if you like.'

'Thanks Chief, I'll do that.' Thanks a bunch. Why don't you call the bloody undertaker while you're at it?

An armoured personnel carrier was approaching the plane. Was this the vehicle that would collect Fizzer and the rest away to safety? Fizzer watched it approaching, as did Nasser and all the rest.

Fizzer said 'By the time this lot is over we'll know each other's faces pretty well I reckon.'

Jacko made no reply as he watched the driver and escort scanning the door of the aircraft. What was he saying to his companion? What were they thinking about? What did they do last evening? Are they fed up and just want to get it over with? Have they a bloody clue what they're doing? Most important, that one. *The sun came out as the waiting column of garbage vans and street cleaning trucks edged slowly forward to harvest the MacDonalds containers, paper cups, crisp packets, cigarette butts and dogshit.*

Already most of the Press were on their way, and the TV and film crews were packing up. Coaxial cables were winched up and away, camera boxes banged shut.

The vehicle edged forward so slowly, it looked almost still. Fizzer noticed that Nasser and the terrs were looking at it as anxiously as he, well, it was hardly surprising in a way, when you thought about it. They were all near enough, in it up to the eyebrows. Funny old world.

In the Tower the Colonel said 'I wonder Mr Manson, Mr Edwards what he will do.'

'We'll just have to see Colonel,' said Manson, 'won't we?' and lit a cigarette. He felt that he deserved one.

CHAPTER EIGHTEEN

SETTLEMENT DAY

If there was one thing that Helen Kershaw valued most of all, it was having the freedom to, 'leave it all behind at the end of the day.' At least, that was what she had said in an interview with Hugo Bath, of *Place and Space*, the flagship journal of Emergent Trends in Contemporary Living.

'My privacy is important to me. This contrasts with a working day which is too full of troubled people and times of commotion. Home has become a place that I escape to. It's where I seek comfort, relaxation and tranquillity; a meeting and a resting place. It's so important to me, that even the hippest things can't tempt me out of my space, you know. That's why I purposely sought for a place in a quiet conventional neighbourhood. I don't want to run into everyone all the time; I need time to refuel, to get a handle on inspiration and to integrate.' All of which explains her natural choice, a conversion in a dinky little street just north of the better end of the King's Road, handy enough for certain shops, without having to be compromised by the proximity of Italian tourists with Barbour jackets draped over their shoulders. There was an organic grocer cum-patisserie nearby, and around the corner, Monkeys, a quiet little club which adjoined an antique shop next door to an surprisingly downmarket pub where you could smell the Old Holborn and reeking urine in the carsey, even as you passed by the open door of the saloon bar. 'Quite a village-like atmosphere, in a way,' Helen reckoned, 'As soon as I saw it I realised that my solution would be to treat the house as a shell, adding only windows at the back, letting the inside become a series of gigantic pieces of a minimalist jigsaw in the raw. Urban dwelling is the way forward for people in tune with the spirit of the age.'

As you entered the hallway of Helen's Town House home you were confronted by a forbidding block of concrete bookshelves which thematically dominated the entrance to the living space abutting a bedroom, itself hidden behind massive library units which provided, 'a cityscape of buildings letting in the light. Stark, uncompromising, a presence.' All in plywood too. The minimalist bit perked up a shade when you got to the kitchen, Miro tiles, white ceramic bottles, and chrome steel, not exactly plain sailing, but a welcome relief from untreated plywood. In the living room you could cop the metal hanging star lanterns, saris adorned with fairy lights, walls lined with black and white photographs of anorectic androgynes, tits like sherbet bags, roll-ups hanging out of their vapid faces. Not surprisingly perhaps, Fizzer had never been invited there for tea and rock cakes.

Waiting for Sylvie, Helen sat fretfully in a Mies van der Rohe Barcelona chair. She sipped moodily at a cup of Lapsang. For God's sake what was wrong with the tiresome bloody woman? She'd sounded very angry on the phone, what was all that about, one wondered? Naturally she had been upset with all that had happened, one would be, but one has to retain some semblance of control, surely. She looked round the room impatiently, taking it all in. Yes, it was time for a change. There was a need for a realignment of themes, and pretty bloody soon at that. She should call Ellie Van Kloop's atelier in Highgate the minute this ridiculous business was cleared up and the ghastly Sylvie was out of the way. The bitch was late, for heaven's sake. How tedious can you get? And yet, Sylvie had seemed like someone with immense possibilities, in so many ways, but things somehow didn't seem to be gelling. And instantly the thought of Sylvie's Lycra encased thighs sent shocks through her guts and bounced off feelings that resonated into others inside, but it wasn't just that, it was the fear, the dead certainty that somehow Sylvie was slipping away. They did that didn't they? Slip away from you and they didn't know that they had been there, or did they? Maybe. What? A clutch in the throat can be good news or bad news. This time it was bad news.

But by the time Sylvie rang the doorbell Helen was back on track as calm, caring and understanding as you like, ready to admit her visitor. One look at Sylvie confirmed that she was probably correct regarding the slipping problem. Another bridge to be burnt, sod it. 'Sylvie darling, Hi, I'm so concerned for you at this dreadful time. It must be awful for you with all your work and responsibilities to have this sort of thing cropping up, just when things seemed to be so right for you. How are things holding up? How are you holding up? I mean, counselling, that sort of thing must be high on your agenda? Had you thought of cognitive therapy?' It would be premature to suggest that her voice might have faltered here, but it might have given that impression.

'I don't think we're looking at counselling are we? For God's sake, Helen what are you saying? This is something more than counselling, way beyond the bloody talking cure,' her patience starting to ebb already, 'There are two hundred people in an aircraft, in it up to the eyebrows, in case you had forgotten; I'm cut in half here, and you're asking me about counselling?' What do I sound like? Fizzer would say that if he could hear me now, hold those platitudes love, for Christ's sake.

Helen replied, 'You should try to relax more darling. It's an acceptance situation really, you know. Like bereavement.' And I had the idea Helen was, what was that I said she was, that time when Fizzer was going on at me about her, and saying she was nothing but a bloody phoney, can't you see that you stupid cow and all? Please God say I didn't call her a free spirit or anything did I, it couldn't be as bad as that?

Helen gazed intently at her, 'Whatever you do you mustn't hide behind your feelings darling, tell me, *I can sense the hurt that must be there*,' or did she mean hide her feelings behind her? For a moment she felt a bit uncertain for a moment there, but recovered. There's nothing like the douche-bag of cliché to settle doubt. How did I get into all this nonsense, where did you leave your brains you stupid cow? That's what Fizzer said, I can hear him now? And now where's his brains? Oozing into the sand on a bloody airfield where the sun knocks you speechless like a drawn sword. Where did I read that?

'It's not a question of anyone needing advice about how to live with an acceptance situation, Helen. Innocent people in the hands of murderers, that's what it is, and I put him there didn't I, that's what I'm talking about. The only person who knew anything about Fizzer going on this flight was yourself, because I told you about it. All I can suppose is that you passed this on. Forget it, I know you did. After all, didn't I did tell you knowing that you'd do just that in the name of freedom. That's it isn't it? And what are you going to do now Helen that's all I'm asking?' And all Helen could come up with was, 'Anger impairs rational thinking Sylvie. You should think about that before you get more confused and emotional about this thing. We have a painful situation here for Fizzer and the other persons involved, and of course one has a concern for their feelings in this respect. But this mustn't deflect us from confronting the situation in regard to the need for political solutions which will determine whether the women of Kurdistan, and other victims of oppression everywhere, are to achieve any degree of self- determination. I'm genuinely concerned that this thing may be inconvenient for other persons. Let's not get too judgmental here though.'

Why don't you top it off with, *regardless of class creed or colour*, you sanctimonious, humourless cunt? She sounds like Gerry Adams talking his face through one of his prepared statements, that's it, of course, I'm wasting my time, she'd be bound to do that. 'You're not saying that you had no part in this, is that it, is that what I'm hearing Helen? Let's have some straight answers.' Christ I'd forgotten, it's one-lawyer-talking-to-another time. Helen replied softly, 'Well of course, I suppose one could say that I accept a degree of involvement in this unhappy scenario, in that I was in possession of this knowledge, but if I passed on such information, I did so in good faith, and in the belief that it would transcend mere personal considerations if placed in the hands of responsible persons. I didn't ask you to tell me, in case you'd forgotten.' Next thing she'll be saying, *well you know darling you can't make an omelette without breaking eggs*, I only followed orders. 'Won't do Helen and you know it. Ever heard of betrayal?' Hardly in a position to say that, me.

Helen laughed, 'I don't think we need go into that one. Come off it Sylvie. You made it clear that you were getting weary of the relationship didn't you? I sensed your anger and the pain there. I thought you were looking beyond it, looking for the development of your needs.' She's right, I handed him over because I was angry about Jan didn't I?

Helen followed up with, 'Sometimes Sylvie being adult means having to shed baggage, if one's needs are fully to be realised in the search for fulfilment.' She'd bloody say that too, would Helen, now beginning to sound like a million people doing commercials for self-realisation. Next she'll be coming on with the accessories of transcendental narcissism, digital technology based life-styles for beautiful people in the fast-track, and how the New Spirituality is meeting the needs of a Godless Age. Helen really believed all this stuff. Life space for the me generation. Load of bollocks Sylvie, that's what Fizzer said, what shit you people all talk Sylvie, did you ever think of that out there in the high moral playground? I mean doing your nut when a *hochgeboren* fruitcake runs off with the grocer's boy, is that your idea of the Cinderella story Sylv? Are they your bloody icons? Because they're not bloody mine. He'd never liked Helen even if he had tried to get into her pants. 'What's the matter Sylvie? Fancy her do you? That it?' Another crass remark for the book. Maybe she had. She certainly didn't at this moment, that was for sure. But she'd liked and admired Helen, to the point of being enchanted almost, that was it. Forget all the bullshit, she was someone to whom you had to pay attention, and had the capacity to pull you in. Like the woman said, *'Attention must finally be paid to this man.'* Was that it? Or was it?

And Helen continued, almost desperate now, 'You are beginning to disappoint me Sylvie. If you go on like this you might even start to bore me. I had you down as someone with a bit extra on board. Someone who was going to make certain major contributions to contemporary scenarios. Now I'm not so sure about that.'

'Being a party to the kidnap and possible murder of my husband isn't on my agenda for successful contributions to anything.' I wonder what exactly the Front means to Helen. There must be more to it. Don't ask, Fizzer always says that, just wait and they'll tell if you wait long enough.

'Helen, the Front. Let me ask you. Why is it such a major big deal for you when it comes down to it? What do you owe these people?'

'Who said anything about owing anything to anyone?' said Helen, perhaps too hastily. That's it. Like Fizz would say, someone has her ass in a sling. That has to be it.

'I don't owe anyone anything Sylvie, you must know that. I pay my way.' She said that calmly, looking straight ahead. She's angry now; she looks as if she might just lose her cool. I don't believe it.

'There's nothing else to say then is there, then Helen?

CHAPTER NINETEEN

GAMBLING MAN

The general feeling was that as usual, Sarno was in his element, and not only that, cooking on gas, as if imminent resolution was outside the door.

'One minute there he was doing his, camp as a line of tents bit, and the next one it was getting Fermat sorted once and for all and while you're at it, put up a paper to the Top Jollies regarding the need to boil their collective heads,' Ted Blunger remarked,' The next thing is, he's on about how no one here should for a moment think that he should presume to crow, but what had he said all-a-bloody long. Jesus Christ, leave it out. Who needs it?'

'As if anyone would, I don't bloody think,' Blunger said to Sandra later in the day in the Lowndes Arms as they waited for the sausage and mash with a pool of gravy in the middle, mushy peas and a side order of crazy chips. Prudently, he delayed telling her about the personal two-step pay rise that had been gaudily announced that very morning by FXS. Why crowd your luck? Women can get funny sometimes, especially where money is concerned. A more appropriate occasion would be preferable.

Sarno's initial reaction to the explanation of Helen's 'little problem', as he would insist on calling it, had been one of pique and irritable tetchiness of the nose-out-of joint variety. And he came on with, 'Blunger, can this be true? I understand that you returned home at an hour that has already given scandal to our newly installed Directrice, and she fresh from the virginal lawns of Cheltenham Ladies Correction Centre, I'll have you know. Have you no shame, I ask myself? I would remind you that this is a Government department, not an escort agency for single professional ladies. The Mata Hari of Somerville was on the phone first bloody thing, I assure you, the famous *embonpoint* positively heaving with anger! Incandescent? Christ alight, Blunger, I'm not sure that the ghastly hag didn't call me "sonny". In your case, it seems that respect for the common decencies was thrown to the winds in the face of a Jezebel, by all accounts. Tell me it isn't true. They'll never let you through the doors of the Twenty Nine again, you know that. Can it really be the case that she peeled off her kit and danced starkers on the Chemmy table?' Sometimes Sarno says such daft things that I wonder if I'd be better off selling double glazing in Walthamstow. I really bloody do.

FX Sarno had looked solemnly at him, 'It's all right Teddy, I could not forbear a tolerant smile after seeing on your face an expression that called to heaven for long deserved recognition of triumphs and the mortification of your enemies. The whole place will be alight with the news by noon, I promise you. I am positively agog. Do tell.' And he did.

'Yes Mr Blunger, forgive me, but would it be all right if I called you Ted? You wouldn't mind would you?' she had asked as they took in the dusky ambience and inviting 'come on in there's nothing to it', atmosphere of the rooms, 'Do you think we might play a few games of poker or something? I haven't played for years of course. Such fun.' Once he'd recovered from feigned surprise at hearing such an unlikely admission, he guided her to the tables. Ms Helen Kershaw, you're talking a right load of old bollocks darling, but you certainly know how to take the piss. I like it. However, Blunger was now near certain that he probably had her on toast. The message was simple enough. Helen knew more about gambling than she'd cared to let on. It was a safe bet that she knew enough, but not enough. This meant that she could be sucked in deep. The signs were there. Already she was trying to sound casual and unconcerned, but it was all too studied. One minute she'd be affecting a laughing nostalgia for the poker games of student days, played with matches, 'what a laugh that must sound,' next switching to half squelched references to the merits of spit-in-the-ocean, versus Cincinnati Hi-Low. There was more to Helen and her experience of games of chance than that. Blunger was certain of it. 'The most dangerous scenario of all as far as your inexperienced punter is concerned involves what my tutor always called "the glib smatter merchants of this world." They're the worst.' He permitted himself this pompous reflection later, as he recounted the story at debriefings, chaired by Sarno who was already claiming him as the prodigal son, 'I always said that one day old Ted Blunger would astonish us all, did I not? Such *brio*.' He smiled upon his unmoved hearers.

Blunger's strategy had simple; his objectives well defined. There was no question of leading Helen into a bent game or any old crap like that. All he needed to know was the lessons that could be learnt from her behaviour at the table. Even the best players have some give-aways in their involvement in something that is only partially a card game. So far all the signs were that Helen, the polymath Ms Supercool, was in one respect at least, as vulnerable as the next. The problem now was how to exploit this without humiliating her to a level where her co-operation would begin to falter. Blunger knew that he had it strapped, he was now approaching 'the apotheosis of Ted Blunger,' as Sarno was to claim it as thereafter, at the same time implying that it was, after all, all down to FX Sarno, 'I mean isn't it what I always said old Ted would come up with?'.

It was the sight of Helen's body-language at the table that had been the clincher. No matter how much you dress it up in sociologic jargon, 'the presentation of the self in everyday life,' and all that stuff, it makes no difference; there are few people, even amongst the best in the field, who don't give themselves away either more or less, as long as you know what to look for.

At the gaming table, weak means strong, confidence, desperation. It all comes down to how you act. And once Helen got started she got it wrong too many ways, looking at the flop when she'd have done better to ignore it, guarding good hands obviously, hands too steady when they should have been shaking, the whole bit. The problem is, whatever you do, however well you think you're covering, you're liable to send out the wrong signals. The best you can do is limit the damage. Blunger reasoned, if she does it so obviously when she's playing she's telling us something. It's funny though in someone like Helen. Maybe that's what she wants, maybe she's saying, 'Look, somebody get me out of this.'

'Quite the psychologist was Ted Blunger on this occasion,' said Sarno, adding, 'though mind you, I always said as much.'

And so Blunger continued, 'We'd got her pretty little ass in a sling. She was going to show us her ass as a bonus. Chief, that's what I realised.' Funny thing though, that was the exact moment when I began to feel sorry for her. The fun wears off a bit when it all; no need to mention that just yet. 'Well, the thing is Chief, to be honest, we lucked out. You see, Sandra was the one who put me on to it. No doubt you'll remember me mentioning her name from time to time, or maybe you don't.' He couldn't resist that shot, bloody Sarno deserved at least that reminder.

'Well, Sandra, she recognised Helen, but she had a different name for her. At the time I thought this had to be a major break through.' As it happened it wasn't quite like that. Blunger said that at the precise instant that Helen realised that Sandra had rumbled her, she went as quiet as a curate who had just farted during an interview with the bishop, but she said nothing. 'If I'd said anything it would have blown the whole thing wide open. No point in letting that happen. In fact Helen never even noticed that Sandra was giving me the nod. I reckon she was too scared to notice anything. Quite a sight, Helen Kershaw looking scared, does anyone believe that? That's got to be rare as rocking horse shit, I'd say.' And FXS positively beamed, 'Ah yes, Mme Sandra, a fascinating person, by all accounts, I always suspected there was much more to that young woman, but I'm interested in her inner thoughts too, Blunger. Her motivations; what's she telling us?' That's bloody rich after his previous comments. *Poule de luxe* indeed. There's no point in telling him what really happened; he doesn't have to know everything.

After this they'd kibitzed at a table where seven-card stud was being played. That was the start of it. Suddenly, Helen said quite unexpectedly, even impatiently, 'I'm tired of watching. Deal me in please.' The dealer looked at Blunger who raised an eyebrow and Helen was in. At this stage Blunger thought it best to leave her to get on with it, and went in search of blackjack. 'Enjoy yourself Helen and don't do anything I wouldn't do.' Jesus, I'm really playing the old fart; I'll be calling her My Dear Young Woman next if I go on like this. And he did too.

'He even bought her five hundred pounds worth of chips I believe,' said Sarno, 'That's what I call style. Good Old Blunger never did anything by halves.' He paused, 'Out of his own pocket, he tells me.' And looked around, positively beaming. Make you sick.

This woman is full of surprises, I wonder what will happen next? As he pondered about this, Blunger became aware of certain familiar and welcome vibrations. Sandra's infra-red sensors had picked him up; they never failed. She looked pretty good, despite a life style that would have exhausted the wearer of the *maillot jaune* in the Tour. *One day I'll take you away from all this, maybe there's a place where we can breathe God's clean air, where people are decent, and a man can walk tall again.*

'Keeping funny company are we then Ted?' she asked, as full of it as you like. I've got to counsel her about that one day. Getting ideas above her station. Some chance. But Sandra was not to be put off. She looked at him directly and he thought, right you can lay off this lark once we get the club going in Manchester, I promise you, young lady. Like you'll be starting with the washing-up if all else fails. We're looking at a class place, not some cheap drinker for oiks in the motor trade and antique dealers from Cheadle, for Christ's sake. Once we break even and make a bit we can buy a nice gaff in The Wirral, wall to wall G and T and not a soul who knows Merleau Ponty from a hole in the ground. You'd get used to the golf and men in funny trousers in no time. Poor sod; how he wished it were true.

'You do know how to pick them, don't you Ted? Come in here with a chick who's left a trail of markers all over town in her time. Nothing personal or anything you know Ted. I'm just saying what I'd heard said, that's all.' I'd better listen up here for a minute, she knows about these things. 'What was that then Sand, I'm not sure I'm reading you? Did you say markers? Was that it?' he asks as casually as anything, 'What's all this stuff about Helen? I mean what are you telling me?' If she says, *don't you realise, you old fool, this kid's dynamite?* I might just do my nut. And another thing, she's no way going to wear gear like that in the club. 'If you don't mind my saying so,' said Sandra,' I'd let her get on with it, then you can enjoy yourself a bit and see what happens, know what I mean?'

'Look Sandra, you obviously know something that I don't. I need to know about whatever it is as soon as possible, like immediately if you don't mind, so let's leave the jollies aside and get on with it. OK? And no crap please about there being no such thing as a free lunch or I'll bloody cash my options and leg it.' A likely scenario, that.

'Since you mention it,' said Sandra, 'why don't you just try asking her if she ever goes to The Black Mamba in Duke Street these days and see what the little cow says to that, that's all I'm saying. And while we're at it, I reckon she's had a nose job as well as tits, and you can tell her I said so if you like. Anyway, I've to go now Ted. I work here you know, in case you'd forgotten, management don't like staff socialising with clients, it's against House Policies and Procedures,' and the bloody ingrate just buggered off, waving her arse at me in triumph, calm as you bloody like and that was it. He sighed pretentiously, 'Women, Christ Guv, I could write a bloody book. Next thing is, I'm back in the blackjack game thank God. And, if I may say so, doing pretty bloody well; the dealer has a ten upcard and I hit till I'm at soft nineteen. It's looking good and I'm thinking that we're looking at a nice little earner this evening when one of Turk's minders is behind me, and he's telling me, *Mr Turk says the broad wants to go over the house limit and will you get it sorted? He doesn't want any old shit. Mr Blunger.*

F X Sarno didn't blink an eyelid, 'Of course Teddy, I understand. I mean he wouldn't want any old shit would he? And what happened after that?' he asked, quite gently now.

'I slipped into the Understanding-Uncle-Guide-Counsellor-and-Friend act and said that under the circumstances, why of course I'd be prepared to OK that, as she was my guest and have a word.' Sarno interrupted somewhat piously, 'Not with any intention of using departmental money, I sincerely take leave to hope.'

'Well, naturally it wasn't going to be with mine was it?' Stupid bugger, what does he think we do? Maybe he isn't stupid, I didn't mean that. 'Well I stroll round and see what's going down. Only bloody mayhem that's all. Thank God I got there. She's having a run in with the dealer, doing her high and mighty act about how she's here as a guest of a very important person from a Government department. As if anyone would give a toss anyway...'

'She was right to say that Blunger, but it was injudicious of her to mention the Government.' He's taking the piss again isn't he?

'...anyway I squared everything with the dealer and thought, now is the time and so I asked her about how were things at the Black Mamba these days Ms Kippax, and she nearly bloody passed out.'

'Who said anything about that place? I don't know what you mean,' she said. So I said, 'Come off it sweetheart. Why don't we go there for a change, it's only round the corner. I haven't been there for years, I suppose it's still open.' Wisely, Sarno repressed one of his, listen everyone, what did I tell you, looks for once, and let Blunger continue. 'From then on it turned out pretty well really.' He sounded almost surprised.

By the time they arrived there Helen had recovered her

normal state of readiness for anything to the extent that Ted wondered if he'd made a mistake and took temporary refuge in false reminiscence, 'Well imagine that, heavens above, I haven't been in this place for many a moon,' and thinking this is going to be a right balls up, I'm losing my grip, it couldn't have been more unconvincing if I'd said, I say, so this is how the other half lives. Face it, there could have hardly been a less likely place than The Black Mamba for the Helen Kershaws of this world. It was a combination of high roll gaming and *maison d'accomo-dation* for the well to do and that was it. Blunger's acquaintance with the place had been confined to an operation in which a foolish Air Vice Marshal was immobilised before he could do any further damage. 'I always find that the wives are the best people to settle things in these matters, Blunger.' F X S had said, 'you can't beat the tweedy Mafia for restoring order in the cuntstruck warrior, though heaven knows what unspeakable privileges the boot faced hags threaten to withhold from them.'

It was flash enough mind you. No expense had been spared in relieving the patrons of their monies amidst an atmosphere of Lucullan splendour. Frescoes, cherubs, gold leaf and all, just like a Bavarian church. Helen looked about as appropriate as a Maoist at a Tory Party Conference in Harrogate until she said disarmingly, 'I used to work here you see,' and relapsed into silence. Blunger let it go and ordered a bottle of house champagne. 'It's all right,' said Helen, 'they won't recognise me. I've seen to that.' Good old Sandra, she'd been right about the nose job. And if it came to that, what the hell had Sandra been doing in a place like this?

Before he'd finished with this speculative rumination, Helen had started to give him the full story. 'Economic forces, Mr Blunger. I don't think I need say more. I think I'd like a stronger drink. What about you?' What came out was nothing new and about as sad as anything you could hear, Blunger reflected. When you owe people money they ask you for favours. They wanted an in to the Anti-Terrorist Unit. Helen got it for them. Just like that. And that's why Abdullah nicked the tape and got shot for his trouble, stupid sod.

'What a story Blunger. You did well there Teddy. It will not pass unnoticed you know.' F X S had never been known to go that far.

'What's going to happen Sarno? What do you reckon next?' Why bother to ask? I know he'll get a result, he usually does. We could wrap it up in a matter of hours. He imagined the scene, 'Thank you Ms Al-Harfi, we'd like you to meet some people and talk things over, so there'll be no need to use your portable. In any case we immobilised it before we came. It's arranged, you see. So if you'd accompany me to the car outside we'll get it all squared away. Diplomatic immunity has been waived.' He wondered if she'd vomit in the lift before or after she'd pissed her knickers. Even Steven usually.

'My prediction is that matters at the Damascus end will be resolved in our favour, even though Mr Edwards will have been obliged to endure a few moments of relative discomfort, which I may add, he is paid to do, and providing that the buffoon Colonel Saad of the Fourth Collapsing Fusiliers, doesn't crash through the scenery in Act Three. My concern now is to see that this end is tidied up. I think that Ms Helen will probably need a change of scene,' he added casually. 'I don't believe it, we can't nick the bloody woman on the basis of a few crappy phone calls and he knows that. And while I'm at it, I'll remind Inspector Edwards to send you a thank you note. I'm sure he'll be grateful.' He smiled.

'I know what you're thinking Teddy. I'm not proposing that she should be placed in custody. I just think that she will feel able to accept inducements that will be offered her to keep her head down for as long as is necessary, after she has identified her friends at this end for us. After which they can be swept under the carpet. We could ask Mr Edwards to do that. After that we can advance her career if need be. Who knows? The same is true of Mrs Edwards. Before you know it Blunger, she'll be on the payroll, a loyal servant sending memos about parking space allotments and giving seminars on race relations at the Training College. Promotion all round. What fun! And we get Mr Edwards for nothing. We can leave the details to the others and have lunch, wouldn't you agree? Who's for the River Cafe? It's heaps better than The Happy Eater, or would you prefer to go to a pub, or I suppose I should say "down the pub"?'

And that was all that F X S would say.

CHAPTER TWENTY

CODA

The sun had rocketed up over the horizon, and the prayer calls had died away after the cut-off that always sounds as if your man has dropped dead half way through the last bit. All of a sudden Fizzer had the idea that he could really fancy a steaming cup of coffee, as if he'd missed out on breakfast earlier; as if they'd been serving hot rolls and scrambled eggs and it was all like that guy in the movie who was pissed off because he'd forgotten to get a cup of coffee at the station on his way to kill the guy, or was it a book he'd read, not a movie?

The early morning air was cool and still; it smelt of woodsmoke and the heady perfume of jet fuel. From the airport perimeter, sounds of traffic drifted across the tarmac, and a few dogs barked cautiously. The inner security cordon was well out of sight, but the armoured personnel carriers of the outer cordon could be seen quite clearly. Small groups of men in combat fatigues stood watchfully at the ready, smoking and gobbing out in the sand, AK 47's slung over their shoulders; they shuffled, stamped and fretted; extra clips taped with dirty strips of band-aid to the magazines, barrels no longer glinting. *Every Friday evening groups of two, three, even four policemen and sergeants carrying drawn staves, were to be found on street corners off Smithdown road, waiting for potential trouble.*

Inside the aircraft it was totally silent now, except for the quiet exchanges of watchful talk between Nasser and his buddies, with Zeinab, aloof and half smiling, shooting glances at Fizzer. And mocking with it in a way. Why does she keep smiling at me? Don't say she's after a quick shag before the shit comes down. What's your problem darling? As if he didn't know. *What will Sylvie do if I get topped? I'd not thought of that had I? Career woman forever or marry some half-arsed copper on the rebound. As long as it's not Dave. Not that I've got anything against Dave. Or become a fucking dyke and live with bloody Helen. That would be a right laugh. Serve me right I suppose. If I could see her again. Just the once really. Just a look really. Funny thing that. Famous last words maybe?*

Behind him Fizzer could hear Mary comforting Liza. Mary had maintained a disapproving mode from the start. Occasionally she emitted the sort of clucking noises that teachers used to make when confronted by pupils whose behaviour had gone from worse than usual to unspeakable. He wondered if she was composing a letter to *The Guardian* examining the whole matter dispassionately and from an informed point non-judgmental point of view. May I presume upon the hospitality of your pages to draw attention to a groundswell of lingering disquiet about inter-racial concerns that troubles many of us in these difficult times of welfare cuts and creeping fascism? *A kiss before dying. I don't want any of these people to die. Even Sir Fartarse and the gorillas. They deserve better. If Jan was here would Sylvie want her to die? Best not to think about that. Pity about Abdullah and all. But he had to go, you could say. I wonder who killed him. Never know I suppose. But it was all a bit hazy by now. Like a dream you might say. That must be it. Like they say it's like in an accident, but it isn't like that, or is it? All these things are like dreams when you come down to it aren't they? It's the death of innocence or is it the innocence of death or is it incense? Incensed with death, may be that's it.*

The Captain called Nasser to the phone. Jesus it was getting all formal now like a bloody law court. If your Lordship pleases, would you mind coming to the phone so we can sort this lot out? Fizzer was watching him hard now, straining after scraps of talk that might tell him something; anything would suffice. It was obvious, this one was the final chat-up, where Nasser sets the final conditions, establishes their acceptance, and gets Manson and the Syrians to agree the arrangements for their departure to whatever place of safety had been agreed.

How Manson must have enjoyed setting that one up, all co-operative, the no-deals policy thrown right out of the window, just the once, mind you, and all the while wondering if he was dropping me right in it. What a bloody stroke! *Understand this, whoever you are, once and for all, we make no deals. Our concern is for the preservation of life. You read me?* Did Manson really do that? But there was no way of knowing now, perhaps best to remember that we're up against people who aren't concerned about our minor rivalries. Why should they be? They go for the big one while we fartarse around worrying about mortgages. If you don't have anything you'll steal anything, even a life, or a used tyre from a parking lot. *Two wrongs don't make a right, surely even chicken-shit liberals like you can take that on board Sylvie. This isn't a meeting of the bloody Hampstead Ethical Society you know...* He watched Nasser, nodding solemnly as he listened to the instructions. Not too strong on smiling, are your actual Nassers of this world. Then he looked out of the window, straining his eyes past the outer cordon, trying to look beyond the wobbling silhouettes of the airport buildings, scanning the dusty caravanserai for any possible glimpses, sounds and hints of normality that might be found out there. A car moved slowly along the perimeter track in the morning haze, but it was an airport car with a 'Follow me' on a sign on the roof in English and Arabic. A taxi would have been a better, a more reassuring, less institutional sight. A few goats had strayed within the perimeter fence, that was a start. Where were they going, he wondered? You might as well have asked a passing butterfly that question. A breeze gusted over the desert, rolling pieces of paper, crisp packets, Pepsi tins and brushwood around as it bore with it across the tarmac a few bars of tinny Arab rock music and the smells of coffee and cigarettes.

The best we can hope for is, that everything is sealed and ready, regardless of what Manson may want. It's the only chance we have. No room for last minute screw ups now. Out of the corner of his mouth, he whispered to Jacko, 'Well sunshine I suppose it's a stay in Beirut next, or Tripoli.' I wonder what Manson will think of that. I mean, like me being in the bag. Best not to ask.

'You could let Sylvie know you met me. Could you do that? Tell her I was all right really. She'd want to know I was all right.' I'm sure she would. I sound like something out of The Dambusters, I'll be asking after the bloody dog next, except that we haven't got one called nigger. They wouldn't get away with that in a movie nowadays.

Jacko replied, 'Time will show Fizzer. Main thing is, we don't need any last minute freak outs from Sir Joss and the Bash Street Kids.'

Great, now he's not even bloody listening to me, and here was I thought he was all set to be my new friend. Big mistake I shouldn't have been taken in by his flash kit. And making jokes with it. Whistling in the dark, that's what I'm doing.

Nasser puts down the phone and says 'They say that we should stand at the door, and you will await my signal to begin the exit. I shall be behind you as we leave. Remember that.'

Thanks for telling me. I'd quite forgotten, how foolish of me. I'll certainly keep my hand on my arse Duckie.

They stood at the door and the captain opened it. Cool morning air from the desert refreshed them all. Fizzer stood behind Nasser; stood dead still behind Nasser with Zohair and Bashir behind. Jacko stood behind them in the aisle guarded by Saleh. And Zeinab, she was right in here, standing like someone out of a Greek chorus or whatever it was. *There's two of everyone Mr Edwards, one inside another.* What was that supposed to mean for Christ's sake? No one's in a rush to be first out ...*scattered shouts and cries, even a few rounds of quiet applause mixed with some quickly squelched laughs, and then, in an instant, a stream of people started to come quickly out...* Everyone's standing behind everyone and no one wants to be first. No, honestly, after you. No, really, you go first, it's my pleasure. If the Syrian army's out there I wouldn't blame them. Some dumb raghead with his shooter jammed on automatic. Hey Sarge what do I do now? *Then the hostages; they came out quickly, that was the thing that amazed him on these occasions. They always come steaming out double-quick, except for the poor buggers who got carried out. And they never look back either, not one tiny glance over the shoulder.*

At this point Nasser signed to Fizzer to start leaving the aircraft ahead of him and it was, so far so good. At the same time Zohair turned unexpectedly, and motioned to Sir Jocelyn and his people to remain where they were. And in that instant, Zohair lost it completely, this was never the time for anyone to do the unexpected, break wind, cough, anything. And so what did Zohair do, but he scores the perfect own goal, his first and last, and no replays in this league. *Fuck you, you're dead is the name of the tune we're playing, would you like to hear it again sunshine? Name that tune Mr Master of the Melowdee.* Nasser was not expecting him to turn, and as he checked, he realised, as he did so, that he'd made a big mistake in a fraction of no time at all. Go to the bottom of the class Zohair. He knows, he bloody knows, now's the time to do him, Fizzer thought, as at that moment Jacko head butted Zohair to the ground and shoved the shooter from his crotch holster into his mouth, calling to Fizzer who picks up a shooter that came skimming across the deck from nowhere. Another thing is I never really liked shooters. *Handle the bloody thing as if you believed in it, it's not afraid of you; you're not going to wipe someone's arse with it the instructor had said, it's for blowing peoples arses away, not wiping them.*

Thirty five seconds.

Nasser is now off his guard, and caught unawares, he gasps as Fizzer decks him in one, and roots him in the face to make sure. Old times sake.

Another thirty seconds. It was all over and not a shot fired. And Mary and Liza are standing each with mini Uzis in their hands. Safety catches forward. Beat that one boychick. Fizzer wonders where they came from. The strange thing was that they didn't look like Mary and Liza any more, no way did they.

Younger and harder, that was it, plus their clothes didn't hang off them like sacks any more either. More muscular and healthier, tighter skin. The social worker and assistant-curator at the local-museum-out-on-the-batter images had been replaced by something keener and heavier. I wouldn't give a roasted fart for the chances of any poor sod who got on the wrong side of those two broads. They'd tie you up, then bloody shoot you, just to make sure. Fuck it why not? Obvious when you thought about it. Always is. Like having a conjuring trick explained. Why didn't I think of that before?

Jacko said, 'OK shitheads, let's have all the guns on the floor or Mr Nasser here goes *fil bayt*,' adding 'tell him Miriam.' to Mary.

Fizzer said quietly, 'What kept you Jacko?'

And all of a sudden he lost patience with the whole crap deal. Too bloody much as it happens. He was tired of it all; tired of being patient, tired of being the great hero, it was time for someone else to do this crock of shit, tired of sweating on his pension, tired of wondering where his life was going and all, and where was Sylvie, and where was his life? He wanted to blow the back of Zeinab's head away with two straight shots into the face, right between open eyes remaining open. Foot and eye. Die, you bastard die. I'm going to kill you murderous Arab whore. That's for the poor bastards you lot top whenever it suits you. Why should the Israelis have all the fun shooting all the fucking ragheads? *...like the tops sliced off soft boiled eggs, revealing shiny pink brain tissue below...*

Zeinab faced him, gun in hand and nearly beat him to it as she said quietly, 'This is from Jan.' Why would she say that? She wouldn't know Jan from the, and there was a white flash and, *Why are you doing this to me Sylvie? That's for all, flash, and the flash and the shit you laid on me with all the birds, flashing, and Jan and that's for the baby you wont let me have and all and everything that you know what I'm saying Fizz. 'Be fair Sylvie' and she says be fair, is this what you call fair as she pulled the trigger again, and his head went out, up and over, it felt like brain salad surgery was that what the thing was called. Talk about a red mist coming down, it made a hang-over look like a wet dream as he struggled with Sylvie for the shooter. What was Sylvie; doing with a shooter? 'Honest Sylvie I never meant all that stuff. I was just fooling around. It didn't mean a thing.'* And he noticed she wasn't wearing any knickers. Arabs don't, that's what Dave said, *they like it up the back Fizz, honest.* The cabin steward came up, 'Would you like to try some of our TWA coffee sir? Jan looked good in the uniform like it really showed her ass up to perfection, plus a VPL that would make your balls go on fire. I'd rather try some of your TWA Tea. Old ones still the best in my humble. *Well, fancy that, a real turn up this is then Jan. Fancy you in the airline business. Got fed up with sucking coppers' dicks was that what it was?* Face it some women really do look better in uniform. That Jan, well she would. *'I suppose I didn't mean a thing' said Jan, 'Well I knew that didn't I. It's just I wondered for a moment there after some crap you came out with last night when we?'* They all say that, what was that you said last night when we were screwing, or was it spewing, what's the difference in a way? It makes you sick, too much of it they reckon. Makes you go blind as I remember. I can always sell matches if it comes to that. No I don't and if I did I wouldn't let on. *Standing on a cliff edge as she spoke.* Well she would wouldn't she? They all look alike when they're going off. Only natural. Strange that Jan and Sylvie looked alike in a way or was it Zeinab. And he'd been right, she had no bloody clit. Good old Dave. They ought to stop that sort of thing; bloody barbaric I call it.

He yelled at her, 'I mean that foot and eye should not lie you understand you Arab bitch god rot you to hell', *I sound as if I might just be cracking up. What was the bloody man talking about, foot and eye? And she still was looking right at him.* All right darling drop 'em, cop yourself a real piece of white meat for once in your life... *and her brains were all over the cabin floor. And she'd shat herself. They always do, it's a well known fact...* In any case they'll be lining up to write her life story. Heroic persecuted Freedom fighter. Some half-arsed bloody Yank will be on to that in no time. Our poor sisters in the gender struggle.

In any case what was all the fuss about? Jan is the cabin staff co-ordinator, clever little sod, how did she get a job like that? Surely she can arrange a clean up. Just a few bits of brain and shards of bone and some shit. Only take a minute. What's all the bloody fuss about? 'I'm calling my supervisor,' Jan said in her best station-house accent, all business-like now. What else? 'I've had enough of this crap.' Trust her to make a bloody fuss. All the same when you come down to it, they really are. 'What seems to be the problem Sir? We aim to give the best service to our customers.' said Helen, if you bloody please. Where did you come from darling? That's great, that is. It would have to be Helen the supervisor, I mean who else? Plus the uniform. Christ, on her it looks good. Make your bloody eyes water. Tits you could die for. Maybe she'll give me a blow-job. *'Excuse me Sir but we seem to have a problem here,' she says all smiling. By now Jan has peeled off most of her kit. 'She gives very good head Sir,' says Helen un-zipping his fly. 'What have we here? Who said size doesn't matter?' She still looked at him and said, 'but not as good as I do.'*

'That's bloody marvellous isn't it Fizzer,' says Sylvie, 'no more than I'd expect.' So Jan says, 'Who's she when she's at home? That's what I'd like to know.' She ignores her, Hey white trash, look at me, I'm a black whore, which, in case you didn't know it, I'm not, at the moment. 'Did you really have to let it happen like that, all those people dead? Is that what you want? Where's this fore play that you're always on about or is it fair ploy?' Not even a greeting, he thought lamely, or do I mean gleeting? She had asked angrily, looking coldly at him, the perpetrator, not pausing this time, 'I thought that the boy wonder settled things without bloodshed, always providing the terrorists are white, isn't that right?' What did you do with this one then Fizz, fuck her brains out, by the look of it. They're on the floor in case you hadn't noticed.' Will she ever shut up? Bloody briefs. All the same. And Helen has to come on a bit strong, well she bloody would wouldn't she? Always the last word like some bloody smartarse mick if she was a man. 'What else can you expect if you marry a barbarian committed to the preservation of outdated bourgeois norms, a capitalist running dog, not to say a lickspittle toady employed to keep a docile working class in order to meet the needs of a larger scale colonialist conspiracy, wouldn't you agree

Sylvie? I mean darling what else can you expect?' But Sylvie wasn't able to give much of an answer what with her brains trickling out of her nostrils like pink KY jelly and all. *'Now look what you've gone and done you ignorant copper,'* said Helen, *'Come here silly boy and I'll let you fuck my brains out too, just to even things up.'* Sylvie chips in with, *'She's right Fizz, it's never too late to change, where did we go wrong, we seem to have lost the way.'* I don't believe it. Nest she'll be taking a smut out of my eye with a handkerchief. *'I'm a doctor actually. It's so silly of me to make a fuss like this. It seems like many months since we met but it was only last week. I'd missed the connection after I changed my book in Boots and had a coffee in the Kardomah. I've been away darkling for such a long time. But now you're back and that's all that fucking matters. I'm fed up with this fucking crossword, to be perfectly honest. And still oozed her brains across the carpet.'* Somebody call housekeeping for God's sake and get them down here double quick... Helen said, 'Don't think that you'll be allowed to get away with this sort of thing, you cheap fascist bastard, you're all the same, it's time she left all this shit behind her, she doesn't need the likes of you Mr Edwards.' Fizzer thought I've had enough of all this shit and pulled the tit again as the back of Zeinab's skull did a Humpty Dumpty. *Tell that to Mr bloody greaseball Arafat. Tell him it's what they call an Oi Vey situation.* If only she'd stop bleeding or oozed tidily like Bergmann, Davis or Joan Crawford. *Honey I forgive you. One day we'll be together. It'll be a better, cleaner world. You'll see.*

Jacko said 'I never saw that, did I, I mean it all happened so quick, felt as if everything was in a dream were you? Was that it? This isn't a Tom and Jerry cartoon sunshine. Knocked out for half a minute and you come back like you went on a whaling trip to the South Atlantic. I never knew what came over me, it's almost as if I was standing outside myself, was that it? Well I've got news for you my friend, the passengers may have noticed an exchange of shots. You'll need to work on that one you know, you bad-tempered sod. You'll have the Police Complaints Authority after you if you go on like this and give you retirement on grounds of ill-health. The only thing might save you is you got a bang on the head. We could get a shrink to plead diminished responsibility. Society is to blame, that's why I murder women, at least I don't try to shag them, while they're alive that is. Could I get some counselling? Be the death of me you will? Don't they teach you nothing at the Police Staff College?' *But Helen still stood opposite, looking all accusing or something, or was it one of the women in the seats behind?*

Fizzer ignored him and said 'Neither did she. Forget it, you could drive a bloody Chieftain tank in here and the passengers wouldn't notice it. Or care.' And Jacko continued, 'Don't crowd your luck. Another thing, I think you'll be needing to take some time off after this lot won't you, I mean the way things are. Perhaps you need counselling?' *It wasn't Helen and where was Sylvie?*

Fizzer said, 'You could be right. All people keep doing lately is, they keep telling me to take time off. Everyone reckons it's the cure for everything. And while we're at it, I suppose I don't need to ask who you work for.'

Jacko replied 'Would it help if I said?'

Almost immediately the stun grenades of the Syrian commandos announced their supererogatory and by now unnecessary arrival, as they swarmed through the floor at the rear of the cabin like rats out of a sewer; a crackle of automatic fire into bodies of the already dead and all the dead are dead again. *The stun grenade echo had bounced and faded, the automatic weaponry stopped crackling and ripping the air, and the silence come down like a fast curtain.*

Another forty five seconds gone.

Inside the aircraft there was near bloody chaos as the passengers got the idea that they had taken in what had happened and were overwhelmed by a sudden onset of freedom. Some even shook hands like it was a French wedding. All knew that they would probably never take it all in though, that nothing would ever be the same again.

Fizzer said to Jacko, 'What's it all about Jacko?' *I really am losing my marbles. No question. It's the drink. Has to be.*

'No time for profundities I reckon.' said Jacko. 'At least the Syrians didn't shoot us. I should know about that and all shouldn't I?'

He laughed at that. 'Look Fizzer, the body bags will be here in no time. These people bury their dead quickly. You'll like that.' And he was right on the last point, how would he know that, thinks Fizzer as he watched the bags being off loaded from an Armoured Personnel Carrier. Trust the bloody Syrians, they were using used bags, well they're a poor country, *at least he didn't say listen pal there's not so much time kid, so here it is,* but I bet he rides off into the sunset. And he waited outside the Embassy and heard Jan laughing and a few cheers, saw Jan with her pants off in the bedroom, heard Sylvie shouting at him, *you lousy shit, that's it then, isn't it? You would have to screw her wouldn't you, you'd screw anything.*

Now here was Jacko getting all formal and then, speaking in another voice again, saying, 'Right then Mr Edwards, my people are waiting for me. It will be soon time to say good-bye, I think. Looking out for the body bags are you, that it?' He laughed, 'I heard you'd done that in the past, isn't that right?' And he signalled to Mary and Liza who looked even more handy again with their Uzis out of the way.

'It's my friends Miriam and Gerda,' said Jacko, now full of piss and vinegar. Unstoppable, you could see that now. And why.

Fizzer said, 'I didn't reckon it was your Auntie Nellie and her friend Vera from Bootle did I? Explanations would be well out of order, I suppose. OK so, I'm not going to ask who you work for but, not that it matters all that much anyway. But it would have been nice to have had it official.' Good coppers prefer the paperwork done right, it's the training.

Jacko replied, 'Shit happens, OK, so I wasn't just on the flight with you by chance; we don't need to go through all that. Let's leave it like that and with the likes of your Mr Sarno. His sort of person likes to play games with the likes of people like you and me. He's the one you should ask maybe. He's also the one you should watch.'

'That sod. I suppose I ought to lose my temper.'

'Take it easy Fizzer. We've all had a hard time here. OK, so I'm sorry about Mr Sarno. He set you up for all this, right? That's how he earns a crust. He has his reasons I suppose. It's market forces. Another day, another buck and a half.'

He paused, 'And another thing, it's time you stopped losing your temper so much, it's bad for the heart.'

'You could say that.'

'Look at it this way. Maybe Sarno had your best interests at heart; after all you'll earn promotion from all this and it'll be down to him.'

'Don't play bloody games with me, Jacko. You've been in the deep end on this one from the moment you boarded.'

'Maybe before. What does it matter? All the same I'd watch the bugger. Bit tricksome? And finally Mr Edwards, there is one point which you might have guessed I suppose, and if you hadn't, now is the time to make it. Our important friend Sir Jocelyn is my property from now on. He goes with us. He owes.'

Fizzer replied, almost angrily, 'It might have been more tactful to arrange that after I'd gone. I'd wondered if that might be the deal but I'd say that it was probably a fair trade off.' Which is better? Sir Jocelyn alive, and Nasser dead, or the other way around?

'One final word,' said Jacko, 'take my advice my son and watch your ass with Mr Manson. He'll never be a busted flush. His sort never are.'

Fizzer replied 'Mazel tov, isn't that what I should say?'

'That's up to you, isn't it?' Jacko smiled. 'Try not to be such an irritable sod. Enjoy. Eat well, live well. At the moment the name is Nick Woodhouse, not that it matters much. You could ask me about it next time you see me.'

That'll be the day; I never liked Westerns anyway. The Man who shot Liberty Vallance was all right. I wonder what the man who shot Ibrahim was like.

And Jacko walked down and out of the aircraft, and away toward the tower. As he walked, he could see Manson coming in the opposite direction and they exchanged glances, looking straight past each other. And Jacko walked on. No greetings were exchanged however, after all Manson wouldn't know Jacko from a hole in the ground would he?

And Fizzer, now approaching Manson, thought sod it why should I say a bloody word? Then, softening, thought, it wouldn't hurt, I suppose. *You may call your soul your own, but we have your ass...* And I was getting to like Jacko.

So Fizzer looked to see Manson looking and he laughed; don't say he's going to apologise about anything. I'm sorry I tried to sell you, but I let it go as the price wasn't right. It won't affect your promotion prospects or pension rights *in any way shape or form though*. I don't think I could keep a straight face. And thought, but he did negotiate me out of here, that's the point. That's what he did. *That's what they pay us for Sylvie. The Common Friend, know what I mean?*

And so when they met, Fizzer felt better in a way, well you would. It didn't matter too much what had happened, that was how he felt right now. And he was pleased to see that on this occasion Manson, for once, was a bit leery. He knows that he's lost this one. Or has he? And if he does know, does he care? Should he care? We all need to save face; it's not just the Arabs.

Manson didn't want to see Fizzer all that much either, but didn't mind perhaps, as there was no ducking it, and anyway did it matter all that much now? And he smiled an official welcoming sort of sod-you-you-pulled-it-off-my son – smile, and said 'Well that's another success for the negotiator then?'

Fizzer said 'Yes, another; you could say that.' And let it go.

'Listen Edwards,' said Manson.

'I hear you but I don't need to listen Mr Manson,' said Fizzer. 'Don't misunderstand me Guvnor. It's just that I've had a bit too much excitement lately, and if you're planning a let's-be-good-friends speech, why not just leave it for now? Why don't we save it for the annual reunion? Forget it. Nothing much changes and it won't. All I want to do now is to get cleaned up and get the fuck out. Also I'd like to go home and pick up on a few things. So you see, whatever we do or whatever we say now doesn't matter too much.' *If anyone tells me to get a life, I'll re-arrange their kneecaps.*

He paused. 'But you see, Mr Manson, you know one thing. You're a good copper and a thieftaker if ever I saw one.' *a hundred years ago at the Elephant, we didn't have time for ethical policing and bloody workshops on community relationships, we just bloody got on with it.* Should I give him the high five maybe? Yo. Maybe not

'I suppose I must be, if you say so Fizzer.' and Manson paused and said, 'And I spoke to your wife, and Mrs Edwards she said she knew you'd make it. She said that.' He smiled again, 'Let's go then.' *Where were you, and what were you doing all that time; I was worried stiff about you? Perhaps not...*

They turned and started to walk towards the terminal building. Three hundred meters away a group of uniformed men stood waiting, but none of them moved. Perhaps they sensed something about the shapes of the two men that walked towards them.

They walked now, straight on, their two shapes joined by whatever it was that joined them both, slowly walking towards the terminal buildings, walking together. Occasionally a laugh could be heard from one of them. And one of them was smoking. But the watching men found that it was hard to tell who was smoking and who was laughing. And even those amongst them who had known them were unsure which was which. Nothing had changed and nothing much was going to change. Fizzer was right. It never does.